A CEREMONIAL DEATH

GLYNN JENKINS

AUTHOR'S NOTE

This is the first novel to feature detective George Ashley and the soldiers and horses of Prince Albert's Troop. It was originally written during the hot summer of 2003 and the events are set in that year.

Readers familiar with the ceremonial life of London will realise that the King's Troop Royal Horse Artillery has been the inspiration for Prince Albert's Troop: I have borrowed, and put to my own use, the Troop's duties, barracks and traditions. There are, though, several differences between the two units; of these, the most important is that the King's Troop has moved with the times and admits female soldiers into its ranks, while Prince Albert's Troop has yet to experience their civilising influence. As a result, the gunners of Prince Albert's Troop are probably more bigoted and reactionary than their real-life counterparts. I have not portrayed any real soldier in this novel: all the characters, military and civilian, are fictional. Similarly, descriptions of Horse Guards, the barracks, the Tower of London and other locations are not intended to be exact.

I am grateful to Staff Sergeant Ben Moore for allowing me to use the picture of him and his horse, Crowthorne, on the front cover of this volume. The picture was taken in July 2010, when SSgt Moore was the senior NCO of F Sub-Section, the King's Troop RHA.

I also owe a long-standing debt of gratitude to WO2 Bryan Elliott, formerly of the King's Troop RHA, for correcting my imperfect knowledge of the world of the mounted gunner. Any remaining errors are my own responsibility.

Glynn Jenkins
Crail, Fife, January 2017

To my Sisters

NOVELS BY GLYNN JENKINS

A Ceremonial Death

A Meet with Murder

Corpus Procession

Friendly Fire

Mediaeval Murder

All these novels feature detective George Ashley, his nephew, Tom, and Tom's comrades in Prince Albert's Troop RHA. They do not need to be read in sequence but those who choose to do so will be able to follow Tom's military career more closely.

CHAPTER ONE

ON GUARD

Every year, towards the end of August, the gentlemen of the Household Cavalry pack their bags – that is, the troopers pack their bags and the officers have their bags packed *for* them – saddle up, and ride off to summer camp. There, living under canvas and having as much equestrian fun as possible, they blow the dirt of London out of their systems. By the end of three weeks the horses are refreshed, the soldiers are relaxed, and large numbers of local females are feeling pleasantly post-coital – so everybody is happy, one way or another.

Meanwhile, Her Majesty's residence has still to be guarded. Monarchs, too, have summer holidays, though perhaps of a rather more inhibited kind than their soldiers, and the Royal Standard rarely flies over Buckingham Palace in August. Nonetheless, the daily round of ceremonial duty continues: gleaming foot guards, secretly sweating in their scarlet tunics, parade at one end of the Mall; at the other, substituting for the Household Cavalry, are the gunners and horses of Prince Albert's Troop Royal Horse Artillery.

*   *   *   *   *

It is twenty past three on a simmering Wednesday afternoon. The gravel on Horse Guards Parade is hot to the touch, so that tourists cutting across it feel its heat through their shoes. Beyond an arch lies a courtyard – the Tilt Yard – surrounded on three sides by buildings and bordered on the fourth by Whitehall. Heat is trapped in the yard and it has an atmosphere which is both clammy and airless. Fortunately, its tarred ground is no longer reached by direct sunlight; otherwise the temperature would be unbearable.

Four sentries are on duty. To the front of Horse Guards, facing across Whitehall, are two "boxmen" – mounted guards, immaculately and authoritatively posed on chestnut horses – the delight of camera-laden tourists, teenage girls and those gentlemen whose preferences are specialised and submissive. Today, these two soldiers face the choice between being fried alive or retreating into their sentry boxes, where they will be suffocated and pressure-cooked. The positions being equally unbearable, they opt for glamour and stand in full view of their adoring public. Cameras fill with over-exposed images, foolhardy children caress the horses and, all the time, the soldiers sit motionless and handsome, receiving the adoration of the public as impassively as statues in a temple.

Within the yard, only slightly less popular, are two dismounted sentries: one by the wooden gates that lead to the guardroom, the stables and the soldiers' quarters; the other under the main arch itself. This is where Gunner Green is standing smartly at ease, his feet slightly apart and at an angle of thirty degrees, his sword in his right hand with the blunt edge of the blade resting on his shoulder.

It is generally reckoned that the boxmen have the best of it. Their duties last only an hour at a time and they come to an end when the four o'clock inspection is completed. After that, the horses return to their stalls and their riders are free to relax and enjoy a drink, to watch television, or to gamble away their salaries over a game of cards. The dismounted guards, in contrast, stand on duty for two hours at a time and must trudge through until nine o'clock. No wonder, then, that the gunners devote hours of tender attention to their kit the night before their round of duty begins, knowing that the four smartest will be selected for mounted guard after the morning inspection. Only the tiniest of details will separate the chosen four from their dismounted colleagues.

A stray thread on the ceremonial saddle cloth had been the undoing of Gunner Green at the inspection. On leading his horse from its stall, he had allowed the cloth to brush against a post and a few strands of cotton had snagged.

'And that is why,' he muses, 'Gunners Gillham and Hall are sitting pretty on their pommels, looking forward to an ice-cold lager within the next hour, while I'm stuck here until five o'clock, and then again from seven until nine. A few bleeding bits of fluff.'

Still, when you only appear at Horse Guards for three weeks in the year – and then only on alternate days – it is quite good fun, whichever duty you have to carry out. Also, the dismounted sentries have a privilege denied the boxmen: they can move. Whenever Gunner Green feels bored or stiff, he can march out to the gate and look out on Whitehall and the Banqueting Hall opposite, or turn the other way and enjoy the view across the parade ground. He does this now, bringing himself to attention and marching the dozen or so paces to the parade ground end of the archway, where he gazes out over the square.

Two American girls squeal with pleasure and take turns to be photographed alongside him. He wonders if they will slip money into the pocket of his breeches, which sometimes occurs with American tourists; or even – as happened to Gunner Watson the other day – a calling card with hotel details and a mobile telephone number. In the case of Gunner Watson this information, wrapped in a fifty-pound note, had been tucked into the back of one of his boots. From there, it had worked its way down to irritate his ankle for the next half hour until he came off duty. The fifty-pound note went part of the way towards making up for the ceaseless ribbing Gunner Watson received when his fellow guards discovered that its invisible donor was a Mr Jonah P. Jackson from Illinois. Mr Jackson's card is now pinned to the notice board, minutely adorned with indecent suggestions. The two girls, alas, lack his boldness and move on, giggling. 'Next time,' thinks Gunner

Green, 'next time...' He pauses for a moment or two, then performs an immaculate about turn and retires to his original position.

*   *   *   *   *

While Gunner Green looks out over Horse Guards, George Ashley surveys the drawing room of the Military Club in St. James' Square. Like the Household Cavalry, Ashley's own club, the Minerva, shuts up shop during August. Its members are given the choice of slumming it across the road at the South India and Minor Schools, or dossing down at the Military. Both clubs have fallen on slightly hard times and are glad of the extra custom. Not wishing to socialise with the accountants and double-glazing salesmen who populate the South India and Minor Schools these days, Ashley has settled himself amongst the present and past ornaments of the armed forces and is wondering whether twenty-two minutes past three is too early for gin.

As the two American girls wander off through the arch and towards Whitehall, leaving Gunner Green with his slight feeling of anticlimax, Ashley decides that it *is* too early. For the next sixty seconds, Ashley and the soldier share the same mild sense of irritation; then, as Gunner Green swings through one hundred and eighty degrees, Ashley, with considerably less elegance, turns to greet his old friend, Frank Raynham. By the time Gunner Green has finished his military promenade and is back at ease in his former position, Ashley and Raynham have decided that three twenty-three is an excellent time for gin.

'What brings you here, George? The Minerva's your usual stomping ground, isn't it?'

'It's having its annual hose-down and your place has offered shelter for the month.'

'Ah – that would explain why I saw a pair of bishops hanging around in the lobby, looking lost. I think they were trying to find the television room to watch the cricket. There's a distinct atmosphere of spirituality and intelligence about the place – we're not used to that here. How's business?' He places a glass of gin, and very little tonic, in Ashley's hand.

'Very slow: all the interesting criminals are spending their purloined riches abroad. Only a cluster of ticket touts, handbag snatchers and confidence tricksters are left, screwing a few dollars out of gullible tourists. What about you? I thought you were posted out in Osnabrück?'

Raynham beams in a self-satisfied manner. 'I was until a month ago. I've been appointed adjutant to the Patties.'

'The Patties?'

'Oh, sorry: Prince Albert's Troop – you know, the ones who do the gun salutes and give royalty a lift to the funeral when they die.'

Ashley is impressed: 'Sounds very glamorous.' He contrasts Raynham's new life with his own: 'I saw them riding to Horse Guards this morning.'

'That's right – we're on guard duty while the Cavalry plays at the seaside. In fact, I'm on my way to see them now; they dismount for inspection at four o'clock and I want to see how it's done in case I ever have to be the inspecting officer. Do you fancy coming along?'

Ashley does. He has nothing better to do, he enjoys watching the ceremonies of London – and Frank Raynham is good company. At twenty-four minutes to four they step into St James' Square, pause as the sunlight hits them full in the face, and then stroll gently towards Pall Mall.

*   *   *   *   *

Gunner Green has marched out to Whitehall, where he is pleased to see his mounted friends looking distinctly moist with perspiration. A child attempts to pat the muzzle of one of the horses and retreats in tears when it bares a vicious set of teeth. Amused, Gunner Green returns to the shelter of his arch before he too begins to sweat. The arch is the coolest part of

Horse Guards, so perhaps those pieces of fluff weren't so bad after all. He is back in his place at twenty-two minutes to four; Ashley and Raynham are crossing Pall Mall, passing the Minerva and stepping into Waterloo Place, and Mark Dawson, one of the junior officers of Prince Albert's Troop, is just turning his charger onto the parade ground.

Dawson, like the mounted gunners he is on his way to inspect, has suffered in the cause of glamour. He has ridden all the way from the Troop's barracks in North London and his whole body is wet. As he straightens up his mare after the turn, he feels another droplet of sweat detach itself from his hair, trickle under the collar of his tunic and work its way down his back. Finally, it rests briefly on his coccyx before dropping into the reservoir that seems to be accumulating between his seat and the saddle. Unlike the gunners, he could have avoided this fate: it would have been perfectly reasonable for him to have travelled in his air-conditioned car, as the officers of the Household Cavalry often do, but young second lieutenants are enthusiastic, and rightly so. Anyway, the public has enjoyed seeing him on his route and he has enjoyed the admiration, so, as long as that reservoir isn't visible when he dismounts, he doesn't mind too much.

He passes through the archway at twenty minutes to four. Gunner Green crashes to attention and salutes with his sword; the sounds of spur striking spur and boot slamming into tarmac reverberate in the natural echo chamber of the arch. They reverberate, too, in the natural echo chamber of Mark Dawson's skull and he draws pleasure from Gunner Green's performance. Returning the salute, he becomes part of the show; as he rides on, both members of the cast feel pleased with themselves, and then feel unaccountably foolish for having gained satisfaction from something as trivial as a salute. In a few more seconds, Gunner Green has put himself back at ease and Dawson has completed his journey through the arch, turned across the Tilt Yard and responded to the salute of the second dismounted sentry. A gunner opens the wooden gates for him, another holds his horse as he dismounts and a third departs to find the bombardier on duty.

Just as Dawson is surreptitiously patting his backside to find out whether the outside of his uniform is as damp as the inside, Ashley and Raynham reach the parade ground.

'You see, the Mall wasn't built until the early twentieth century and before that Horse Guards was the only approach to both palaces – Buckingham and St James's, that is. Now that we've got the Mall, with the great vista down it from Admiralty Arch, it seems that the sentries are guarding nothing at all, but it's still the official entrance, really.'

Ashley already knows this, but he allows Raynham to continue, enjoying the obvious enthusiasm of his friend for his new posting. A few moments later, he shares Raynham's satisfaction when Gunner Green, ever alert, recognises his new adjutant and the arch echoes again to his salute. Raynham, having assumed that his civilian clothes and comparatively recent appointment would offer anonymity, is pleasantly surprised. Gunner Green correctly interprets his adjutant's thought and feels self-congratulatory once more.

On the Whitehall side of the arch a large crowd has gathered for the approaching ceremony. A genial policeman and a rather less genial female colleague are keeping the spectators behind a line on the side of the square opposite the entrance to the stables.

'We'll stand here.' Raynham heads towards one of the corners which are out of bounds to the public, to the obvious annoyance of the policewoman. She is about to march across to reprimand them when her partner, an old guardsman himself, shakes his head. Sulking, she takes revenge on a Japanese tourist who has placed a foot over the magic line. He understands not a word of her objection and takes a photograph of her. This annoys her even more.

'In a moment, the gunner under the arch will march out and take up a position opposite us. Then a lance bombardier – that's the artillery equivalent of a lance corporal – will come out from the gate and bring the two mounted sentries into the square. After that, the duty bombardier brings out the rest of the guard and then the inspection can begin. Dawson should march on exactly as the clock chimes four.'

Gunner Green carries out his part to the letter: 'Out of the arch, turn towards the crowd, three more paces, and – Halt! Pause – just long enough for them to get the camera out but not long enough for them to take a picture. About – Turn! Stand at – Ease!' An entirely fictional drill sergeant gives the commands inside his head. The bystanders take photographs, most of which are blurred shots on the turn or rather unsatisfactory views of the back of his head. Gunner Green, safely facing away from his audience, risks a small grin to Gunner Scott, his fellow sentry at the gate. Another camera clicks close behind him and the grin becomes larger as he wonders if Mr Jackson of Illinois is there, snapping away at his ceremonially presented buttocks. Such a photograph should be good for fifty quid any time... Then he sees Captain Raynham in the far corner and his grin disappears in a flash.

'Any time now.' Raynham looks at his watch, then up at the Horse Guards clock.

A minute or so later: 'They'd better get a move on.'

But nobody appears. Raynham swears softly.

Ashley notices that the gunner who had been grinning a moment ago, is looking concerned. There are sounds of activity from behind the gates.

Two minutes to four. Raynham observes the seconds passing on his watch. One minute to four: still nothing.

The clock begins to strike the hour.

A soldier appears, no busby, no sword. He walks – almost runs – over to the policeman. There is a passing of information – a question – an answer. The crowd picks up on the tension and a soft buzzing begins. The policeman gives hurried instructions to his colleague and follows the soldier back towards the gates. Raynham, too concerned even to swear, intercepts them.

'What is it? What's up?'

There is a look of relief as the soldier recognises his adjutant. For a fraction of a second he has the instinctive urge to leap to attention. Instead he says, 'Sir, I think you ought to come and see.'

The three go through the gates. Ashley wonders whether he should follow but decides that tact decrees otherwise. He hears the policewoman telling the crowd that the inspection has been cancelled and watches them disperse, slowly, and in bad humour.

Gunner Green and his fellow guards wish somebody would tell them what is going on. There are no standing orders headed "Action to be taken in the Event of a Ceremonial Disaster", so they stay exactly where they are. Gunner Green is feeling rather less pleased with himself now.

A minute passes, no more. Another soldier, also with no sword, but this time wearing his busby, emerges and approaches Ashley.

'Mr Ashley, sir?'

'Yes?'

'Captain Raynham asks if you would come through, sir.'

And so now Ashley, too, goes through the gates, leaving behind the familiar Tilt Yard and entering the private world of Prince Albert's Troop.

*   *   *   *   *

Past the guardroom, the canteen and the bar. Glimpses of abandoned swords and head dresses seen through doorways. Through the small inner yard where the gunners mount up and dismount and past the harness room. Another sword propped against the doorpost. Into the stable – half a dozen or more soldiers crowding around at the far end, creating a Babel of sound. Raynham's raised voice: 'Get back! And for God's sake, shut up!' The policeman speaking calmly into his radio; Mark Dawson vomiting onto the straw in an unoccupied stall.

9

In a far corner, beyond the stalls, yet another soldier. It is as if he has fallen forwards in the "at ease" position. His feet, immaculately booted and spurred, are the regulation distance apart. His hands rest behind his back. Unlike the soldiers gathered around him, he has no dress tunic over his green vest. His braces hang loose around his breeches.

And he has no head.

CHAPTER TWO

AFTERMATH OF MURDER

Ashley sat in the study of his Lonsdale Square apartment. Around him, covering most of the carpet, were newspapers; and covering most of the newspapers was Prince Albert's Troop. The Troop filled pages 1, 2, 4 and 5 of the *Star*; similar amounts in the *Mail* and the *Express*; rather less in the *Mirror*, the *Guardian* and the *Independent* and rather more in the *Telegraph*. The *Times* and the *Sun* were unknown quantities. Edward, Ashley's assistant, had a taste for the Murdoch press and had taken them into the kitchen, where he was making tea.

The macabre death of Bombardier Simon Cooper may have been a personal tragedy; it was certainly a huge embarrassment to the army and marked a crisis for the Troop in particular – but it was God's gift to the newspaper industry. In a holiday season devoid of political news or celebrity scandal, every hack in London had gnawed away at the story until only the bombardier's skeleton seemed to be left. Each dog then chewed on his favourite bone. The *Star* saw the incident as the latest in a series of military disasters rocking the armed forces; the *Guardian* and the *Independent* used the occasion to argue for the abolition of ridiculous empty ceremonial, hinting even at the end of the monarchy itself. The *Telegraph*, taking an approach exactly opposite, shored up the establishment, printed as many full-colour pictures of the Troop as it could get away with, and filled Ashley in on almost all the things he wanted to know.

The Troop had been just one of many units of Horse Artillery when Prince Albert had arrived in England. Stationed near Windsor, they had greeted him with a salute in the Great Park, firing off their guns with such style and aplomb that he had adopted them as his own. Queen Victoria, denying her bridegroom nothing, had ordered that the unit should be henceforth known as "The Prince's Own Troop". When it was pointed out to her that they would certainly be nicknamed "The Potties", she had changed her mind, christening them instead, "Prince Albert's Troop" – and so they have been "The Patties" ever since, which is slightly less embarrassing. There was even talk of kitting them out in the cherry-coloured breeches of the Saxe-Coburgs but that honour finally went to the Eleventh Hussars. The modern-day gunner regards this near miss with considerable relief.

As the army became increasingly mechanised, exchanging horses for armoured vehicles of every description, George VI issued a decree establishing Prince Albert's Troop as the ceremonial battery of the Royal Artillery. The Patties moved to a barracks in north London, riding out to fire salutes on all state occasions. (Here, the *Telegraph* paused to devote a column and a half to a list of Real Birthdays, Official Birthdays, Commemorations, State Visits and other events adorned by the Troop.)

To them was also granted the privilege of escorting any Royal or near-Royal remains to Westminster Abbey: a special gun carriage is maintained for the purpose, pulled by a team of black horses rather than the Troop's usual chestnuts. (And here the *Telegraph* included photographs of the funerals of Lord Mountbatten; Diana, Princess of Wales and the Queen Mother.)

Finally, said the *Telegraph*, the Troop is internationally famous for its Musical Drive, in which six teams, each of six horses, manoeuvre their First World War guns (capable of firing a thirteen-pound shell for a mile and a half) in patterns of increasing complexity. The article went on to castigate the government for abolishing the Royal Tournament, which had always featured the Musical Drive as one of its highlights.

Most of us enjoy reading what we already know, and much of this information was vaguely familiar to Ashley. Still, the article had filled in a few gaps and it provided a useful frame to the extraordinary picture which had been in his mind since yesterday afternoon.

It had only taken about five minutes for more police to arrive. In that time, Raynham had ordered the soldiers into the canteen, sent the lance bombardier to bring in the mounted guards and dispatched Mark Dawson to the lavatory, where a gunner could sponge down his tunic. Ashley had spent the time taking in as much detail as possible.

The first thing he noticed was that the bombardier's hands were not simply resting behind his back; they were strapped together at the wrists, with what Ashley took to be some piece of equestrian kit. It was not, perhaps, the most efficient way of securing a man's hands but it had clearly been adequate for the purpose.

Second, lying in a stall several yards away (explaining why it had not been spotted at once) was the bombardier's head. It could not possibly have rolled there; it must have been thrown, or even kicked. Its mouth was gaping and its eyes staring. The brutal clash of arterial blood on the yellow straw conjured up images of Tudor executions on Tower Hill, or the beheading of Charles I only a few yards away outside the Banqueting Hall. Ashley wondered whether this had inspired the murderer to choose such a particularly bloody way to end a man's life. Had the killer held his victim's head aloft afterwards, proclaiming – or just thinking – 'Behold the head of a traitor,' before flinging it into the vacant stall?

Ancient beheadings had involved an axe and a block. Ashley had looked around for the necessary apparatus for decapitation, but there was nothing in sight that could have substituted for a block. There were, of course, ceremonial swords all over the building. Would it be possible to behead a man with a sword but without a block? Was a ceremonial sword sharp enough for the job? Ashley had approached the torso as closely as he dared; to his untrained eye, it seemed that a single stroke had sufficed. Was it that easy to remove a head? Didn't he remember taking a lurid pleasure in his early schooldays, on hearing that it took three blows of the axe to end the life of Mary, Queen of Scots and – was it? – as many as five for the Duke of Monmouth?

Finally, he had looked at the blood. The pool by the neck and shoulders was just as he would have expected and there were individual splashes for quite a distance in front of it and against the wall; presumably, these had projected out as the body slumped forward and hit the floor. But there were other small patches, spattered seemingly at random, all around the body. If they had spurted out in the act of decapitation, whoever had done the deed must be marked. To his surprise, he found himself hoping that precautions against this had been taken; it would be a shame to plan such an elaborate death, only to be caught so easily.

When the team of police arrived, their first instinct seemed to be to get Ashley and Raynham out of the way. They might have let Raynham stay when he told them that he was the senior officer present, but he blew his chances when he added, 'And my friend here is a private detective'. They were ejected immediately and sent to join the rest of the soldiers in the canteen.

They had left the stable and entered the small inner yard, where Gunners Gillham and Hall, finally relieved, were dismounting. The lance bombardier who had brought them in was helping Gillham to untack, so Raynham lent a hand to Hall, loosening the horse's girth and unbuckling the bridle. These he took into the harness room and Gunner Hall, knowing that the stable was now out of bounds, put a head collar on his horse and looked around for a cloth or sponge to wipe some of the sweat from its eyes and muzzle.

Ashley had watched the soldiers dismount, then lost himself in speculation. Could a mounting block have been used? The one in the yard was concrete and fixed, but perhaps there was a wooden one somewhere? Perhaps…?

His thoughts were interrupted by a furious whinny from Gunner Hall's horse. It rose up, kicking out with its hoofs and did its best to tear itself away from the young soldier. To his credit, Hall just managed to keep hold of it. It pulled away again, its metal shoes clattering violently on the cobbled ground of the yard. The harder Hall tried to steady its head, the more determined it became to tug away. Raynham and the lance bombardier rushed out of the harness room. The lance bombardier took in the situation and seized the head collar just as Hall, his wrist now agonisingly twisted, had been about to let go. The lance bombardier led the horse to the other side of the yard and began to calm it, leaving the gunner standing stunned, apparently torn between nursing his damaged wrist and examining the cloth in his other hand. It seemed to be the cloth that had caused the outburst.

Hall lost interest in his wrist as he unrolled the material. Towards the centre there was a large, fresh bloodstain.

*　*　*　*　*

There were eight gunners in the canteen. If they had been talking, they stopped when Ashley and Raynham entered, and leapt to attention. Ashley noticed that two wide-eyed lads, who looked remarkably similar, were wearing green overalls and lace-up army boots, rather than ceremonial uniforms. The remaining six had either unbuttoned their tunics or removed them altogether; Ashley now began to perceive the gunners as eight apprehensive individuals rather than as a body of identical toy soldiers, capable of only group emotions. Raynham signalled them to sit again and he and Ashley fell into plastic chairs. Gillham, Hall and the lance bombardier arrived, removed their busbies and tunics, then joined the group.

It was the lance bombardier who broke the silence. 'So, what happens now, sir?' he asked, voicing the question for the whole group.

15

'I've no idea, Lance Bombardier Burdett,' said Raynham. 'This is outside my range of experience. Can you tell us anything, Ashley?'

'Well, if it's anything like other murders I've been involved with, we wait.' Ashley perceived the instant interest of the soldiers with a small feeling of satisfaction. 'I think you should all be aware that I'm a detective, but a private detective, nothing to do with the police. Murder is rather like war is said to be: ten per cent thrilling, dangerous excitement and ninety per cent hanging around not doing very much at all.'

'And we've had our excitement,' suggested a blond-haired gunner.

'Precisely. The police will photograph the body from every conceivable angle; they'll comb the area for as long as they feel like it; a doctor will do whatever it is that doctors get up to – and then, when they think that we've sweated it out long enough, they'll see us one by one. It's a long, slow and very boring business.'

'What will they ask us, sir?' This gunner, clearly very nervous, could have been no more than seventeen years old.

'Personal details, of course – name, age, that sort of thing. Then they'll want to establish timings – what you were doing and when. They have to try to recreate everybody's movements as accurately as possible.'

'That'll be a job and a half, sir,' said the lance bombardier.

'Some parts will be easy – obviously, your stretches of duty will fall neatly into place, once they've understood the routine. It's the bits in between that will be difficult – when you went to the stable, the harness room or the canteen. They need to know precise times and, of course, we can rarely be that exact. People forget what they did, or they muddle the order.'

Ashley considered for a moment and then added:

'And whichever of you committed the murder – will lie.'

The reaction was everything that Ashley had expected. Where twelve pairs of eyes had been entirely directed at him, they now looked anywhere else; at each other, at the floor or the ceiling. Chairs scraped on the floor as the soldiers shifted in their seats. Ashley knew that he had created an atmosphere of mistrust. Even Raynham, who knew that Ashley couldn't possibly suspect him, looked awkward.

'I'm sorry to say such an unpleasant thing, but you may as well be prepared. The police will certainly be working on the hypothesis that one – or more – of you is responsible. You'll all be under suspicion until the case is solved. That's the most unpleasant aspect of a crime – if it isn't solved, a lot of innocent people suffer.'

The silence lasted a long time. Finally, Raynham asked, 'Where's Dawson?' Then, turning to the blond-haired gunner, he continued, 'Lang, you were looking after him, weren't you? What have you done with him?'

'I gave him a good sponging down, like you said, sir, then he went off to the guardroom. I think he was a bit embarrassed, sir.'

'Get him in here. No point in his being stuck by himself. We're all in for some embarrassment soon enough.'

'Yes sir.'

When Lang returned with Dawson, Ashley noticed that the lieutenant had sensibly removed his tunic, too. Unlike the gunners, in their green vests, he wore a collarless white shirt. Without his tunic and cap, he looked very young, barely older than the gunner who had asked a question a few minutes earlier, though he must, thought Ashley, be nineteen or twenty. More, if he had been to university before joining the army.

'Come in, Mark, and sit down. Don't look so forlorn – I nearly threw up myself.' Raynham's lie did the trick. Dawson looked sheepish and blushed, but he sat down in the group and was obviously glad to be with the others.

'Thanks, Frank. I telephoned the CO as you told me. He's on his way over.'

'Oh, that'll be nice, sir.' A tall, thin gunner managed the first grin of the afternoon since Gunner Green had smirked across the Tilt Yard.

'It will be *very* nice, Gunner Chadwick,' agreed Raynham. 'Anyone here suffering from constipation? Because, if so, you're in for one hell of a cure…'

Raynham's assessment, if not literally accurate, exactly captured the spirit of the commanding officer's arrival. Ashley and the soldiers indoors were unable to witness Major Benson's approach; had they seen it, they would have been impressed. His car swept onto the parade ground, scattering gravel and a few lingering tourists. He had headed towards the centre arch at an illegally fast speed, alarming Gunner Green who, for want of anything better to do, had returned to his old post. At the last moment, the major had decided that navigating the arch itself at fifty miles an hour was a bad idea, so braked and skidded dangerously on the gravel, ending up only inches away from the massive stones of the archway.

'Bloody hell, it's the Bulldog!' Green had sprung to attention as the major leapt out of the car and strode towards him.

'What's going on, Gunner Green? Any idea?'

'None at all, sir – I've been on stag since three o'clock. All I know is that Captain Raynham's in there, and so are the police, sir. Sorry, sir.'

'All right, Green. I'll see that you're relieved as soon as possible.'

'Thank you, sir.'

Ashley had been amused by his own urge to clasp his arms to his side and stand rigidly to attention as the major entered. He stood up with the rest, only just preserving his civilian identity.

'Right then – yes, thank you, you can all sit down again – who's going to put me in the picture? Raynham?'

'As I understand it, sir, the men were all ready for the four o'clock inspection but, with five minutes to go, Bombardier Cooper was nowhere to be seen. Dawson sent Gunner Sorrell to search the harness room and the stable and Gunner Watson to search the upstairs quarters. And – Sorrell found him.'

18

The very young gunner nodded: 'At the far end of the stable, sir, where all the buckets and brooms are. Hands tied behind his back with a spur strap and his head nowhere to be seen, sir.'

Raynham continued: 'So Dawson went to see for himself.' (Rather unwisely, as it turned out, thought Ashley, though Raynham didn't mention this to the commanding officer.) 'And sent Lance Bombardier Burdett to fetch the duty policeman.'

Lance Bombardier Burdett took up the narrative: 'Coming back, sir, I saw Captain Raynham and asked him to come in. Then a bit later Gunner Carlton was sent to fetch in Mr...?'

'Ashley,' said Raynham and introduced him.

'Sorry you've been caught up in this,' said the major.

'Ashley's a detective, sir, and an old friend – I thought his presence might be of assistance.'

'Ah, I see – and has it been?'

Ashley spoke for himself: 'Not much, I fear. The police arrived very quickly and I was shooed in here straight away. I imagine they're going over the stables now.'

'I see.' Benson turned back to Raynham: 'Have the horses been fed yet?' There was a sense of relief as the major dealt with practicalities.

'No sir – with the police in the stable...'

'Bugger the police, those horses need feeding. You backroom boys,' The two green-clad gunners stirred from their open-mouthed daze. 'That's right, Smith and Smith, come with me and we'll see to it. If the fuzz tries to kick up a stink I'll point out to them that they have no jurisdiction here and can be booted out in a trice. Frankly, I'd rather have them than the Redcaps any day, but they don't know that. Let's go.' The whole room stood as he moved towards the door. 'Oh, and those two chaps outside need relieving. We'll keep the show looking as normal as possible. And by normal, I mean a bottle of whisky on that table by the time I get back.' The major and his escort disappeared.

Lance Bombardier Burdett nodded at two soldiers whom

Ashley now knew to be Gunners Sorrell and Chadwick. Then Raynham said, 'Not Sorrell – he's had enough for today. Sorry Barker,' he turned to a dark-haired gunner who had hitherto been silent, 'I'm going to ask you to slum it on foot for a couple of hours.'

Gunner Barker gave a good-natured grin, which seemed to display a certain amount of relief. 'No problem, sir – I'd rather be outside than hanging around in here doing nothing. I just need to get my kit from the harness room, sir, and then I'll be ready.'

When he was gone, Burdett and Chadwick spent a few moments donning tunics and busbies and gathering up their swords. They quickly checked each other over and left the canteen. Two minutes later, the three soldiers marched smartly through the wooden gates and went through the ritual of relieving the sentries as though nothing had happened.

CHAPTER THREE

AN INTERVIEW WITH THE POLICE

Ashley was quietly pleased with the way he had dealt with the police. It wasn't often that he got the chance to make a CID inspector look foolish, and he found himself looking back on the interview with considerable satisfaction.

They had, naturally, kept him waiting until last. It was nearly ten o'clock before Ashley had been summoned to the harness room, where Inspector Cowan of the Metropolitan Police had set up his headquarters.

Major Benson, having put the inspector firmly in his place concerning his legal position and authority, had insisted on sitting in on all his men's interviews: he wasn't going to have them bullied into any statements they might regret. The thought of his presence terrified the soldiers but they were grateful to him all the same. When Gunner Lang emerged from the harness room and Ashley was ushered in by a police sergeant, the major remained in his chair.

'Perhaps, Major Benson, since we've now finished our preliminary inquiries with your men, you'd like to get away?' But the major, to Cowan's obvious annoyance and to Ashley's amusement, was perfectly content to stay for the final session.

'I'm sure this gentleman is quite capable of standing up for himself – still, I'd be most interested to hear what he has to say. Would you object, Mr Ashley?'

'Not in the least, sir.' Ashley sensed an important ally. Besides, there was a small surprise he had up his sleeve in case he needed to pull the inspector down a peg or two. If he made use of it, it would be good to have an audience.

Inspector Cowan loathed private detectives. By this stage of the evening he also loathed interfering commanding officers and soldiers who were so determined not to incriminate any of their friends that they seemed to have been wandering around all afternoon with their ears covered and their eyes closed. He was in no mood to do Ashley any favours.

'Your full name, please?'

'George Frederick Thomas Ashley'

'And your date of birth?'

Ashley realised that he was in for a war of attrition. Inane question would follow inane question until, he supposed, Cowan considered him to be ground down.

'Fifteenth of November, nineteen sixty-eight.' He toyed with the idea of adding at random, 'It was a Wednesday', but decided against it.

'Your address?'

'54B Lonsdale Square, N1 1EN'

'And your pro...'

'Have you forgotten so quickly, Inspector? Captain Raynham told you that I was a private detective.' First point to Ashley?

'Oh – I had assumed that was just a hobby.' Score equal. Ashley just managed to suppress a scowl.

'Could you tell me in what capacity you were present today?'

'I was here at the invitation of Captain Raynham.'

And so it went on: tedious, barely relevant questions. Cowan was determined neither to ask Ashley's opinion on any aspect of the crime, nor to give him any information. He established the time that Ashley had arrived at Horse Guards and exactly when he went through the gate; he made an assistant write down a detailed list of telephone numbers and email addresses where Ashley could be contacted. He extracted, in as much detail as possible, Ashley's movements over the next few days: 'In the unlikely event that we might need to contact you'. Ashley made most of this part up, doing his best to give the impression that his week was divided between titled ladies and high-ranking government officials. He didn't expect Cowan to believe a word of it, but it all had to be written down.

After half an hour, Cowan brought the interview to a close; 'Well, Mr Ashley, I don't think we need to keep you here any longer.'

And then he made his mistake: 'Unless you have any questions you would like to ask us, of course?' It was a formality; he said the same thing a dozen times that evening, but he had given Ashley the opening he needed.

'Just one thing, Inspector. I wondered if anybody thought to tell the doctor he should check for bruising behind the victim's right knee? It will have been inflicted before death, not like the marks on the head itself. They were caused afterwards.'

For one second, Ashley enjoyed the sight of Cowan's discomfort, then he left the room.

*   *   *   *   *

'I don't get it,' said Edward, who was lounging on the sofa in Ashley's flat. 'That is, I see that you made Cowan look stupid in front of his team, because he treated you like a fool – and yet you had noticed something important that he had missed. But how did you know about the bruising? He still had his trousers on, didn't he?'

'Who? Cowan?'

'No, the body, idiot.'

'Well, breeches, rather than trousers, but otherwise you're right. I guessed at the bruising behind the knee because the easiest way to make a man kneel down is to kick him there. I'm no expert on beheading, I'm glad to say...'

'Let me guess – but you know a man who is.'

'I do, as a matter of fact. Nonetheless, even with limited knowledge, I'd bet you a large sum of money that you can't behead a man when he's standing up. Assuming that our bombardier wasn't co-operating, and didn't therefore kneel of

23

his own accord, it's pretty likely that he'll have received that sharp kick behind his knee.'

'The right one?'

'It's always possible that we have a left-handed murderer, but I'm pretty sure that the soldiers are trained to control the reins with their left hand and carry the sword in their right. The chances are, therefore, that the killer stood on the left of the bombardier and, unless he wanted to get in the way of the sword, his assistant...'

'Assistant?'

'Of course – you don't think all this could have been done by one person do you? The assistant would have stood behind, and to the right, of the victim. Hence the likelihood of bruising behind the right knee. Brilliant, is it not?'

Edward considered. 'Now you've explained it, it doesn't seem so brilliant after all.'

'That's rather like Winnie-the-Pooh saying to Eeyore that he can read the sign once Eeyore has told him what it said. And he was a bear of very little brain: also called Edward, incidentally.'

Edward took revenge by dipping a finger in his tea and flicking a few droplets in Ashley's direction. They fell short and spattered the front page of the *Daily Mail*.

'All right, Christopher Robin, tell me about the post-mortem damage on the head.'

'Actually, I think I'm Owl rather than Christopher Robin; Christopher Robin was genuinely wise and sensible, whereas Owl was just an old fraud. The damage to the head is child's play: it couldn't possibly have rolled all that way, so it must have been propelled there. The force of the impact on landing is very likely to have caused some grazes or scars. If it was kicked – and some odd instinct keeps telling me that it was – the kicking will have caused some more. If we're in luck, the doctor's report will confirm all this and our friend Cowan will have received a lesson in humility.'

'And where do we go from here?'

'Unfortunately, the answer to that very reasonable question is: nowhere. Cowan would rather lick up Lieutenant Dawson's voluminous pile of sick than invite me on the case. Her Majesty's armed forces will leave things to the police, civil or military, and we will be left to follow it in the newspapers, with perhaps the odd snippet from Captain Raynham. A shame really – it's quite the most interesting crime I've come across in years. Is it too early for gin?'

'By about two hours.'

'Ah well. Any chance of some more tea then? And have you been down to check the post yet?'

The post was pretty much as usual: too many bills and circulars; not enough letters bringing work or money; a whining letter from Ashley's sister.

'Anything interesting?'

'An all-too-small cheque from a not-suitably-grateful client. He now accepts that the wife you have been trailing so successfully for the last week is not having an affair, but is, in fact, attending a weight-watcher's class secretly, in the hope of being able to fit into a bikini before the summer is out. Does the poor woman have any chance of achieving her ambition?'

'Not a hope. Milkshakes and cream buns after every session. Anything else?'

'My sister complains that my nephew, Tom, has been awarded the most appalling grades in his latest set of exams and is refusing to return to school for the Upper Sixth. Without actually saying so, she manages to imply that I should do something about it. I, apparently, am the only one he ever seems to listen to. God only knows what makes her think that – I just tell the boy to do exactly what he wants.'

'And therefore he always follows your advice.'

'Good point. Do you have the diary there, Edward?' Edward stretched out from the sofa, which he had reoccupied on returning from his errand, took the diary from a small table and slid it across the floor to Ashley, who opened it.

'We can cross out our suspicious husband, so that means

we have the rest of the day free.'

'And tomorrow – and next week.'

'Well, perhaps something will come along. In the meantime, I have a whim to see an expert on the not-so-subtle art of decapitation. Put your shoes on, Edward – we're going to the Tower of London.'

*　　*　　*　　*　　*

'And so, ladies and gentlemen, imagine the emotions of the unfortunate nine-day Queen, when she saw the headless body of her young husband being brought through *that* gate!' Yeoman Warder Albert Gillick was in full flow. He pointed dramatically, and thirty-two pairs of American eyes followed the direction of his finger.

'The morbid procession passed into the chapel of Saint Peter in Chains.' Sixty-four eyes swivelled round towards the chapel, 'Where the unfortunate Dudley was laid to rest among countless other victims of the wrath of the Tudors. And then Lady Jane began the preparations for her own execution…'

The party of elderly people from Carefree, Arizona, was lapping up every word. Yeoman Warder Gillick stood on the very site of the scaffold and they clustered around, separated from him by a low chain. Most of them, quite reasonably, had only the vaguest idea of English history: Lady Jane Grey could have been Mary, Queen of Scots or Marie Antoinette, for all they knew or cared. Still, it was all very romantic and the grizzled Warder, with his Tudor uniform and ceremonial mace, looked magnificent. His account swelled to a climax: Lady Jane, blindfolded, groped for the block and the next second, his arm raised, Gillick held aloft an imaginary severed head. Several ladies, incongruously, applauded.

'Thank you, ladies, thank you. In a moment, Yeoman Warder Watkins will take you over to the Wakefield Tower, where his late Majesty, King Henry VI was brutally done to death by Richard, the hunchbacked Duke of Gloucester, afterwards King of England. In the meantime, if anybody has any questions, I shall do my best to answer them.'

A cheerful lady in enormous sunglasses wanted to know if a guillotine had ever been used in England. 'No, madam, the English aristocrat met his end resting his upper-class head on a good English block, and had it neatly severed with an English axe, wielded by the sturdy arms of an honest English executioner. The guillotine, as you will be aware, is a nasty French contraption, a device invented by a nation too squeamish and effeminate to wield a weapon properly.' This final comment provoked instant applause from the whole party; one ex-military type even ventured a rebel yell. Thus, Yeoman Warder Gillick's one-man show came to a triumphant conclusion.

'And now, ladies and gentlemen, here is Yeoman Warder Watkins, who will escort you to the Wakefield Tower. Thank you, sir, but we are not supposed to accept – well, if you insist – thank you too, sir, madam…'

As Gillick shiftily pocketed a fistful of notes, Ashley and Edward walked over.

'Gillick, you rogue, if degrees were awarded in bullshit, you'd pass *summa cum laude.*'

'Mr Ashley, sir, what a delight to see you! And this is…?'

'Edward, my assistant, who has just believed every single word of that nonsense you were peddling to the tourists.'

Gillick grinned wickedly: 'Well, sir, strictly speaking, the facts were largely correct, though I may have adorned them with a few dramatic illustrations.'

'All your own work?'

'Oh no, sir – the trick of standing as if holding a bleeding head has been handed down from warder to warder for generations. The bit about the French was all mine though. Went down well, didn't it?'

A few minutes later, they were sitting in the tiny front room of Gillick's quarters: one of a dozen small houses built into the side of the moat wall. This he shared with four ghosts and Mrs

Gillick, 'Who is not such good company, but better at doing the housework.' His wife being out, Gillick disappeared into the kitchen and came back with three bottles of ale and two mismatching glasses. 'You're in luck – you'd have only had tea if she hadn't been out making a nuisance of herself somewhere. Her latest fad is that she wants the ghosts exercised.'

Ashley had a brief vision of four spectres in baby reins being taken for a good brisk walk by the formidable Mrs Gillick.

'I said to the Padre, leave the ghosts alone, but if you know a prayer that will make *her* disappear, I'll be the first to say "Amen".' He gave Ashley and Edward a glass and a beer each, then took a good pull at his ale, straight from the bottle. Refreshed, he tugged at his tunic and stepped out of it. Resplendent in his buckled shoes, and a string vest, he joined Ashley and Edward at the diminutive dining table.

'You need to know, young Master Edward, because Mr Ashley will have been far too modest to tell you, that you are working for the best detective, private, or otherwise...' (Gillick paused to sniff contemptuously as he thought of some of the "otherwises" who had crossed his path over the years), '...in London. In England, probably. A few years back, when you were still in short trousers and he wasn't that long out of them himself, he got my son out of a very nasty spot of trouble. I've been grateful to him ever since, and even Mrs Gillick has got him on her very short list of "People She Approves Of". So, Mr Ashley, assuming that you didn't just call on me to admire my fancy dress costume...'

'Splendid as it is, your supposition is correct.'

'Then what can I do for you?'

'You can tell us, if you don't mind, as much as you know about the process of decapitation. None of your anecdotal rubbish; we need the solid facts.'

Gillick beamed and his string vest expanded with importance. 'I'll do better than tell you, sir – if you can hang on until just after five o'clock, I'll *show* you.'

CHAPTER FOUR

THE EXECUTION OF EDWARD

At five past five, Ashley and Edward were waiting patiently outside the Martin Tower. After their liquid luncheon with Gillick, they had spent a pleasantly hazy afternoon exploring some of England's more spectacular history. They had 'done' Henry VI, the Princes in the Tower, and a whole host of Tudors who lay buried in the chapel. They had viewed the Crown Jewels and explored the Fusilier museum. In short, they had been everywhere except, at Gillick's special request, St. Martin's tower.

At four o'clock, they had headed for the tearoom. Over a pot of sweepings from the floor of the tea factory, Ashley had written a jolly postcard to his wayward nephew (the picture showed the execution of the Earl of Essex) and a consoling one to his sister (Lady Jane looking tragic and resigned). Edward, with no family to speak of, had guzzled most of the tea and eaten two cream cakes. By a quarter to five, the tourists had started to drift away; at ten to, the party from Carefree, having denuded the gift shop of T-shirts, baseball caps and replicas of the Crown Jewels, had staggered towards their bus. By five o'clock itself, the Tower was practically deserted.

Gillick arrived barely a minute after Edward and Ashley. He was now dressed – to Edward's obvious relief – in a perfectly respectable set of corduroys and a blazer with a hideous regimental badge on the left pocket. He had a regimental tie on as well: Ashley was rather disappointed to note that not only did the tie correctly match the badge, but that both indicated accurately the unit in which Gillick had actually served. With Gillick was another man, similarly dressed, but a shade smarter in every respect. There was no badge on the blazer and his silk Hussar tie was distinctly classier than Gillick's polyester memorial to a none-too glorious career in the Corps of Transport.

'This, Mr Ashley, is Major Charles Hicks, Deputy Constable of the Tower. He knows everything there is to know about removing heads from shoulders.' They went through the formalities. Major Hicks seemed to be an affable sort. ('He used to be plain Charlie Hicks before they gave him a quartermaster's commission, since when he's come over all posh', volunteered Gillick.) He was spending his retirement at the Tower researching for a book, to be called, *Heads You Lose: Decapitation in England 1450-1750*.

'The Constable is taking a holiday at Frinton, Mr Ashley, so you've come at just the right time. He's a very worthy man – Cavalry, of course – but has no interest in the supernatural or the more macabre aspects of history. This is regarded as a sad failing by most of the residents of the Tower. My own house boasts three ghosts, including that of Lord Hastings who, for reasons best known to himself, frequently perches on the Ali Baba basket while my wife takes a bath. The Constable has seven ghosts in his house and has never seen a single one.'

All the time he was delivering this speech, the Deputy Constable was sorting through an enormous key ring. He selected a key of middling size and tried it in the door of St Martin's Tower. There was a satisfying sound of ancient but well-oiled bolts shunting around and the door yielded. The major led the way upstairs, continuing his monologue: 'He would have taken a very dim view of us inviting you into the Martin Tower after hours, whereas his predecessor wouldn't have dreamed of giving an evening's entertainment without offering to show his guests the instruments of torture. It was surprising how many of them wanted to try being strapped to the rack.'

They reached a landing where beyond a rope, tantalisingly

out of reach of the general public, were sets of thumbscrews, a brazier with branding irons, a curious ladder-like arrangement with large and vicious spikes and, of course, the rack. Major Hicks continued upwards, without pausing: 'Of course, to those of us whose interests are more sophisticated and, er, *terminal*, shall we say, these are just childish playthings. It was often sufficient merely to show the victim the instruments of torture to achieve one's purpose.'

Edward gave Ashley a glance, which he accurately interpreted as 'What sort of mad-house have you brought me into?' Ashley responded with a shrug, and a lop-sided smile, which could be translated as: 'It's too late to back out now,' so they followed Major Hicks up the stairs. The next landing contained only two items, combined into a single exhibit: behind a Perspex screen was an executioner's block and, leaning against the block, was an axe.

'Now there, gentlemen, you see a display which has obsessed connoisseurs of death for generations. I'm told that the late, great Albert Pierrepoint would visit the Tower once a year and spend at least an hour in this chamber.'

'It must have been like a writer of prose being introduced to poetry,' Gillick observed, wistfully. He gave a sigh to make his string vest ripple. 'Er, you did say, sir…?'

'I know I did, Gillick. It's completely out of order, of course, but as the Constable is away and given that our interest is purely *professional*…'

The major reached into his trouser pocket and brought out a much smaller key. He fitted this into a lock in the Perspex screen and slid the barrier to one side. With Gillick, he crouched down to enter the chamber and they carried the block and the axe out onto the landing.

Ashley, who had been half regretting coming here a few minutes earlier, now began to feel himself strangely drawn to these two instruments of death. A sideways glance at Edward showed him that he, too, was staring in fascination. Ashley asked a tentative question: 'And these – actually…'

'That's right, sir,' said Gillick proudly. 'This is not some silly replica like you might see in Madame Tussauds: this is the real thing. This very block and this self-same axe were used to behead Lord Lovat...'

'Ninth of April, seventeen forty-seven,' interjected the major. 'The last man in England to suffer death by decapitation. A crowd of over ten thousand turned out to watch, and so many climbed onto a gallery erected for the occasion that it collapsed, killing several spectators. Lord Lovat is said to have been very amused by this episode. As you can see from the number of axe marks on the block, it must have been used for several other executions as well.'

'And,' Edward spoke for the first time, 'How did they actually, er, *do it*?'

Full of enthusiasm, Gillick and Hicks both began to explain. Strictly speaking, the warder should have given way to his superior, but the major politely backed off.

'Well, Master Edward, you will observe that the top of the block is carved out on either side. That side which is nearest you has a very large hollow, to accommodate the shoulders of the condemned. The far side has a similar, but smaller, niche for the chin. The neck, therefore, rests on the central ridge, thus facilitating its efficient severance. If, young sir, you'd just like to...?'

To his own astonishment, and to Ashley's amusement, Edward found himself kneeling in front of the block, his hands resting on its two sides: 'What shall I do?' he asked.

'The very words of Queen Jane herself!' cried Gillick, triumphantly. 'Just lean forwards, sir, and – there!' Edward's shoulders and chin fitted neatly into the hollows. As he asked his next question, he felt his Adam's apple quivering against the two inches of wood with which his neck had contact. Had Lord Lovat and the others experienced the same sensation on this very block?

'What do I do with my hands? Would they be tied behind my back?'

'Good Lord, no sir! Only the upper classes are accorded the privilege of being beheaded. As an aristocrat, you are expected to be a willing participant in your own execution. There is no need, therefore, for you to be bound in any way. The custom was that you would say a prayer in the position you now hold and, when finished, you would extend your arms outwards, thus showing your executioner that you were ready to receive the fatal blow.'

Edward stretched out his arms as if he was playing a game of aeroplanes. As he did so, he felt the weight of his head pull down on the far side of the block, so that the pressure of the ridge on his neck became greater. 'Like this?' he gurgled.

'Precisely sir!' said Gillick, while the major made appreciative grunting sounds. 'And now consider the overall picture, Master Edward. You are on Tower Green, surrounded by a crowd of thousands. A high platform has been erected for you so that as many as possible may view your spectacular transition from life to death. On one side of you stand the Constable of the Tower, a clergyman and a select group of friends. On the other side is your executioner, whom you have just forgiven for the bloody act he is about to perpetrate. You are staring into a wicker basket containing straw and sawdust. The crowds fall silent – the drums begin to beat...'

Edward found himself so caught up in the situation that his heart became one of the drums, pounding its rhythms against his ribs, faster and faster; sweat began to stream down his forehead, dripping onto the stone floor beneath; the ridge of the block pressed ever harder against his neck, so that breathing was becoming impossible. His eyes began to water, blurring his vision. He felt he could hear the soldiers beating their drums at an ever-increasing pace and with ever more violence.

And then... He could not believe what he was thinking.

Do it! Come on, do it! I want it to happen! I want to see the floor rising towards me – to hear the blood gush out of my own neck and feel the hot liquid spattering my head! Hold it aloft and let me hear the cheers – DO IT!'

Ashley said calmly, 'Are you all right, Edward?'

The spell was broken: there was no crowd, there were no drums...

'We can stop if you like.'

They had stopped. Edward had staggered up from his position and had actually used the block as a seat. With his feet apart, his hands on his knees and his head slumped forward, he obeyed Ashley's instructions to breathe slowly and deeply. Gradually, the world came back into focus. He lifted his head and was aware of Ashley, gazing with real concern into his eyes. Then he saw Gillick, remorseful and worried, and Hicks, shifting awkwardly on his feet. Ashley passed him a handkerchief and Edward accepted it gratefully, wiping the perspiration from his face.

Hicks cleared his throat and made a very sensible suggestion: 'I think we should all go back to my house for a drink.'

*　　*　　*　　*　　*

Major Hicks' house was larger and grander than Gillick's. Much of the furniture was of great age and value, and the pictures on the wall were genuine Tudor portraits on wooden panels. 'It all comes with the house,' he said, as Ashley and Edward stared about them. 'Got my own stuff in store. Here, sit down and drink this.'

Edward found himself holding a balloon glass almost a third full of brandy. He took a good-sized gulp and felt much better.

'The Tower is an extraordinary place,' mused Hicks, 'And, come to think of it, after everything that's happened here, it would be remarkable if it wasn't. The atmosphere can have very strange psychological effects. Warders and the other resident staff get used to it gradually, but I'm afraid we rather threw you in at the deep end. Sorry about that.'

'I'm sorry too,' added Gillick. 'If I'd realised the effect I was

34

going to have, I'd never have asked you to kneel down.'

Half way through his brandy, Edward was feeling more relaxed about the whole thing. He was even beginning to enjoy the attention. 'Have you ever tried that experiment before?'

'No – and we shan't be trying it again. You, Master Edward, are the only person ever to have knelt down at that block and lived to tell the tale.'

'The strange thing is, I was so – *hypnotised* is the only word I can think of – that I desperately wanted to go through with it. Were you actually standing over me with the axe poised?'

'Thank goodness, no. I was getting rather too caught up with the whole thing as well – if I'd have lifted the axe, I'm not sure I could have trusted myself. I was, however,' and here Gillick became his former cheerful self, 'Planning to conclude my act by grabbing your hair and making as if to hold your head up, like I did for the tourists this afternoon. Oh, they'd have loved to have seen that, they would.'

'I think,' said Edward, thoughtfully, 'that I should have been violently sick all over the block.'

Gillick beamed: 'Oh sir, they'd have *adored* it!'

*   *   *   *   *

Several drinks later, the evening was becoming very genial. Hicks and Gillick seemed to be competing to see who could tell the best Tower ghost story, and Edward egged them on by gasping in all the right places and asking detailed questions. More than once, Ashley suspected that the two, Gillick especially, were improvising their answers, but who cared? Then an anecdote and a bottle of wine came to a simultaneous end and there was a lull.

'I'm conscious of the fact, Mr Ashley, that you came here for scientific information and all we've given you is one failed demonstration and a whole lot of gossip. Before we sink into oblivion…,' (here, there was the satisfying sound of a cork being drawn) '…is there anything you'd like to know?' The major sniffed the cork and trickled a small amount of wine into his glass; he tasted it, smiled approvingly, then poured for Ashley and Edward before filling up his own. Gillick was drinking beer, accumulating an impressive collection of empty cans by his chair.

Ashley devoted a moment to the new wine. 'Yes, there are one or two things I'd like to know. But I'm not so sure the demonstration was a complete failure. I know it was pretty awful at the time, especially for Edward, but it's given me a very good sense of what an execution must have been like. Now, I'm interested in a recent murder, as you've probably realised…'

'Not yesterday's Horse Guards case? Dreadful thing, of course, but fascinating, absolutely fascinating.'

'Precisely. I now think I understand – as far as it's possible – how it must have felt to have been involved. That gives me an insight into the minds of the people who were present, which could prove to be very valuable. If you could add to my psychological understanding by helping me with some factual information, I'd be very grateful.

'In the first place, there was no obvious sign of an axe and a block. I haven't been allowed to look around the place carefully but I'm assuming that the murder was committed with a sword. Is that likely?'

'By far the best way of doing it,' said Hicks. 'The axe can be bloody clumsy, actually – the weighting is all wrong. There were a lot of botched executions using an axe. As long as the sword is sharp enough, and the hand steady, it should be very efficient. When Henry VIII had Anne Boleyn beheaded, he sent to France for an expert swordsman.'

'He was a bastard, but my God, he had style,' said Gillick, appreciatively.

'Would you need a block?'

'No, absolutely not; you'd be likely to strike the far edge of the block with the blade and be unable to sever the head properly. Also, the downward stroke implied by the use of a block is natural to the axe, but less so to the sword. The sword stroke is most effective from right to left (assuming a right-handed executioner) with only a slight downward action.'

'Could a modern ceremonial sword do the job?'

'Only if it had been sharpened to a much higher degree than normal. You *can* behead with a blunt axe or sword, but it's a very messy and time-consuming job. The other point to make here is that continental swords were quite large affairs, with the hilt grasped in both hands. A ceremonial sword can only be held with one hand.'

'Is that a problem?'

'Probably not, as long as it was sharp enough.' Hicks stood up and experimented with a number of imaginary sword strokes, some two-handed and some with just his right hand: 'Not much in it, one way or the other.' He sat down again. 'Does that help?'

'Enormously. Just a couple more questions, then I'm done. How long do you think it would take to sharpen a ceremonial sword to the point where it could become an efficient beheading weapon?'

'That's tricky. If you had a proper sharpening wheel set up, probably not more than fifteen minutes – but that's unlikely. My guess is that you'd have to do it by hand with a whetstone and that would take a long time. Well over an hour, possibly two or three. Even more, maybe. Sorry, that's outside my experience.'

'Not to worry, it's good enough to be going on with. I'm sure you're right about not having a proper wheel set up. Do you think it would be easy to spot that a sword had been sharpened in this way?'

'Hmm, tricky again. Obviously, if you were to get close enough, the answer would be yes, especially if you were looking out for it. But from three or four feet away? Probably not. Much would depend on the skill of the person sharpening the weapon.'

Ashley considered: 'I think that we can be sure that at least one of our killers is a very skilled person indeed.'

CHAPTER FIVE

TAKING ON THE CASE

By the weekend, Edward was feeling rather proud of his strange experience. When Ashley returned to the flat after a Saturday morning exploring antiques in Camden Passage, he was amused to hear Edward's voice speaking boastfully:

'That's right, *the one they really used to use* – it was *weird...* I thought it was actually going to happen... Just imagine it – all your blood *spurting out...* Well, that occurred to me too...'

The voice was coming from the kitchen, so Ashley turned into the study, shut the door, and relaxed into one of the armchairs. Although Wednesday's murder was still very much on his mind, there was little point in exploring it further. The case was in the hands of the police, and that was that. There had been nothing to learn from Friday's newspapers; these had continued to trumpet the scandal but had been noticeably lacking in details. This morning, the murder had been knocked off the front pages by an announcement from a minor starlet, that she was leaving her footballer husband to set up home with the goalkeeper of a rival team.

Having run out of available friends, Edward joined Ashley in the study and poured gin. 'No post, no news, no work, nobody called and nothing's happened,' he announced cheerfully. 'How was your morning? Anything good at the market? Cheers, by the way.' He took up his usual supine position on the sofa.

'Cheers. I looked at some swords but didn't learn anything we didn't already know. I nearly bought a present for my sister...'

38

'Gobstoppers?'

'Don't be rude. It was a rather fine *art deco* brooch that would have gone very well with one of her outfits and would have cheered her up a bit. But it cost a lot of money – and I don't have that much at the moment.'

'And when *you* don't have any money, *I* don't,' observed Edward nonchalantly. 'Famous private detective George Ashley gives a financial sneeze: Edward Montmorency de Vere Radford, his valued assistant and cultural advisor, catches financial influenza. Are we completely broke?'

'Almost – and I thought your middle name was Jason?'

'Well, I made up the "Montmorency de Vere" bit.'

'Yes, I suppose I would too, if I was called Jason. No – don't throw that cushion, I'll spill my gin. Did you make up the bit about "valued assistant and cultural advisor" as well?'

'I read it in a colour supplement somewhere. I thought it sounded rather good.'

'Well then, valued assistant, what shall we do? What do you advise?'

Edward mused. 'As I see it, there isn't going to be any more work until the crooks and society ladies come back from Benidorm. So we could: a) go on holiday ourselves – except we haven't any money; or, b) dump ourselves on your sister, free of charge – except that she hates my guts.'

'I can't think why.'

'Don't interrupt: c) we could give up detecting altogether and get a job stacking shelves in Waitrose – it would pay the bills and we'd probably get to meet a nicer class of customer. Finally: d) as your cultural advisor, I could suggest that you sell the Widgery to tide us over for a bit. Any of those any good?'

Ashley contemplated the moorland landscape scene above the fireplace. Like everything of any value in the flat and, indeed, the flat itself, it had been a legacy from his godfather. He was rather fond of it: 'I'd rather not sell the Widgery unless I really have to. On the whole, I think that we should combine option b) with option c) – *I'll* go and stay, free of charge, with my beloved sister, and *you* can go and stack shelves in Waitrose to pay off the bills. How about that?'

'That would *not* be a good idea,' said Edward, emphatically.

In the end, they came to a decision of sorts. If the Monday post brought no work, they would devote the mornings of the week to putting the flat in order: a long-neglected task. In the afternoons, they would visit such galleries and museums as had no admission charges and have tea at the Military Club; in the evenings they would eat in frugal style at home.

'Which means cutting down to one bottle of wine,' observed Ashley, dryly.

'Each?' asked Edward, hopefully.

'Hmm…'

*   *   *   *   *

By half past nine on Monday morning, the only way to put off the housework was by arguing over who should carry out which task. Ashley thought it entirely reasonable to expect Edward to begin with the fridge, the oven and other ghastly parts of the kitchen, whilst he himself would spend the morning going through the drawers of his desk, putting papers in order. Edward, in contrast, argued that cleaning the fridge was no task for a young man of impressionable years and that it should be left to a gentleman of maturity, whose natural development was in no danger of being warped by the experience. They compromised: Edward would clean the fridge if Ashley pulled an equal weight by washing up. If work was going well, they would allow themselves to break for gin at eleven o'clock.

Then the telephone rang. It was Raynham.

'Hello George, may I come over? It's about this blasted murder, of course. The commanding officer wants you to take it on, if you will.'

*   *   *   *   *

At half past ten, the fridge was still mouldy, the rancid pile of washing up still teetered menacingly by the sink and Raynham, an impressive figure in his service uniform, was sitting on the sofa putting Ashley in the picture. Anticipating the riches to come, Edward had gone out to buy limes for the gin.

'Cowan, needless to say, is getting nowhere. He's been charging about trying to bully the chaps into telling him things and they've all clammed up like nuns on a vow of silence. Soldiers don't mind taking a bit of hard talk from their own kind, but they're not prepared to take it from outsiders. To make matters worse, the Military Police keep trying to get involved, so there've been some almighty rows between them and Cowan – during which nothing has been done about the actual crime.'

'Sounds healthy.'

'You don't know the best bit yet; first thing this morning, the Queen rang.'

'Really? I take it that this is not to be regarded as a Good Thing? She wasn't just ringing to invite you all to tea?'

'Absolutely not. Of course, it wasn't the Queen in person; it was one of her secretaries. The CO took the full blast but I was listening in on my extension. Apparently, Her Majesty is in a filthy temper, mainly because this all happened in the first place, and then because it hasn't been cleared up straight away. A load of Commonwealth leaders are arriving in September and if the matter isn't closed by then, she's going to cancel their gun salute – she says she doesn't want her guests greeted by a bunch of murder suspects.'

'If one believes half of what one reads about some Commonwealth leaders, it would be entirely appropriate.'

'Well, there is that. The CO made the entirely reasonable protest that the matter was in the hands of the police and asked what he was supposed to do – and the reply came back, "It is Her Majesty's wish that you shall do whatever is necessary." There was then a dark hint that, if things weren't sorted out – soonest – the whole unit might be posted up to Catterick.'

41

Ashley winced: 'Nasty.'

'*Very* nasty. Anyway, that's why I'm here: the Bulldog was impressed with the way you put one over on Cowan last week. He wants you to come and stay in the Officers' Mess for a bit – for however long it takes you, in fact.'

'That would be a new experience,' Ashley savoured the prospect.

'Does that mean I can tell him you've agreed?'

'I think it does, but I have to ask one awkward question.' Ashley shifted uncomfortably; he always hated this bit.

'If you mean what I think, your fee is all arranged. The CO is an old boozing chum of the Adjutant-General and he got on the phone to him straight away. Just put your bill in and the MOD will pay.'

'That's rather good. It will be nice to get some of my income tax back.'

'Absolutely. The Bulldog suggested that the A-G might sneak your fee from a budget he disapproves of and the A-G said that was the best financial suggestion he'd heard all year. You're going to be paid by the Armed Forces Equal Opportunities Programme – so make sure you put in a big claim.'

*   *   *   *   *

Half an hour later, suitcase in hand, Ashley stood on the pavement of Lonsdale Square with Edward, Raynham and three young boys. These last were gazing alternately at Raynham and his army Land Rover in awed fascination. Edward was juggling sulkily with two limes.

'Is he taking you away?' asked the bravest boy.

'Not for very long,' Raynham smiled, then took custody of Ashley's suitcase and heaved it into the back of the Land Rover.

'They've found out that Mr Ashley is a Dangerous War Criminal,' said Edward and three pairs of childish eyes widened. 'He is responsible for Numerous Atrocities.'

'And I think I'd better go before I commit another,' said Ashley, climbing into the passenger seat. 'Don't forget about the fridge, Edward.'

The Land Rover roared away, drowning out Edward's response. 'I thought of bringing a driver along,' said Raynham, 'but this way we can talk without our conversation going around the whole barracks.'

'Good. Are you in a position to fill me in on a few details or do I have to liaise with the odious Cowan?'

'We rather assumed you'd like to work separately from him. Right from the start, the Bulldog has insisted on having copies of everything, in case the Redcaps really do move in. Cowan didn't like giving them to him, but wasn't given a choice. You can see them when we get to the Mess but I've read them as well...'

'So Cowan doesn't suspect *you*? Since you couldn't possibly have done it, I assumed you'd be top of his list.'

'As to whom he suspects, God only knows. Actually, I shouldn't think he realises I've had access to anything – he has no understanding of what my job involves.'

'Presumably Major Benson sees nothing that hasn't already passed over your desk?'

'Exactly; so I know pretty much everything that Cowan knows. Ask away and I'll do my best.'

Ashley spent a moment organising his thoughts and then said: 'Three small but important details and then one big chunk of information. First of all, where was the sword?'

'In Cooper's own scabbard in the harness room.'

'A nice touch.'

'It'd been wiped clean, of course, but there were detectable traces of Cooper's blood on it and the blade had been sharpened.'

Ashley digested this information and then asked: 'Could anyone apart from the twelve gunners and the lance bombardier have been involved?'

'Cowan doesn't think so – not that that means anything, of

course. Nobody could have come through the main gates without being observed. There's a back gate which is hardly ever used and it's possible that somebody might have come through that way.'

'Was it locked?'

'Yes, and bolted on the inside. I say that it's hardly used, but this being the army, of course, it's regularly cleaned and the lock kept well oiled. So there were no useful signs of broken cobwebs or recent use of a rusty lock. Cowan checked for fingerprints, but didn't get anything useful.'

'Naturally. Who has a key?'

'We know of three keys: one in the guardrooms at Horse Guards, another in Knightsbridge Barracks and the third back at our place.'

'So reasonably, but not necessarily easily, accessible. Did any of them show obvious signs of recent use?'

'No.'

Again Ashley paused for thought. 'Well, it doesn't sound promising, but it's worth bearing in mind. Now, the last of the small questions: how did the killers prevent themselves being spattered with blood?'

'They wore coveralls – those big green overalls which will fit over your smart kit when you've a messy task to do. There are always sets around. The backroom boys wear them nearly all day, but even the sentries slip them on if they want to check up on their horses or buff up a piece of equipment. There were two bloody ones folded over the partition wood of the last stall.'

'That all fits. Now the big one; tell me about the doctor's report.'

'The doctor used fancy descriptions of bones and muscles of course, but the long and the short of it was that death, as you would expect, was caused by the severance of the head from the shoulders in a single stroke with a sharpened object, such as a sword. The stroke appeared to have been administered by a person standing slightly behind and to the left of the victim.'

'Does that mean we can immediately eliminate any left-handed soldiers?'

Raynham confirmed what Ashley had already thought: 'No. All sword drill is done with the right hand because, when mounted, the left hand is required to control the reins. Any left-handed soldier would be able to wield a sword with his right hand – though whether he could do it with the force necessary, I couldn't say.'

'I see. And do we have any left-handers amongst the suspects?'

'Lance Bombardier Burdett and one of the Smith twins – not that I suspect either of them, of course.'

'Sorry, it's an unpleasant term. Why only one twin? If you mean the two chaps in the green coveralls, they looked identical to me.'

'Yes, they were two of what we call the "backroom boys"; there are four altogether. They don't go out on guard, but look after the horses and help the other chaps with their kit. For the four o'clock inspection, two of them – Watson and Carlton, last Wednesday – get into ceremonials to make up the numbers and the other two – the Smith twins – stay behind. The twins are what's called "mirror image" rather than identical, so one is left-handed, the other right-handed. There are lots of other minor differences between them as well. We've become quite good at telling them apart.'

'Fascinating. All right, go on with the doctor's report.'

'As you guessed, to the annoyance of Cowan, there was a large bruise behind the right knee, inflicted before death, and considerable scarring of the head itself, inflicted afterwards. The doctor said that this couldn't have been caused simply by the head falling onto the floor. It *could* have resulted from the impact of landing on the other side of the stable, assuming that it was thrown fairly hard.'

'Did the doctor go on to hypothesise that the head might have been kicked?'

'I was just about to say it. Not a pleasant thought, is it?

Killing a chap in cold blood is bad enough, but to play football with his head…'

'I know. All I can say is that Edward and I had an elaborate introduction to the art of beheading on Thursday and the psychology of the situation is very disturbing. I'll tell you about it over a drink some time. I don't think one can expect normal patterns of behaviour to predominate. Is it too much to hope that Cowan searched for bloodstains on all the boots?'

'He made a visual check on the soles straight away – predictably, lots of people had them. They'd all crowded round, if you remember. He didn't check the uppers until the doctor made that suggestion about the head being kicked across the stable.'

'By which time, any trace had been removed and about ten layers of polish added?'

'Exactly – he found nothing. Do you want anything else from the doctor's report?'

'Two things – blood other than that on the head and the body, and his suggested timing for the killing.'

'The act of decapitation had caused a considerable amount of blood to flow from the neck and head…'

'I remember it well: it was all over the place. I should have been more specific: was the positioning of other blood consistent with the Bombardier being killed on the spot where he was found, or had he been killed and then moved out of sight? Before you tell me, I'll guess that he was killed where we saw him. Am I right?'

'The doctor was pretty sure of it.'

'Good. I didn't get long to see things, but I think I would have noticed the initial splashes being in the wrong place and then any trail leading to the new position. What about timing?'

'According to Cowan's sergeant, who is quite a good sort, doctors are notoriously cagey about this…'

'I know,' said Ashley, with feeling. 'They're scared of being too specific and then hearing that there's evidence that the body was alive and well half an hour after the official time of death.

Because of that, they tend to give the largest span of time possible, just to cover themselves. You can see their point, I suppose, but it's not much help in catching a murderer. What timings did he suggest?'

'Probably, and he stressed the "probably", at some time between a quarter past two and a quarter to four.'

'Sounds pretty useless for our purposes. Can we eliminate anyone?'

'No one at all. There was a complete change of sentries – both mounted and dismounted – at three o'clock, taken by Lance Bombardier Burdett. Cooper could have been killed before the new guard went out or after the old guard came in. That doesn't take into account the backroom boys, who were around all the time – as was Lance Bombardier Burdett, other than when he was on the guard change. Thirteen suspects, to use your term, and apparently no way of eliminating any of them. Any more medical questions?'

Ashley pondered: 'I don't think so; not at the moment.'

'Good, because here we are. Welcome to the headquarters of Prince Albert's Troop Royal Horse Artillery.'

Raynham swung the Land Rover into the barracks and an armed sentry saluted with his rifle. Once again, Ashley had the sensation of leaving behind familiar things and entering the arcane world of the Troop.

CHAPTER SIX

THE OFFICERS

Raynham pulled up the Land Rover outside an ivy-clad, neo-Georgian building. Its restrained, classical beauty contrasted harshly with the surrounding functional army architecture (nineteen-sixties, Ashley guessed). As they alighted, a Mess orderly appeared at the door.

'Good morning, sir.'

'Morning, Robin. This is Mr Ashley, who will be staying with us for a few days.'

'Yes sir, so I understand. How do you do, sir? Do you have any luggage?' He was deferential, not subservient, a distinction which pleased Ashley. Raynham answered on his behalf: 'In the back.'

'Very good, sir – I'll take it up to Mr Ashley's room. Lunch will be ready in twenty minutes, sir; Major Benson hopes that you will join him and the other officers for drinks in the morning room.'

'Thanks Robin.'

'Thank you, sir.'

The morning room, where they found Major Benson and four other officers, was just to the left of the main entrance. As they walked in, a second orderly appeared with a tray containing two ample glasses of gin and tonic; 'Major Benson said you'd be needing a drink, Mr Ashley, sir.' Ashley took the drink gratefully and then turned towards the commanding officer, who was heading in his direction. The room had fallen silent.

'Mr Ashley, we are all *very* glad to see you.' The major shook Ashley's hand warmly and then brought him into the small group of officers. Ashley noticed that they were wearing different orders of dress, presumably appropriate to the duties they had been carrying out that day. The major himself was in his brown service uniform, like Raynham, except that he was wearing trousers and shoes rather than breeches and riding boots. He had also removed his leather Sam Browne belt; out of the corner of his eye, Ashley noticed Raynham doing the same thing, placing the belt on a table where there was already another, together with a selection of caps and berets.

'Gentlemen, Mr Ashley, as you all know, has come to help us pull through the present crisis. I'm sure that you will all do your utmost to make him feel welcome and will co-operate with him in all matters pertaining to the investigation of the case. Now, Mr Ashley, you already know Frank, of course; you've also met Dawson briefly...'

Ashley smiled and shook hands with Mark Dawson, who today was dressed in combat shirt and trousers, looking significantly more composed than when Ashley had seen him last. In succession, he met Captain Richard Shaw, the riding master, and Lieutenant John Dutton, both of whom were wearing open-necked khaki shirts with breeches and riding boots; finally, he was introduced to Second Lieutenant Justin Fox, who looked even younger than Mark Dawson. Fox was the only officer not to be in uniform: Ashley thought, not for the first time, that it was remarkable how a soldier in civilian clothes still managed to look military; whereas, presumably, if he ever had to put on a khaki tunic, he would still look utterly civilian.

The major interrupted his thought: 'Now, Dutton here, Fox and Dawson are the bachelors of the unit – along with Raynham, of course – and they all live in. Shaw and I are married – hence the grey hair and various symptoms of premature ageing – so you won't see so much of us round here in the evenings, except when we can escape occasionally. Well, gentlemen,' Benson caught the eye of the orderly at the door, 'shall we go through?'

Luncheon was a civilised affair. They helped themselves to soup from a silver tureen, which was placed on a side table and presided over, Ashley noticed, by the orderly called Robin. Then they sat down at a magnificently polished table, laid out with silver cutlery, cut glass jugs containing iced water, and place mats adorned with the crest and motto of the Troop. Ashley found himself seated between Benson and Dutton.

'How has morale been in the unit?' he asked Benson.

'The men have been pretty subdued since Wednesday, as I'm sure you'll imagine. We're a close bunch – just over a hundred and fifty men and six officers – so everyone feels the effect of something like this in a way that you probably wouldn't get in a larger outfit. Then that oaf Cowan blustered in on Thursday, putting everyone's back up and creating a lot of resentment, which didn't help matters. Fortunately, a lot of the men managed to get away for the weekend, so there was a feeling of things starting to get back to normal this morning. Also, we've got a bit of a show-jumping competition coming up this week. In the circumstances, I nearly cancelled it, but Frank argued that it would be good for the men, and on the whole I agree with him.'

Ashley nodded: 'That sounds sensible. Will the murder have an effect on recruitment, do you think?'

Here he had hit a nerve. Benson frowned before replying: 'Almost certainly, especially if it isn't cleared up very quickly. We've had an instance already: about twice a year, we invite small groups of lads to do a three-week work experience with us. We do our best to give them a good time – though we work them pretty hard as well – and it's not uncommon to pick up a few recruits as a result. We were due to have a group of eight coming in on Wednesday and four of them have now cancelled. The loss of even one or two new chaps in a year can make a big difference to a small unit – we're stretched to the limit as it is. Which reminds me of something I need to talk to Frank about, if you'll excuse me?' Benson leaned across the table towards Raynham; Ashley heard them discussing arrangements for the arrival of the four remaining cadets. He turned to the man on his right.

'It's Mr Dutton, isn't it?'

'That's right – John Dutton. I live in, as the CO said, so we'll be seeing quite a bit of each other over the next few days. In fact, I've been deputed to give you a tour of the barracks after the meal, if you'd like one.'

'I look forward to it. Have you been with the Troop long?'

'I've done a year. Before that I was in Germany for three years – you probably know that we're part of the Royal Artillery.'

'Yes, I did know, but I'm not sure I understand how it works.' Ashley's tone invited an explanation, so Dutton continued. 'It's slightly different for officers and for the men. An officer has to join the Troop through the Artillery. We can say at the beginning that we'd like to come over here for a while, but there's no guarantee that it will happen. On the other hand, if you join in the ranks, you can specify that you want to ride with the Patties and then spend your whole time here. Similarly, there are lots of gunners who never do anything on the ceremonial side of things. However, it's perfectly possible to swap over for a couple of years. A chap from the Troop might want to try a bit of "real soldiering" or a gunner might like the idea of learning to ride and doing something a bit more glamorous for a change.'

'It sounds good. How does it work in practice?'

'If the soldier is adaptable – and most of them are – it works very well. He spends a couple of years doing something completely different and either returns feeling refreshed, or he likes the new way of life sufficiently well to want to stay. The only problem is that he might have lost his place in the promotion queue – and that means a lot to a soldier. On the other hand, if a chap isn't adaptable, it can be a bit of a disaster. A gunner may like the idea of sitting smartly on a horse while the general public takes photographs and thinks he's wonderful, but he doesn't necessarily realise that the whole business of looking after a horse can be backbreaking work and that learning to ride is jolly difficult. He arrives here, within a few weeks decides that he hates horses and everything to do with them – and finds he is stuck here.'

'Very awkward.' Ashley pondered the point that Dutton had just made; then an idea occurred to him. 'Do you happen to know if any of the chaps on duty last Wednesday had come over from the Artillery?'

'As a matter of fact, I do. There was just one.'

'And that is?'

Dutton paused; 'That is – or rather, *was* – Bombardier Simon Cooper.'

*   *   *   *   *

To a civilian, an army barracks is a fascinating compilation of strange buildings, strange equipment, strange routines and strange customs. The inanimate objects, even those unconnected with the art of war, have a distinctly military look to them; and as for the soldiers...

A soldier neither moves, speaks nor thinks like a civilian. He conducts his life according to set routines and patterns; these control his eating in the canteen and drinking at the bar as much as his appearance on parade. Far from turning him into a thoughtless automaton, these fixed disciplines give him a confidence and self-assurance almost unknown to the civilian. He knows exactly how he is required to behave on all occasions; he is aware of his precise place and function within his section and of his section within his unit; he has been thoroughly trained to carry out the tasks allotted to him; and he understands himself to be an important part of an important profession. Over and above all this, he knows himself to look far smarter and to be fitter and healthier than any civilian.

Ashley found himself musing on this all through his tour. Whether they were in the harness room or the forge; the riding school or the gun park, they found men working methodically and efficiently at their tasks. Although they called Dutton 'sir', there was a surprisingly relaxed atmosphere, for officer and men treated each other with equal respect. He was impressed that Dutton knew the name of every soldier they met. As the tour went on, Ashley became aware of a niggling feeling that he couldn't quite identify. He usually associated such instinctive feelings with a detective's "hunch" but, to his surprise, he gradually realised that he was feeling a strong pang of regret that he had no part in the way of life he was observing. He wanted to be there, in the harness room, rubbing polish into a bridle; in the forge, sweating under a huge leather apron, as a shoe was beaten into shape; in the gun park, wearing ugly green coveralls, lying under a gun to grease an axle. Even the lad who held the horse while its shoe was fitted had exuded a sense of purpose and of belonging.

Ashley pulled himself together. He *had* a purpose – to solve this case, so that these people could continue in this strange, rather wonderful way of life. Anyway, he told himself, he'd have made a rotten soldier.

In the gun park, their last destination, Ashley had been surprised to recognise the young soldier who knelt beside a gun, tightening wheel nuts with a spanner.

'It's Gunner Sorrell, isn't it?' he asked. 'Not on ceremonial duties anymore?' Sorrell, large-eyed, and glowing from his exertions, gave Ashley a smile of recognition. 'Hello, sir – no, none of our team is up at Horse Guards any more. The CO said he didn't want us being picked on by the press, so he put us all back to our normal duties.'

'That's right,' added Dutton, dryly. 'We had to train up a new team in twenty-four hours – it took some doing, I can tell you.'

'I heard you were up all night with them, sir,' said Sorrell cheerfully, 'And that Gunner Chambers fell asleep on his horse all the way down Baker Street.'

'Well, it's not entirely accurate, but you're not far wrong, Sorrell,' admitted Dutton. 'Though Gunner Chambers is usually half asleep on his horse at the best of times. Still, we coped – that's the main thing.'

'Yes sir.'

'A good lad that,' observed Dutton, as they went out of the park and onto the parade ground. 'Sad story too: his parents were killed in an accident when he was very young. None of his relations wanted him so he went into a home about a mile from here.'

'Not a nice start to life,' sympathised Ashley.

'No. Then one day, the headmaster at the home asked if they could have a tour here as a treat, and he fell in love with the place. The kids were given a ride and had a go at grooming their horses afterwards – all the things you can imagine. That must have been when he was about thirteen or fourteen. Anyway, next thing, he was hanging around the gate all the time to see the horses come and go, and bunking off classes to see the salutes in the park. The head came along and asked if we could find a way of keeping him at school; so the CO at the time promised him he could come in on Saturdays and help out – but only if he brought a letter, confirming that he'd been at school on the previous five days. He signed up with us on the first day he legally could, which was about six months ago.'

Ashley found the story genuinely touching. 'I'm glad the tale has a happy ending.'

Dutton looked suddenly grim. 'Well, it was happy enough until Cooper came across him. My God, he picked on that boy…'

Ashley would have liked to follow up Dutton's last remark, but at that point Justin Fox came out of one of the stable blocks. He had changed out of his combat shirt and trousers and was now splendidly, if self-consciously, dressed in a set of blues. Following after him, leading the officer's charger, was Gunner Green.

'Ah! The young soldier off to the wars!' enthused Dutton. 'It's very brave of you, Justin, to ride over to Horse Guards – you know what happened when Mark rode over on

Wednesday. You drove last time, didn't you?'

'Yes, but I thought it would make a change.'

'Besides which, sir,' said Green, happily, 'Mr Fox's Mummy and Auntie Rita are going to be watching today and they've brought the video camera with them.'

'You treacherous bastard, Green!' Fox blushed, as Dutton whooped for joy.

'Sorry sir – my father's mother was Welsh, so I can't help it. Would you like to stand on the mounting block, sir?' Green held onto a stirrup, so that his officer could climb into the saddle.

'And if your father's grandfather had stuck to sheep, like the rest of his kind,' Fox put his left foot into the near side stirrup, 'I wouldn't have to put up with such a lippy groom.' He swung his leg over and eased himself into the saddle. Green fussed around him, tweaking a rein here and adjusting a stirrup there. 'I know, sir, but you'd find that life became very dull. Hang on a second, sir, you've smudged your boot on the stirrup.' He pulled a duster from his coveralls, wiped the smudged area vigorously and stood back to admire the effect. Not satisfied, he leaned over and breathed heavily onto the leather. It clouded up and he instantly recommenced rubbing it down with the duster. Ashley found himself deeply entertained to see the officer being groomed as carefully as the horse. He had a vision of Green picking out Justin's hoofs and giving him a quick rub down with a handful of straw when he returned from his ride.

Finally, Green was satisfied with both horse and rider: 'Okay, sir, I think you'll do very nicely.' Justin gathered up the four reins into his left hand. 'Thank you, Green. See you, Dutton, goodbye, Mr Ashley.'

'Don't forget to smile for the camera, Justin,' Dutton smirked, 'And send Auntie Rita our love. Older members of the Troop still have fond memories of that night of passion she gave them after the Coronation.'

'Oh, sod off, Dutton!' Justin found himself laughing and

blushing at the same time. 'I'll be back just before six o'clock and if there isn't a bloody stiff drink waiting for me, I'll set Aunt Rita onto *you*.' He rode on, recovering his dignity in time to return the salute of the sentry at the barrack gates, then passed out of sight.

Dutton turned his attention back to Ashley. 'I've shown you all the usual sights. Is there anything else you'd like to see?' It occurred to Ashley that this was a rather stupid question, since he hardly knew what else there *was* to see – so how could he tell if he wanted to see it? He smiled and replied, 'I think, if you don't mind, I'd like to spend a few minutes chatting with Gunner Green.'

'Of course. Green, you remember Mr Ashley, don't you?'

'Yes, I do sir; you were with Captain Raynham last Wednesday, weren't you, sir?' Ashley acknowledged this.

'I'll be off then,' said Dutton. 'They serve tea and toast in the Mess at about four; most of us will be there – shall I send your excuses or will you join us?'

'I'm not sure – could you be prepared to send excuses, just in case? And thanks, by the way, for the tour. Very interesting.'

'My pleasure. All right Green, thank you.' Green, having left his head dress in the stable, had snapped to attention, rather than saluting. 'Carry on. See you shortly, Mr Ashley.' Dutton headed back towards the Mess, leaving Ashley and Green together.

CHAPTER SEVEN

THE GUNNERS

A detective has to guard himself against forming friendships with the people he is investigating. Ashley was aware of this; he held out for about fifteen minutes before deciding that he liked Green very much and hoping that the gunner wasn't involved in any way with the murder. Green probably wasn't particularly bright in any academic sense, but he was quick-witted and sensible, and he had that knack, so useful in the army, of making fun of people and situations while staying firmly on the right side of the line dividing respect from rudeness. He also had the ability to put Ashley at his ease within seconds; it was only after a short while in Green's company that Ashley, relaxing, realised he had been feeling tense ever since his arrival in the barracks.

They went back into the stable block from which Green had emerged. 'I just need to tidy up the stall, sir, and then we can talk away. If you'd like to sit, I can offer you a luxurious choice between a bale of straw and an upturned bucket.'

'Which is the less uncomfortable?'

'The straw, sir; Major Benson always opts for it when he's feeling sociable. The junior officers tend to go for the bucket to show off the fact that they don't have piles – and they don't have their own batman to pick the straw out of their uniform like the major does.' Ashley didn't have piles or a batman either, but he opted for the straw anyway. He perched on the end of a bale and watched Green going about his tasks; tidying away grooming equipment, raking over the straw and topping up the horse's water. Green was in identical coveralls to the ones

Ashley had seen Sorrell wearing a few minutes earlier. He tried to imagine the two of them at Horse Guards, standing over Simon Cooper's headless body, their olive green clothing splashed with blood; but it was very difficult. Would Sorrell have had the courage and ability to kill? Would Green, even supposing him to have been badly treated, ever *want* to kill? Ashley answered both questions with a probable negative. On the other hand, if he swapped the names around, perhaps the answers would change as well.

'There, sir, all finished.' Green unbuttoned his coveralls and stepped out of them – a process, Ashley noted, which took five seconds at the most – revealing his everyday riding uniform underneath. This comprised khaki shirt and breeches, the Troop's green and cherry coloured stable belt (Ashley guessed that the cherry band was a legacy from Prince Albert) and boots which, while very smart, were clearly not the ones worn on ceremonial occasions. Matt, rather than gloss described their polish best, Ashley thought. Green was wearing them without spurs; these were in his upturned service cap on the straw bale next to Ashley. Looking at them, Ashley was reminded of the strap that had bound Cooper's hands. He picked one up and held it in the palm of his hand.

'Did you realise, Gunner Green, that Cooper's wrists were bound with a spur strap?'

'Yes, sir. I didn't see it myself, of course, because I was still on duty, but Gunner Carlton told me – he noticed it when they'd all been looking at the body. A new one, he said.'

'A new one? Was he close enough to see that?'

'You wouldn't have to get very close, sir – look.' Green took the spur from Ashley's hand and began to remove the strap from it. Ashley saw at once that there were kinks in the leather where it had been threaded through the metal; a detail that one of the Troop would be able to spot at once. 'Are these things easy to come by?' he asked.

'Dead easy, sir – if you break a spur strap you can just sign for another set, as long as you bring the broken one with you to prove you're not fiddling the system. You then get issued with a new pair, leaving you with a spare strap.'

'You're used to working with tack and buckles – do you think it would be a simple thing to bind a man's wrists with one of these?'

Green contemplated his own wrists and looked at the strap. 'I think you'd need to put an extra hole in, sir. Look, if I do the strap up to its smallest hole, I can still get my hands in and out quite easily.' The soldier demonstrated.

'So I see. Do you know where we can get hold of an old one and play around with it a bit?'

'There's bound to be one in the harness room, sir. There's also a kettle there. It's meant to be for softening up wax, but mostly it gets used for making tea, if you fancy the idea, sir?'

'Do they still put bromide in army tea?'

Green smiled: 'If they do, sir, it's not working.'

'Then I fancy the idea.'

In the harness room, they found a spare spur strap, a kettle and mugs, and Gunners Lang and Barker. Ashley recognised Lang by his brilliant blond hair and remembered Gunner Barker as the soldier who had "volunteered" for an extra duty on the day of the murder. Barker, with dark eyes and prominent cheekbones, seemed a more subdued character than his colleague. Dressed like Green, except that Barker had stripped to the waist, they were working on a bridle and saddle respectively; Ashley discovered that they were regarded as the two best polishers in the Troop.

'It can be quite a little earner, sir,' said Lang, cheerfully. 'Most of the lads are fine at the everyday spit and polish, but there's a particular skill in getting things up to a really gleaming standard. Some of them can bull away at their kit for hours without making any difference beyond a certain level.' He paused to spit with pinpoint accuracy on a part of the bridle and then rubbed in more polish. 'This is Gunner Boyd's kit, sir. He's at Horse Guards tomorrow and is desperate to be one of the boxmen.'

'For the first time in his life,' interjected Barker. 'He got lucky at cards, sir, and decided to invest his winnings.'

'How very sensible,' said Ashley. 'Presumably several hours less work for him today and then, if he's successful, a much easier and more pleasant day tomorrow.'

'That's about it, sir – not a bad result for fifty quid.'

'And we did his boots as well, as a gesture of goodwill,' added Lang, in the manner of a second-hand car dealer. He nodded at the most brilliantly glistening pair of riding boots Ashley had ever seen, standing in their wooden trees on a bench. Ashley was too impressed to say anything other than, 'Gosh!' After a moment, he added: 'They look as though they're made from melted liquorice.'

'It's not a bad bliff, is it, sir?' Lang lapsed into the slang of the Troop. 'The expression we tend to use is, "Shining like an otter's turd".' The gunner grinned, as if the joke was all his own: 'Not that I've ever seen one, of course...'

'But it conveys the idea admirably.'

'Exactly, sir.'

Green prepared four huge mugs of tea (two teabags per mug and several heaped spoons of dried milk) and handed them round: 'There you go, sir – if you don't like sugar, don't stir it.' Ashley observed Lang and Barker stirring their mugs with half an old riding crop and did the same when it was offered to him. The tea, virtually orange in colour, was every bit as appalling as he had anticipated, but there was a pleasant feeling of camaraderie in sharing it with them. He watched Green seat himself on a work surface with an action not unlike mounting a horse, contemplated a similar attempt and decided that he'd probably do himself a mischief. Instead, he just leaned against the same surface. Barker and Lang continued their work.

'How much longer will it take?' asked Ashley. 'To my untrained eye, it looks amazing already.'

'You're not far wrong, sir,' replied Lang. 'Ten minutes at most – we'll be finished by the time you've drunk your tea.' As if to show that he was nearing the end of his task, he breathed rather than spat on the leather and then gently rubbed it with a cloth.

'I've got a bit longer to do on the saddle', said Barker, expectorating what must have been ninety percent army tea onto the pommel. Ashley half expected it to sizzle, as if strong acid had been spat onto it. Barker continued: 'Blondie works faster than I do.'

'But you've got more stamina than I have,' pointed out Lang. 'Up half the night he was, sir, when the Troop were first at Horse Guards – must have made himself a fortune.'

'But you're taking things easier today?'

Barker continued rubbing polish into the pommel. When it was finally gleaming to his satisfaction he answered Ashley's question. 'That's right, sir. I'd got a bit behind on the payments on my car, but they're up to date now, so I've eased off on the extra bliffing in the last week. You can only do so much of it before the thrill wears off.'

Ashley agreed. He turned around an idea in his mind for a few moments and then said, 'When you've both finished, I wonder if you'd care to lend me a hand with a little experiment – it won't take long.'

Lang, who was already hanging up a gleaming bridle and starting to put his polishing kit away, smiled and said, 'Of course, sir; what would you like us to do?'

Ashley held up the spur strap. 'I want two of you to try to bind the wrists of the other one with this strap. I need to see how quickly and efficiently it can be done.'

Green gave a broad grin; 'Well sir, you *do* think of interesting things to do in your spare time. Come on, Blondie, give us your limbs.' Green eased himself off his perch and Lang held out his arms, crossing them at the wrist. Green wrapped the strap around them, then took it away again. His finger now marked the place where an extra hole was needed. Opening a drawer in the workbench, he rummaged around with one hand until he found a small gimlet. With this, he bored an extra hole into the leather. He tried the buckle in the hole, then gave a good tug to the resulting loop. 'That should do nicely. Round you go, Lang.'

This time, Lang put his hands behind his back while Green slipped one end of the strap through the buckle and pulled it tight up to the new hole. Immediately, he undid it again: 'Too loose.' He made a second hole, about half an inch away from the first, then repeated the process. Lang was bound fast.

'I think I preferred it the first time', he observed, amused.

'How long do you think it would take you to get out of that, Gunner Lang?' asked Ashley. 'Could you just snap it, do you think?'

'If it was an old one, I probably could, sir, but this new one would hold for a long time. I noticed it was a new one that – well, you know.'

'Yes, I do,' agreed Ashley. 'Now, that's stage one of the experiment – yes, you can let him go now, Gunner Green – the second stage is more fiddly. If we assume that your bombardier didn't want to have his head sliced off, we must also assume that he didn't politely hold his hands behind his back like Lang just did. Either he was overpowered, therefore, or he was taken by surprise. In either case, he could have called out – but as far as we know, he didn't. We must also assume, in that case, that somebody stuffed something into his mouth. That's a lot of work for two people, yet there were only two bloodstained coveralls. Do we have to imagine a third person, who then stepped right out of the way, or could two have managed it, do you think?'

Gunners Green and Lang showed that they could be quick witted. All this time, Barker had been putting the finishing touches to Boyd's saddle. Green caught Lang's eye and, suddenly, they shot forward, Green forcing violently into Barker's mouth the cloth which had been used to polish the bridle, while Lang seized Barker's wrists, holding them crossed behind his back. Green then grabbed the spur strap, wrapped it around Barker's wrists and pulled it tightly up to the second hole. In the shortest possible amount of time, Barker had been silenced and immobilised. Ashley could have cheered.

But then something happened which changed everything.

Without waiting for any instructions, Lang, his hands on Barker's struggling shoulders, kicked his friend behind the right knee. Barker sank down to the floor.

Ashley gaped at the appalling tableau in front of him. Facing away, Barker, trembling all over, knelt exactly as Simon Cooper must have done. Holding him in position with a hand on either shoulder, Green and Lang faced Ashley, both grinning.

Green was the first to realise that Ashley was shaking almost as much as Barker: 'Is something wrong, sir? Are you all right?'

Ashley forced himself to speak. Addressing Lang, he said, slowly and quietly: 'How did you know that Cooper had been kicked like that?'

At first, Lang was obtuse; the first four or five words of his answer came out cheerfully and naturally: 'I didn't sir, I just…' and then the sentence dried up, his mouth open for a word that never came. His eyes widened in horror as he realised the implications of his action and he began to gabble: 'No sir – really – it was an instinct – you can't think…' He fell silent and stared fearfully into Ashley's eyes, tightening his clutch on Barker's quivering shoulder.

It was Barker who brought Ashley back to reality; he began to shake in spasms and to make choking sounds behind his improvised gag.

'Oh God!' Ashley exclaimed: he flew forward, barging the frozen Lang aside, leaned over Barker's shoulder and tore the cloth from his mouth. In the same instant, Green grasped the situation and thrust a bucket in front of the kneeling form. In a series of violent jerks, Barker, his wrists still tightly bound behind his back, emptied his stomach into the bucket, while Green and Ashley held his shoulders steady.

Barker retched six or seven times, gasping for breath

between each spasm, while sweat literally ran down his forehead and his back, so that his whole, shaking, upper body was wet and glistening. At last there was nothing to come except a translucent stalactite of bile and saliva, which hung from his lower lip, defying attempts at removal. It quivered as he gulped for more air.

Suddenly, Green remembered that the strap had yet to be loosened. He swore, and unlatched the buckle in a second. Ashley, observing the livid red dents cut into Barker's wrists, fully expected the gunner to lash out at them the moment his hands were free. He was utterly unprepared for what actually happened.

Barker sat back on his haunches, put his hands to his face and broke into uncontrollable sobs.

* * * * *

Half an hour later, Ashley left the harness room and headed towards the Mess. He felt chastened and ashamed. These three decent, guileless young men had welcomed him into their private world and he had rewarded them by bringing suspicion, pain and guilt into their lives.

It was only Green who had displayed any common sense. As Barker had howled, and Lang and Ashley had looked on uselessly, he had dashed from the harness room, returning moments later clutching a towel and a bottle of whisky. The towel he had draped around Barker's wet shoulders; he had then poured the remains of Barker's tea into the bucket and half-filled the mug with whisky. He had crouched down beside Barker, and gently persuaded his friend to take the mug into his hands: then, with his right hand supporting the base of the mug and his left hand steadying the back of the trembling man's head, he had made him drink.

At length, Barker had stood up and Green, taking the two ends of the towel, had gently pressed them over his face: partly to dry him, Ashley realised, and partly to hide his immediate embarrassment. When Barker, after a few moments, had taken over control of the towel and begun to wipe his face more vigorously, Ashley had known that it was time to say something.

'I am so sorry – please forgive me,' had seemed utterly inadequate; Green's, 'Adam, we've been shits – sorry,' was a bit more to the point. Lang had managed to second Green with a monosyllabic, 'Yeah,' and had then added a final, dismal, 'Sorry,' to the collection.

When he could no longer pretend to be wiping his face, Barker had lowered the towel and looked up. 'No – it's not what you think. Not the pain or,' he had nodded towards the stinking bucket, 'that. It was something else…'

Ashley had known. Like Edward, four days before, Barker had been touched by the extraordinary emotions connected with sudden and violent death. But it had been worse for Barker: he had known the person who had been so suddenly seized, gagged and bound, kicked to his knees and then murdered. Barker had turned his red eyes on Ashley: 'I know, now, exactly how he must have felt.'

CHAPTER EIGHT

PLANNING AHEAD

The guest room in the Officers' Mess was an awkward mixture of utilitarian furniture and some rather stylish ornaments. Bed, desk, chairs, chest of drawers and wardrobe were obviously standard army issue: ugly, uncomfortable and, sadly, indestructible. In contrast, half a dozen very fine Campion prints, illustrating glorious episodes in the history of Prince Albert's Troop, hung on the walls. On the chest of drawers there was a remarkable piece of abstract art, made from empty shell cases and other military flotsam of the type that must have accumulated in every First World War trench. Finally, a bronze gunner sat proudly on his horse, in front of the looking-glass above the fireplace. In addition to all these things, there was a good rug on the floor, some books and an important-looking folder on the desk.

Ashley fell into the only civilian piece of furniture in the room; a large, sagging leather armchair, obviously seen as too ancient for use downstairs. It was time, he felt, to take stock of the situation: dispassionately, if possible. 'Keep to the facts,' he thought, 'and leave out your gut instincts – for the moment.'

So: known information about Bombardier Simon Cooper.

One: he was a transfer from the regular artillery and, from the sound of it, an unsuccessful one.

Two: according to Dutton, he had spotted Sorrell's vulnerability and had taken advantage of it. It sounded like the classic tactic of a bully. Why had not Dutton or some other officer intervened?

Three: not just one, but two people wanted him dead –

twice the usual number. Standard causes of murder: sex, jealousy, money, blackmail. Speculate on these later.

Four: the murder was premeditated. The killers would have had to work out the manoeuvres of gagging and binding, the preparation of the sword and the spur strap.

Five: details and manner of the murder – everything pretty well established except the precise time.

Known information about Gunner Lang.

One: significant fact – he had exactly copied an aspect of Cooper's killing, which he could not possibly have known. Co-incidence? Speculate later.

Two: not good in a crisis. Could he have coped with murder?

Three: brilliant polisher. Not likely to be relevant.

Known information about Gunner Barker…

This was not getting Ashley far, but it was calming his mind; the incident in the harness room was beginning to seem less dreadful. It was his job to establish facts, and experiments had to be part of that process. Without them, the murder would remain unsolved and the Troop would live in a state of distrust and suspicion for years. Therefore, back to:

Known information about Gunner Barker…

There was a knock at the door and Robin entered. He was carrying Ashley's dinner suit and black shoes and looked very amused by something.

'Hello sir. I've pressed your suit and given your shoes a quick polish.' By this, Robin meant that he had brought them up to a shine almost worthy of Gunners Lang and Barker. 'You'll find all your other clothes in the chest or the wardrobe. Major Benson asks me to tell you that there are only three Mess rules that need concern you.'

'And they are?'

'One, sir, black tie is worn for dinner. Two, it's never too early for gin, and three – if he sees those brothel creepers in the Mess after six o'clock in the evening, he will personally tear them from your feet, sir.' Robin smiled triumphantly; reporting the words of one's CO can in no way be interpreted as insubordination.

Ashley contemplated his old, comfortable suede shoes mournfully. 'Do I get the impression that your commanding officer doesn't approve my taste in footwear?'

'I think, sir, he appreciates that a detective finds it useful to work in soft shoes,' said Robin, tactfully, 'But he assumes you won't be doing too much sneaky-beaky in the Mess in the evenings, and should therefore be shod like an officer and a gentleman.'

Ashley smiled. 'He's quite a character, your CO.'

'The Bulldog – absolutely terrifying, sir,' said Robin, approvingly. 'If his kit isn't cleaned exactly as he likes it, there's hell to pay.'

'And that's your responsibility, is it?'

'Yes, sir, I'm his batman. My name's Robert, really, but the junior officers started calling me Robin and it sort of stuck. Even my mother calls me Robin now. Anyway, the CO lives out – though he's dining in tonight, because you're here – so he says my main priority is to look after you while you're here, sir.'

Ashley rather liked the thought of this; Edward was a good detective's assistant, when there was any work, but he was sadly inadequate when it came to keeping the master looking up to scratch. It would be nice to spend some time in a world where shirts were ironed, beds were made and shoes were polished by someone other than one's self. For the first time in a couple of hours, he started to feel cheerful.

A useful idea came to him. 'Tell me, er…'

'Robin, sir – I've got used to it.'

'All right, Robin – what were you doing last Wednesday afternoon?'

'The day of the killing, sir?'

'That's right.'

Robin considered. 'I had my meal in the Mess kitchen with the chef and the two other Mess orderlies – John and Colin. Then we served at the officers' luncheon until two o'clock.

After that, Colin and I got Mr Dawson's uniform ready for him to ride over to Horse Guards. Strictly speaking, he's only a junior officer and should do his own kit, but Horse Guards is pretty important, so we offered to do it for him.'

'Very decent of you,' observed Ashley.

'Well,' admitted Robin, 'It did get us out of the washing up. We finished the uniform by half past two – it doesn't take long when there are two of you working at it – and got Mr Dawson into it by a quarter to three. We saw him off and then, to be honest with you, we went back to the kitchen and played poker until four o'clock.'

'"We" being?'

'Chef, John, Colin and me, sir. Chef won – he always does. Anyone who can pass off frozen chicken nuggets as *Morceaux de poulet en croûte* isn't going to have too much trouble convincing you that he's got a pair of aces in every hand. I wonder why we keep playing with him, sometimes. Anyway, at four o'clock, I served the tea and at about twenty past four, I took that telephone call from Mr Dawson. Then…'

Ashley interrupted. 'That's fine. So, I can take it that from about two o'clock through to four o'clock you can easily prove that you were here, in the presence of one or more witnesses?'

'Yes sir, as you say, easily.'

'Good. You're the first gunner I've spoken to whom I didn't have to worry about being a suspect. Sit down and tell me everything you know about Bombardier Simon Cooper.'

There was a fair bit. Robin hadn't had much contact with Cooper himself ('thank goodness') but a small barracks is like a village especially, Robin explained, if you happen to work in the Officers' Mess. 'All the chaps like to buy us drinks in the bar to get the latest Mess gossip and in return we get everything back from them.'

Ashley made a mental note not to say or do anything in Robin's hearing which might get back to a suspect. He asked him to continue.

Simon Cooper had served about ten years in the Artillery

before transferring to the Patties. His promotion had dried up in Germany and this was popularly assumed to be the reason for his requesting a transfer: 'It's not much fun, sir, when people who signed up after you are being made sergeants and staff sergeants and you're stuck as a bombardier – and let's face it, no-one was ever going to make him a sergeant. Mr Dutton was over in Germany with him for a few years and he said that Cooper wouldn't get any more promotion because of his reputation as a bully.' This reputation had preceded him to England. He was particularly noted for hating "high fliers": those who were likely to outrank him one day. 'I think the tactic was to make their lives so unpleasant, sir, that they'd leave before they got promoted.'

'Did it work on anyone?'

'Not here, sir, he was only with us six months, so there wasn't time. But he picked on Green, Barker and Chadwick like mad. They're the ones we all think will most likely get made up to lance bombardier when vacancies come up.'

'Why didn't they complain?'

Robin shrugged: 'Complaining like that just doesn't happen much in the army, sir. And also, there are ways of picking on somebody which feel like bullying, but which you can't prove. Telling someone his saddle's not been done well enough and throwing it onto the floor, so that it takes hours to get the scratches out – that's a rotten thing to do if the saddle was fine, but you haven't got any real evidence that you've been unfairly treated. I'm sure you can imagine the sort of thing, sir.'

Ashley could. 'How did they react to it?'

'Gunner Green just laughed it off, sir. He said that he knew he could do his job far better than Bombardier Cooper and could ride a lot better than him too, and that was all that mattered.'

'Was Cooper's riding bad?'

'Dreadful, sir – worse than mine, even. All right, he could stay on his horse from here to Whitehall, but that was about it. He'd never dare be part of anything risky like a gun salute or the Musical Drive. He hated horses, and they made life difficult for him in return.'

'What about the other two gunners? And Sorrell?'

'I don't know about Sorrell, sir – I wouldn't be at all surprised to hear that he'd been picked on, but I never heard of it. I think Barker and Chadwick found him quite difficult to cope with, sir. Not many people are as resilient as Gunner Green. I see you've been chatting to him today, sir.'

'Gossip travels faster than I realised.'

Robin smiled: 'It's not that, sir – but you've still got some straw on the seat of your trousers. Major Benson sometimes goes to talk with him; he says that he gets more common sense out of Green in five minutes than he gets out of the Ministry of Defence in a year, besides which, Gunner Green makes him laugh. I think the Bulldog's got him earmarked as the senior NCO in years to come. I'll get rid of the straw once you're changed into your evening suit, sir.'

'Thanks Robin, that's been very helpful.' Ashley looked at his watch: it was half past five. 'Is there a bathroom on this passage?'

'The bathroom just opposite is for your use, sir. Would you like me to run you a bath?'

Ashley beamed at the thought of such luxury. 'And did you say that it was never...?'

'... too early, sir? Would you like your gin brought here, or shall I leave it next to the bath, sir?'

Ashley thought that gin with his bath would be an excellent idea.

*   *   *   *   *

The bathroom, according to Robin, was the one Major Benson kept for his own use when staying in the Mess: it boasted a distinctly unmilitary array of bath salts, bubble baths, body lotions and other luxuries, along with a plastic duck and an apparatus for reading a book while wallowing. Next to the bath itself, a vast, enamelled, claw-footed affair, there was a mahogany occasional table, on which stood a bowl of *pot-pourri* and a coaster with the Troop crest on it. So, Major Benson liked to drink in the bath as well. Ashley decided that a good read would be useful; he selected the least dull-looking history of the Troop from the small pile on his desk and returned to the bathroom.

Robin had correctly guessed that vast amounts of bubbles were the thing after a hard day's detection. Ashley sank into them and was just beginning to unwind when Robin brought in his gin. Ashley found himself half embarrassed, half amused. Never having had the luxury of a valet before, it had not occurred to him that this easy attitude to nudity was a natural part of the relationship.

'Don't mind me, sir,' said Robin, placing the gin on the coaster, 'I'm invisible at times like this.'

'If only I were too.' Ashley took a grateful sip. Robin had given the tonic bottle the mildest of punishments.

'Once you've seen the Bulldog in the bath, sir, with his stomach rising out of the water like a Pacific atoll, nothing else will ever really frighten you. I'd give anything to stick a model coconut tree in his navel and take a photograph. I'll take your clothes, sir, and bring in your dressing gown and slippers.'

Half an hour later, Ashley was feeling completely refreshed. He had read an interesting chapter of his book, outlined some plans for the next couple of days, and had then devoted useful thought to the most difficult aspect of Cooper's death. This involved establishing the exact timing. If only he could do that, many suspects could be eliminated at once. Finally, he had concluded that there was probably not much significance in Lang's act earlier that day. You didn't have to be either the murderer or a brilliant mind to realise that a smart kick to the back of the knee was the easiest way to bring a man down.

In thinking this, Ashley was vaguely aware of the fact that he rather wanted to find reasons to clear Lang of suspicion. He had taken a liking to the blond polisher. But then, come to think of it, he had liked everyone so far. Lang, Green, Barker, Sorrell, they had all been straightforward, open, uncomplicated, friendly people. What a shame Cooper couldn't possibly have cut off his own head.

When he returned to his room, he found Raynham, lounging in the leather armchair. Raynham had half changed into his evening clothes; he wore black socks and trousers, but his dress shirt was open at the collar and he had no jacket. His hair was neatly combed and still wet from washing.

'News from the mortuary,' he announced. 'Cooper's body – and head as well, I presume – has been released. Funeral on Thursday morning.'

'Will it be a full military affair?'

'Almost certainly not. At the moment, the family is insisting that they don't want any military presence at all – and I suppose you can't blame them, in the circumstances. On the other hand, they might change their minds, so I've put Chadwick on standby to sound the Last Post and *Reveille*, just in case.'

Ashley had been trying to picture Chadwick since Robin had mentioned him. Then he remembered a very tall gunner asking a question in the canteen on the day of the murder; there had been a pair of crossed trumpets embroidered onto the sleeve of his tunic. An idea occurred to him, and he smiled.

'I know what you're thinking,' said Raynham. 'It would make for a very fine piece of dramatic irony if Chadwick turned out to be one of the murderers, sounding the Last Post at his victim's funeral.'

'Victorian melodrama, perhaps, rather than Shakespeare – but, yes, that was exactly what was crossing my mind.'

'We wondered about using one of the other trumpeters, but Chadwick is easily the best. Anyway, as I say, he's only on standby, he may not be needed.'

'Will anybody else be attending? And, if so, can I scrounge a lift?'

'Sure, the CO and I will be going. The plan is that we travel in his Jaguar, with Hall driving.'

'Hall? Is he the one whose horse panicked at the bloody cloth?'

'That's the one. Chadwick, if needed, will sit in front with him, so it might be a bit of a squash in the back with three of us.'

Raynham pondered the logistics of the journey. 'We could solve the problem by letting Chadwick double as driver, but last time he was in charge of a Land Rover he got his spurs caught up with the pedals and took out the barrack gates and half the wall of the garden opposite.'

'I hope he didn't break his embouchure?' Amused, Ashley pictured the trumpeter's lips impaled on the windscreen wipers.

Raynham smiled at the thought: 'No, but considerable damage was done to army property, and the garden wall – not to mention the underwear of a little old lady who was watering her begonias at the time.'

'Well, let's leave him in the passenger seat then; I don't mind squeezing up if you don't.' Ashley decided to move the conversation on. A reference in the regimental history had puzzled him. 'What is tent pegging, Frank? It was mentioned in the book I read in the bath.'

Raynham was momentarily taken aback by the change of subject and then replied: 'It's one of the traditional old equestrian skills. A block of wood is placed in the ground and you have to spear it with a lance as you gallop past. It doesn't happen often these days. They used to place a lot of emphasis on that sort of thing up to about a hundred years ago. There were other things called "pig sticking" and "cleaving the Turk". The old-fashioned skill we still use is to do a simple series of jumps while removing one's tunic.'

'Sounds dangerous.'

'Well, frightening rather than dangerous. Once you're used to it though, it doesn't half build up your confidence. If you're interested, you can see some on Friday – we've got a bit of a competition coming up. I think I heard the CO telling you that he thought of cancelling it, but decided that it would be good for morale. Anyway, how's your day been?'

'Very useful, though not without its traumatic side.' Ashley told Raynham about the episode in the harness room. The adjutant was disinclined to worry.

'I shouldn't fret too much about Barker and Lang – they're both sensible chaps. They'll have a few drinks in the NAAFI this evening, get a good night's sleep, and be fine in the morning. Green will keep an eye out for them, too.'

'He's a good man, Green', interjected Ashley.

'Very good,' Raynham agreed, 'Only don't let him make tea for you.'

'Too late.'

'Bad luck. Yes, we've been talking about his promotion this morning.'

'Really? Tell me.' Ashley was genuinely interested, not merely polite, so Raynham gave him the details.

There had been talk of promotion in the air before the Troop took over duties at Horse Guards. One sergeant was leaving to get married and another was transferring to Germany for a couple of years. This left, obviously, two vacancies, which would have a knock-on effect through the ranks. Then recent events had left a third vacancy…

'And the problem is,' Raynham sighed, 'that several of the likely candidates for promotion are now under suspicion of murder. Can you imagine the time the press would have if they found out that we'd actually promoted one, or even both, of the killers?'

Ashley nodded: he could.

'Now, the obvious person to promote to Cooper's position is Lance Bombardier Burdett. He's a good, reliable chap and will do the job infinitely better than Cooper ever did. But we can't make him up straight away, because from three weeks on Wednesday, he's baby-sitting the four cadets on work experience. It should have been eight, if you remember, but four dropped out after the murder. Now that's a full-time job for three weeks – at least, it is, if you want to get any recruits at the end of it – and, in the meantime, his section needs a bombardier. The Bulldog and I have been going over possibilities all day, until our brains exploded about half way through the afternoon. Then we bunked off and went for a ride round Regent's Park.'

Ashley considered Raynham's dilemma. It occurred to him that some part of this situation might be turned to his advantage. It could transform one of his vague bathroom ideas into a working proposition. 'Tell me,' he asked Raynham, 'of all the people at Horse Guards last Wednesday, who would you say was the least likely to be involved in the murder?'

There was no hesitation: 'Green. I've only been here a very short while, don't forget, but my instinct is that he's an excellent chap. I know the CO thinks very highly of him too.'

'Good. I trust the judgement of both of you. I don't know him well, but I'd say he was the last person I'd ever suspect of any serious crime. Now, obviously, I've no idea what you're going to do about your two sergeants...'

'Well, they're not off until September, so there's less urgency with them.'

'But I might have a solution to the other problem, which could aid me in my work as well, if you and Benson think it's a good idea.'

'Let's hear it, then.'

Ashley outlined his idea. Raynham was silent for a moment, and then said, 'I think it's worth trying, and I'm sure the CO will agree. I'll go and sound him out while he changes for dinner.'

Raynham left the room. Ashley opened the wardrobe and rummaged around until he found his mobile. First, he rang Edward with instructions for the next day.

Then he rang his nephew, Tom.

CHAPTER NINE

EXERCISE 'BOMBARDIER COOPER'

It was getting on for eleven o'clock on Tuesday morning. At Horse Guards, the old guard had ridden out to await the arrival of its relief. Back at the barracks, an instructor was giving a jumping lesson to some of the more advanced gunners in the riding school; in the gun park, a team busily dismantled and overhauled the six guns in preparation for the next salute; Ashley sat upstairs in the Mess, wading through the folder of Cowan's notes and reports.

Acting Bombardier Burdett surveyed with satisfaction the work in progress before him. It was going well – he'd give the men a break shortly.

He had been summoned to the adjutant's office early that morning and told of his promotion. He was only "acting" bombardier until the present crisis passed over, when, as Raynham had put it, 'We hope to be able to confirm the appointment.' By this, Burdett correctly assumed, the adjutant had meant that as long as he wasn't arrested for murder, the job was his. Promotion meant that he had handed over the task of minding the four cadets to Green, now similarly promoted to acting lance bombardier. That was less of a problem than Raynham had envisaged. Burdett had done the job several times and had compiled a file containing the whole three-week programme. Green was now studying it in the harness room, over a mug of his famously awful tea.

Meanwhile, Burdett had been given a new task. Spread out in front of him was a labyrinth of poles and mine tape. Four gunners, Watson, Carlton and the Smith twins – the backroom boys of last Wednesday's guard – were mocking up an outline plan of the Horse Guards complex. As Burdett watched, great lengths of mine tape gradually took on the outline of the stable, the canteen, the guardroom, and so on. Burdett stood in the most recently formed enclosure; as he looked around him, Smith One stepped over a length of tape and placed a post with the sign HARNESS ROOM next to him.

'I think you've just walked through a wall, Smith One,' Burdett observed, cynically.

'That's nothing, Bomber,' Smith One smiled broadly, 'Carlton's just destroyed a sentry box with a single kick. He doesn't know his own strength.'

Burdett turned to view Carlton tangled up in mine tape. 'Let's take that break, shall we?'

Over tea in the real canteen, the four gunners quizzed Burdett.

'So, Lance, sorry – Bomber – why don't we just go over to the real Horse Guards if Mr Ashley wants to do a re-enactment?'

'The fact, Carlton, that I have just been promoted to the dizzy heights of acting bombardier, does not mean that Mr Ashley has chosen to confide his innermost thoughts in me. Still, if you want my guess, I'd say that he wants to do a run-through without being in the public eye.'

'And away from that sod, Cowan.' Smith Two had been given a particularly nasty time by the Inspector. 'He's around Horse Guards all the time, they say. According to Robin, who got it from Bombardier Croft, he walked right into a pile of shit up to his ankle over the weekend.'

'I heard that too,' volunteered Watson. 'Crofty told me it was difficult to tell which was the shit and which was Cowan.'

'Shame they didn't shovel him up.'

Burdett let the banter go on for a bit and then said, 'My other guess is that Mr Ashley would like an overview. We could probably go down after dark to Horse Guards and walk everything through without being noticed, but if Mr Ashley was in the stable, for instance, he wouldn't be able to see what was going on anywhere else.'

'So, we've all got to move around like we did on Wednesday, while he watches us?' Smith One, the brighter twin, began to catch on. 'It'll look like a giant game of *Cluedo*.'

'Oh, Gawd – can you imagine Sorrell as Miss Scarlet?'

'About as much as I can imagine you being Professor Plum, Watson. Now, we've got a bit more tape work to do. Then we've got to distribute various props around. We need a couple of tables and lots of chairs in the canteen; a table representing the work surface in the harness room, and buckets and brooms and that sort of thing in the stables. Oh, yes, and has anyone got a football?'

'What do we want a football for?' Smith Two had barely enough brains to make his body function.

Burdett looked grim for a moment and then said, 'I'll give you three guesses, and here's a clue: we're going to draw a face on it.'

∗   ∗   ∗   ∗   ∗

'I must be,' observed Edward, importantly, 'the only person ever to be decapitated twice within the space of a week.'

'You know you love the attention,' said Ashley. 'Besides – and seriously for once – I'm assuming it won't be so traumatic the second time around. Yesterday's little bit of theatre was as unpleasant as our episode at the Tower, in its own way, and I don't want to put another chap through that. Do you mind?'

'As you say, seriously, no I don't mind. I'm sure I'll be fine this time.'

'Good. For most of the exercise I've borrowed the bombardier from yesterday's guard. He knows all the routines, of course, which you wouldn't. Then for the murder itself, we'll substitute you. I'm afraid it means that you'll have to get yourself into the same kit as him.' Ashley grinned; Edward was possibly the least military person he had ever met.

79

'And what kit is that?' Edward narrowed his eyes and looked suspiciously at Ashley.

'Oh, you'll see...'

It was a quarter to two, fifteen minutes before the re-enactment was due to begin. They walked out of the Mess and contemplated the work of Burdett and his team. The mocked-up game-board version of Horse Guards was on a reduced scale; even so, it still took up the parade ground and spilled over the riding track and towards the Mess. Outside the Mess door, they walked between two oblong areas of tape; these were each labelled SENTRY – MOUNTED. They then stood in a square area with a post in the middle. On this was written TILT YARD. Turning left towards the real parade ground, they passed through a non-existent wooden gate, walking successively past GUARDROOM and CANTEEN on the right and HARNESS ROOM on the left. They then passed through INNER COURTYARD and into an area marked STABLE. Various other smaller details had been picked out; the back entrance, tucked away in the inner courtyard, the lavatories and the stairs up to the soldiers' accommodation. Burdett's liberally scattered props also aided what Ashley remembered being called "the willing suspension of disbelief" in literature lessons at school. It was really rather impressive.

The new acting lance bombardier appeared from a stable block, walked straight through one of the imaginary Horse Guards walls and over towards Ashley. 'Hello sir. I've spoken to Gunner Lang and he's cheered up quite a lot since yesterday – especially now he knows that you don't regard what happened as serious evidence. He's quite happy to play second murderer, if that's what you want, sir.'

'Excellent, thanks very much. Now this, Lance Bombardier Green, is your victim.' Ashley introduced Edward. 'Bombardier Croft has kindly agreed to play Cooper for most of the mock-up, but I don't want a repeat of yesterday's drama with Barker, so Edward here will swap over for the actual kill.'

'Jolly good sir. I'm sure he'll die like a true professional.'

'I've had enough practice', observed Edward, dryly.

'Do you think, Lance Bombardier Green, that you could get Edward kitted out like Cooper was when he died? Ceremonial kit from the waist down and just a vest and braces from the waist up? It will all help to make the situation more realistic. Is there time to do that?'

Green looked Edward up and down and gave a broad smile. 'If you don't mind us being five minutes late, sir, I'll take him to the dressing up box now. When you next see him, I can promise you, sir, you won't know him.'

'You're just saying that to please me...,' suggested Ashley, as Green and Edward walked through another wall and off towards Green's quarters.

By five minutes to the hour, everybody except Green had assembled in the area designated TILT YARD. Ashley had given detailed instructions about their order of dress. There was, he had decided, no need for everybody to have to make the effort of getting into full ceremonial uniforms. The sentries and Burdett, therefore, were in their everyday riding outfits. They were also wearing combat jackets and carrying swords. The four backroom boys were in their green coveralls. Watson and Carlton had theirs over their riding kit, ready to change at the appropriate time. Only Bombardier Croft was dressed exactly as if for Horse Guards itself. Ashley greeted him as he approached.

'Thanks for going to all this effort; it's good of you to give up your time.'

'That's quite all right, sir. It sounds as though it's going to be rather good fun, actually.'

'Yes; it's an odd thing but walking through a murder usually *is* rather good fun. It can be like a badly put together Amateur Dramatic Society's annual production. More to the point, one can discover an enormous amount from it.'

'I'm sure, sir. Anyway, glad to be of use to you. Here comes the CO, sir, if you'll excuse me.'

The gunners had formed up in three ranks; there was a

81

Green-sized gap in the second rank, owing to both his promotion and his temporary absence with Edward. Bombardier Croft moved to a position behind the impromptu parade and Burdett called the assembled men to attention as Major Benson appeared at the front door of the Mess. There was a unanimous crunching of boots. Once again, Ashley had to make a conscious effort not to leap into the same rigid pose. Burdett performed a smart about-turn and saluted his commanding officer.

'Good afternoon, sir. The former guard party is assembled as instructed, sir.'

'Thank you, Bombardier Burdett. Stand the men easy.' Burdett saluted again and turned back towards the gunners.

'Guard, stand at – ease!' The same satisfying sound of boots striking the ground. 'Stand easy.'

The gunners visibly relaxed; Ashley felt himself doing the same. The major moved forward to address the gathering.

'You have all, by now, met Mr Ashley who, as you know, is here to help us bring this whole sorry affair to a conclusion. He has, very properly, asked me to remind you that he is a private detective and a member of neither the civil nor military police: you have, therefore, absolutely no legal obligation to answer any of his questions nor, indeed, to take part in the present exercise. Therefore, although I should like to think that you will all co-operate to the best of your ability, I tell you now, that anyone unwilling to walk through the events of last Wednesday afternoon may leave the area and no conclusions will be drawn from this action.' Benson paused: it was a little like that awkward moment in weddings, when a member of the congregation has the chance to bring the service to a shuddering halt.

Benson asked, 'Does anybody wish to leave?' Nobody moved. After a few seconds, Burdett ventured, 'I think, sir, that we're all very keen to do what we can.'

'Good – thank you for that. Mr Ashley, the men are all yours. Carry on, Bombardier Burdett.'

Burdett carried on by bringing everyone back to attention and saluting once more before Major Benson turned back into the Mess. It was as well that the major left when he did, for the next moment Green came round a corner, grinning from ear to ear. With him was a half-embarrassed, half-amused Edward, dressed according to instructions. Gunner Carlton gave a great whoop of joy, which became general. The two Smiths wolf-whistled.

Unused to the strange art of walking in stiff, waxed riding boots and terrified of getting his spurs caught up, Edward was waddling along, looking like a duck who had offered to act as surrogate mother to an ostrich egg. Once Hall had suggested loudly to Green that he must have performed an anatomically inappropriate act on his new friend, and Green had responded that Hall was merely jealous, the new acting bombardier decided it was time to call for order. 'Right, that's enough of that, we've got work to do. Shut up, Gillham, yes, you can have him later, if Mr Ashley doesn't want him back...'

'You've got to admit, Mr Ashley, sir – he does look lovely', said Green, proud of his handiwork.

'He does indeed – if only we had a camera.'

'That's all sorted, sir - I've taken dozens of pictures already, though I'm not sure the camera can do justice to that walk.'

Ashley decided that it was time to get down to business.

'Now gentlemen, I'm delighted that you've given my assistant such a warm welcome, but perhaps we can be serious for a moment. Bombardier Burdett and his team have, as you can see, mapped out for us a very good representation of Horse Guards. First of all, I'm going to ask him to walk us through it and then we will gather in the area representing the canteen where there are plenty of chairs set out. We may as well sit comfortably for the briefing.'

Ten minutes later, they were all gathered around a couple of tables in the imaginary canteen. Ashley was pleased to see that, now the exercise was getting underway, everybody was intent on getting it right. Edward's exotic appearance was forgotten and he was taking notes at Ashley's side.

'Now, according to the doctor's report, Bombardier Cooper was killed at some time between a quarter past two and a quarter to four. Frankly, I don't think that tells us anything we couldn't have worked out for ourselves. We know that there was a changeover of the two boxmen at two o'clock, which he commanded, and that he was found dead shortly before four o'clock. The heat of the day was such that standard medical methods of being more specific about the time of death did not necessarily apply; for example, his body was still at a relatively high temperature and his blood was only partially congealed.'

Ashley paused for the men to take in the information, then continued: 'You all outlined your movements between two and four o'clock that afternoon to Inspector Cowan. I spent some time this morning combining your separate accounts into a single chart, giving the movements of all of you in sequence. I propose using that this afternoon as a sort of script, which will tell us where to move in our turn. Any questions so far, or is that clear?'

Nobody spoke: it seemed to be clear.

'Good. Now, from this chart, I can already see that there are times of fairly busy activity; in particular, there is one around the three o'clock changing of all the sentries and another marking the preparation for the four o'clock inspection. Around them, there are two relatively quiet slots. I am working on the fairly obvious hypothesis that the murder took place during one of these lulls. The first was from about a quarter past two until twenty to three; the second from a quarter past three until just after half past.

'During those two periods of relative inactivity, by far the most popular place to be was the canteen. There were refreshments available in there and there was a Test match on the television. According to your independent statements, Bombardier Cooper did not tend to keep company with the rest of you and would normally relax in the guardroom, where there was also a television. Any questions at this stage?'

Gunner Hall wondered whether it was possible that the murder might have been committed during one of the active periods: 'Under cover of all the moving around, if you see what I mean, sir.'

'That's a good point.' Ashley made a note of it. 'And one of the uses of re-enactments like this is that they enable us to establish exactly that sort of thing. For the purposes of this exercise, I'm going to place the murder in the second period of relative inactivity, but that's simply because I've got to put it *somewhere*. Hopefully, by the end we shall all be a bit wiser.'

He looked at his watch: it was time to bring the briefing to a close. 'Right, just a few final details. First, if I'm to take your accounts as the exact truth, I must congratulate you all on having cast-iron bladders. Nobody mentioned going to the loo, or any similar little wanderings of the type we often make without thinking anything of it – going upstairs to look for a cigarette lighter, taking a mug of tea to someone in the harness room or stable – that sort of thing. Now it may be that this walk-through will jog your memories; if so, I need to know. Just stick your hand up and we'll add it to the chart.

'Second, the one person who didn't get the chance to tell us his movements was Bombardier Cooper. They, of course, are the ones we all want to know. So, if at any stage you find yourself thinking, "Oh yes, I saw him then, coming downstairs", or something like that, then again, just stick your hand up. As you know, Cooper will be played by Bombardier Croft. He's dressed in full uniform to make him stand out, so keep an eye on him and try to see if what happens today fits with your memories. For the actual re-enactment of the murder, Edward here will take over the role.

'Third, and last. You all have swords, caps and jackets. The cap represents your busby and the jacket, your tunic. Behind the scenes, these were often left in different places. Try to be exact in your placing of these items. It's sometimes in a tiny detail that the truth can be discovered. Final questions anyone?'

There were none. All the soldiers looked alert and earnest.

'Then let's begin. Gentlemen, it is just coming up to two o'clock last Wednesday afternoon. Gunners Gillham and Hall are in their boxes waiting to be relieved; Gunners Sorrell and Chadwick are also on duty, standing at their posts. Just behind the wooden gate, Gunners Lang and Barker are mounted and Bombardier Cooper is about to march them out. The four backroom boys have seen them onto their horses in the inner courtyard and are now awaiting the arrival of the old sentries to help them dismount. Gunners Green and Scott are in the canteen, watching the cricket, as is Lance Bombardier Burdett. Will anyone who was not carrying a sword at this time or not wearing a busby and tunic please place those articles as nearly as possible where they were at the time.'

As Ashley spoke, the soldiers moved to their correct positions until everyone was accounted for. Then Ashley said, simply: 'Two o'clock.'

Exercise "Bombardier Cooper" had begun.

CHAPTER TEN

EDWARD IS EXECUTED AGAIN

Lang and Barker moved into the make-believe tilt yard, followed by Croft. The two gunners took up positions about ten paces behind Gillham and Hall, while the bombardier moved forwards, into an imaginary Whitehall. Standing on the real steps into the Officers' Mess, he nodded to the old sentries. They advanced and turned in towards each other and then into the yard. At the same time, Lang and Barker moved into the sentry boxes. Gillham and Hall faked a dismount in the yard and led their invisible horses back through the non-existent gates. Burdett moved and stood by the entrance to the canteen to watch the sentries enter.

It would have been all too easy for the soldiers, without the theatrical props of horses, bridles and saddles, to have made light of these moments; instead, they went through their movements with as much precision as possible. Once again, Ashley found himself impressed with their self-discipline and commitment.

'Good. Gunners Gillham and Hall then move into the inner courtyard. Where did Cooper go?'

'He followed us through, sir.'

So Croft also went into the inner courtyard, where Smith One removed a phantom saddle and bridle from Gillham's supposed horse and Watson did the same for Hall. They then departed for the harness room, while Smith Two and Carlton led the horses through to the stable. Gillham and Hall deposited their swords, service caps and tunics in the canteen before returning to the stable to check their horses.

'Which stalls did you put the horses in?'

'Front two on the left, sir,' said Carlton. 'The four duty horses are always nearest the door.'

'And Cooper?'

'Off to the guardroom, sir.' Gillham's tone was dismissive: 'He never hung around longer than he had to.'

'That's right.' Burdett confirmed both observations. 'As he walked past me he said, "You can do the next one – I want to watch the cricket".'

'All right.' Ashley was pleased with the additional information. 'Just remember that it's very important to let me know when you see him next. Now, gentlemen, after that activity, our first lull is about to begin. Most of you complete your tasks and return to the canteen, to watch the cricket. Smith One stays in the harness room, cleaning the two bits and organising the saddlecloths. He then goes to chat to his brother, who is just finishing in the stable and they join the others in the canteen just in time to see Trescothick complete his century. We know that this took place at eighteen minutes past two. No movements are recorded until twenty to three, when the backroom boys began their preparations for the next change over. At about that time, Gunners Smith One and Watson headed for the harness room and Smith Two and Carlton, followed shortly afterwards by Gillham and Hall, headed for the stable. Before we put that into action, can anyone remember leaving the canteen for any reason at all?'

Gillham put up his hand: 'I went to check up on my horse at about half past – he'd been a bit frisky earlier.'

Green's hand was up as well. 'Scott and I went for a pre-duty pee at about the same time, sir.'

'How long were you away?'

'Perhaps a couple of minutes, sir – it was functional rather than sociable.'

'Did any of the three of you see anything significant?'

No one had, so Ashley went on. The three o'clock changeover, taken by Burdett, was similar to the earlier one, except that the two dismounted sentries were relieved as well. In effect, this meant that the only person not busy, one way or another, between a quarter to three and five past, was Cooper himself – if, indeed, he was still alive at that time. After about five past three, Sorrel and Chadwick, who hadn't had to worry about horses, were able to relax in the canteen. There, they were joined about ten minutes later by the backroom boys and Burdett. Barker and Lang went to the harness room to see if it was worth touching up the shine on their bridles ready for the next morning. Lang had decided that his was fine and returned to the canteen, but Barker put in a few minutes' work on the part of his bridle nearest the bit.

'I took a mug of tea to the harness room, for Barker,' Lang pointed out. 'Not that he drank it, the ungrateful sod.'

'Sorry, Blondie, I was engrossed in my work.' Barker grinned, his dark eyes coming briefly to life.

Lang had returned to the canteen straight away and Barker had joined the others there shortly after twenty past three. Ashley continued his narrative.

'And so, gentlemen, we have our second lull in activity. We're going to break our re-enactment at this point and perform the murder itself. I remind you that there is, as yet, no firm evidence as to the precise time of death, so there is no particular significance in placing it now – but we've got to put it somewhere in the afternoon and this is as likely a point as any. Therefore, the four sentries on duty are not off the hook, any more than those within the building stand under any increased suspicion. Perhaps you'd all like to come through to the stable area and stand where you can see, without getting in the way of the action.'

Everyone moved and re-assembled in a group about half way up the imaginary stable. Green and Lang, abandoning their previous roles, moved into the space behind the far left-hand stall and began to slip on coveralls over their uniforms.

'For the purposes of this re-enactment, Lance Bombardier Green and Gunner Lang have agreed to act as our killers. I need hardly say that this fact has no significance in terms of the investigation. Many, if not all of you, will have realised that we have to hypothesise two killers. In evidence of that, two pairs of blood-stained coveralls were found folded over the partition of the last stall. To carry out the deed, the murderers required a sword, a cloth to use as a gag and a spur strap. We don't know how Cooper was lured to the end of the stables – perhaps one of the killers came with him, or perhaps it was a pre-arranged meeting. However it was, we're pretty sure that the killing itself went like this…'

Edward, managing to walk comparatively normally, came into the stable. His audience separated, allowing him to pass through. When he reached the last stall, Green and Lang leaped into action exactly as they had done before. It took two seconds to ram the cloth into his mouth; in another five, his wrists were bound behind his back. It was the work of a moment for Lang to kick him into a kneeling position. Green used that fraction of time to seize the sword. He raised it – Lang leapt back – there was a flash of light as the gleaming sword caught the rays of the sun – and Edward fell forward. The whole process had taken twelve seconds.

The soldiers were wide-eyed. Sorrell was twitching nervously and even Barker, who had known what to expect, looked stunned. Smiths One and Two had their mouths gaping symmetrically; Burdett's, in contrast, was tight shut, his teeth clenched. Ashley left the performers frozen in position and moved over to the audience.

'Quite disturbing to watch, isn't it? No matter how much you try to imagine the scene of a murder, seeing it acted out in front of you is always shocking. Particularly, in this case, the speed and violence of the whole thing. Bombardier Cooper passed from a state of freedom to the state of a headless corpse in less than a quarter of a minute. Does anyone have anything to say?'

'Only – blimey!' suggested an awed Smith One. Most of the others nodded agreement. The silence of the soldiers was in strong contrast to the enthusiastic applause of the American tourists five days before.

Ashley continued: 'What follows is partly speculation, but it must be fairly close to the truth. Come a bit closer, so that you can see more clearly.'

The soldiers moved in. At a nod from Ashley, Green and Lang continued their performance. Lang stooped and picked up the football which Burdett had left as a prop. 'We think,' said Ashley, 'that he pulled the cloth away and passed it over so that it could be used to wipe down the sword.' This being impossible to act exactly, Lang simply stared at the football while Green removed the gag from Edward's mouth and began to wipe imaginary blood off the blade of his sword. 'We also think that one of the killers was so overtaken by some strong emotion – rage, hatred, or perhaps even self-loathing – that he either flung or even kicked the head away from him.'

Lang decided on throwing the football, which ricocheted off a post in the direction of the gun park. Somehow, the ludicrous sight of this substitute head bouncing along as no real head ever could, served to emphasise the fury of the action. The soldiers followed the ball with their eyes, until it came to a halt on the soft riding track.

Lang and Green removed their coveralls carefully and folded them over an imaginary partition. They walked through the group of soldiers and out of the stable. In the inner courtyard, Green suddenly became aware of the bloody cloth in his hand. He rolled it into a ball and threw it behind the mounting block.

'That's the cloth I tried to use to wipe the sweat off my horse!' exclaimed Hall. 'No wonder it reared up.'

Lang and Green continued on their way. Lang went straight to the canteen, while Green went into the guardroom and substituted Cooper's sword for his own. Then he, too, joined his comrades.

Gunner Watson broke the silence: 'They could have done all that in the time it takes to go for a pee.'

'That's right,' confirmed Ashley. 'A well-planned killing can be over very quickly. Of course, they may have had to lie in wait for some time but, equally, they could just have popped out for a couple of minutes. You'd think that they were off to the loo, just as you say, and in that time, a murder might have been committed. Shall we resume our re-enactment, gentlemen?'

The rest of the exercise continued. At about half past three, Carlton and Watson climbed the imaginary stairs to change into ceremonial uniforms, ready to make up the numbers for the four o'clock inspection. A real Mark Dawson appeared in time to play his part as inspecting officer. He dismounted in the inner courtyard and Smith One tethered his charger to a make-believe ring on the wall. Shortly afterwards, the others began collecting swords, head dresses and tunics. By five to four, they were assembled, ready to march out for inspection, and by five past four they were gathered around Edward, who all this time had been lying, face down, on the ground.

'And that, gentlemen, is that,' said Ashley. 'Before we all go our separate ways, I have two things to say. First, I hope that walking through the afternoon has helped you all to have a better understanding of the circumstances surrounding the murder. Second, it's not uncommon that dramatic presentations such as this serve to jog the memory in such a way that you realise you have some information which might be of use. If this is the case with any one of you – now or later – please make the time to speak to me or to Captain Raynham as soon as possible. Remember, while this case goes unsolved, you all live in an atmosphere of suspicion and mistrust; the sooner we can correct that, the better. Does anybody have any questions?'

If Ashley was hoping for the sudden remembrance of a crucial clue, he was disappointed. The soldiers made eye contact with him and with each other, but remained silent. After an awkward interval, he thanked them and gave them permission to leave.

The group dispersed in various directions. Edward and

Green headed off to the acting lance bombardier's quarters; Ashley and Dawson made for the Mess; Bombardier Croft went to his room to change out of his ceremonial uniform. While Burdett and the backroom boys remained to dismantle their model, the remaining gunners made for the NAAFI. Within a few minutes, four separate post-mortem discussions were taking place.

* * * * *

'Was it useful?' asked Dawson, as he and Ashley sank into armchairs.

'If you mean, "Did it lead me directly to the murderer?" then no,' replied Ashley. 'On the other hand, it gave me several ideas to chase up. Also, it's quite possible that one of the chaps will now realise that he saw something significant that day and will come forward.'

'Soldiers, of course, hate doing anything that might be regarded as sneaking on each other.'

'Granted, though one hopes they'll appreciate the difference between, say, a bit of pilfering from the quartermaster's stores and cold-blooded murder.'

Their conversation was interrupted by the appearance of Dutton. In contrast to Dawson and Ashley, he seemed unnaturally cheerful. 'Great fun, Ashley – I watched the whole thing from my office window. Was that really how it was done, do you think?' He fell into a chair beside the other two, removed his spurs, and rested his booted feet on the coffee table.

'I'm pretty sure of the details of the actual murder. Other facts have yet to slot into place.'

'Having seen the re-enactment, I'm left wondering why they had to behead him. Wouldn't it have been easier to run him through with the sword?'

'It's a good question – and I don't pretend to know the answer. There are various possibilities: perhaps they thought that beheading leads to certain death, whereas people recover from stab wounds; or maybe they regarded Cooper's death in some quasi-judicial way and liked the thought of a method which suggested a mediaeval execution. Then again, perhaps they just had a morbid blood lust – many people seem to be strangely drawn by the concept of beheading.'

'I can vouch for that,' said Dawson. 'It was absolutely revolting to see, but even when I was throwing up, I was almost, well – *excited* by the whole thing.'

'That's right,' Ashley agreed. 'I've now witnessed one headless body and three mock executions and they've each been oddly compelling. Last Thursday, I went to see an old friend at the Tower of London…'

Dutton and Dawson listened, fascinated, to Ashley's account of the episode in St Martin's Tower.

*   *   *   *   *

'What do you think, Bomber?' Smith One, threw an armful of jumbled mine tape into a black plastic sack.

'Yeah – do you think he knows who it was?'

'Who do *you* think it was?'

'You must have some idea, surely?'

The last three questions were from Smith Two, Carlton and Watson respectively. Burdett considered, and then said, grimly: 'No, I don't have any idea who it might have been – but I bet I know who Mr Ashley has got at the top of his list of suspects.'

'Who, Bomber? Come on, tell us,' demanded an excited Smith Two. His brother, however, had correctly interpreted Burdett's frown.

'You stupid twit, Chris – he means *us*. Don't you, Bomber?'

'I'm saying nothing. Come on,' Burdett changed the subject. 'We've still got lots to do. One and Two, get all those signs gathered up. Carlton, dump this sack by the bins. Watson, start stacking the chairs.'

The discussion was at an end.

94

Green was making two mugs of tea. Edward had tried to remove his riding boots by himself, but had given it up as a bad job. He was now sitting in the army's idea of an easy chair, surveying the room: there were no pictures on the wall, nor a hint of a suggestion that Green's quarters had been personalised in any way. Green registered his inquisitive gaze and said, 'I only moved in this morning. As a gunner, I had to share a room, but now I get my own place.' He handed a mug to Edward. 'They say the first promotion is the best you ever get – no more menial duties, and your own room. I just hope your boss can clear everything up as soon as possible so that it can be properly confirmed – otherwise, it's back to sharing accommodation with Carlton the Phantom Snorer.'

Edward took a sip of tea and realised that he should have said he wasn't thirsty. 'I'm bound to say, you and the other chap killed me very stylishly. If I ever need to be beheaded properly, I'll give you a call.'

'Well, we'd had some practice, yesterday. We really traumatised Adam Barker – I felt guilty about it afterwards, but he's all right now. You were much calmer about the whole thing.'

Edward did his best to look important: 'Well, once you've laid your neck on the execution block at the Tower of London, a simple slice of a sword is easy to cope with…'

Green was a good listener; he gasped in all the right places and asked all the right questions. Edward became so caught up in his own story, which somehow got mixed up with other bloodthirsty anecdotes from Yeoman Warder Gillick, that he allowed a second mug of repellent orange tea to be placed in his hand. Eventually, he decided it was time to get back to Ashley.

'How do I get out of these things?' He looked down at Green's best riding boots. There were scratches in the polish where the boots had come into contact with the parade ground.

'There's a knack to it, but first you have to take the spurs off. Don't worry about the scuffing, I'll get Adam or Blondie on to them. All right...,' Edward had unlatched and removed his spurs, 'Give me your right foot.' Green grasped the boot by the heel with one hand and under the ball of the foot with the other: 'Now you tug towards you and I'll pull away...'

* * * * *

'I reckon it was you, Scott, when you and Green went for your pee at half past two.' Hall had turned detective in the NAAFI. 'You were looking distinctly shifty, I remember, now.'

'Scott always looks shifty – it's his eyebrows.'

'You mean eye*brow*, singular – he's only got one – it goes all the way across.'

'Further proof of guilt! Come on, Monobrow, own up.'

'Yeah, yeah, Green and I did it,' said Scott sarcastically. 'Green did the chopping and I mopped up the mess with my eyebrow. Happy now?'

There was silence for a few moments and then Lang suggested that Sorrell had done the whole thing by himself: 'Cooper wouldn't present any problems to a big strong lad like Sorrell.'

'It was all too easy,' Sorrell admitted. 'I bunged one of my nappies in his mouth and then he knelt down as good as gold while I sliced his head off.'

A detailed forensic conversation followed as the gunners discussed the finer and bloodier points of decapitation, and the psychological state of both the victim and his assailants. Yeoman Warder Gillick would have loved it.

CHAPTER ELEVEN

REVEILLE

It is twenty-five minutes past six on Wednesday morning. Gunner Chadwick is standing by the riding track that encircles the parade ground. He is wearing his khaki service uniform, breeches and best boots, which Lang has polished to a mirror-like brilliance. In his right hand, he holds a long, valveless cavalry trumpet, which is hanging from a cord on his left shoulder. At exactly half past, he will march into the centre of the parade ground and sound *Reveille*.

The daily life of Prince Albert's Troop is punctuated by music. The soldiers are bidden to rise, to parade, to eat and to retire by patterns of notes which have evolved over the centuries and which are as familiar to them as the spoken order. In infantry regiments, such calls are given on a bugle; the cavalry favours the older, more majestic trumpet, with a larger range of notes and infinitely more elaborate calls. Prince Albert's Troop, an artillery unit, regards itself as neither infantry nor cavalry and reserves to itself the right to use both instruments. Defying all logic, the bugle is used for mounted calls (when the trumpet hangs silently on the musician's back) and the trumpet is reserved for the parade ground. No one is able to tell how this situation came about: the Troop now takes it for granted. The *Reveille*, therefore, will not be the familiar, short Remembrance Day call, but the magnificent concerto proper to the cavalry trumpet.

As the seconds pass, Chadwick contemplates the events of the last week. He does not even try to be sorry that Cooper is dead. Cooper had made it his business to render his life as unpleasant as possible, devising torment upon torment in the hope of goading him into a rash and foolish response, which would delay or even prevent his promotion. Chadwick smiles with satisfaction when he considers that Cooper, hoping to incite a small, readily punishable action, instead incited two people to murder. He wants the case closed, because he does not want his promotion delayed any longer than necessary; but he would be quite happy for it to go unpunished.

He looks at his watch: two minutes to go.

*   *   *   *   *

Smith Two, with that instinct that awakens us before the alarm clock rings, is lying in bed, contemplating the same events. His limited powers of thought do not make him less susceptible to emotions, and Smith Two is about as miserable as it is possible to be. He relies on his brother's intelligence implicitly – and his brother says that Ashley suspects them. Inspector Cowan had as well, and had done his best to bully and muddle Smith Two into a bewildered state. In his confusion, he could have said anything, had not Major Benson been there to look after him. Will it be long before the hand of a policeman is on his shoulder and he is bundled into a van, his wrists bound, like Cooper's? Perhaps it will happen this morning.

Then Smith Two thinks about what he knows. He is desperate to talk to somebody – but to whom? Not to Ashley or Raynham, because he cannot bear the thought of the consequences. Not even to his brother, because this would merely inflict his burden on the person he loves most in the world.

Smith Two regards Gunner Barker, with whom he shares a room, sleeping soundly in his bed. The peaceful sight of his roommate only makes his own dilemma seem worse. Somehow, it inspires him to a decision; in the remaining seconds before the trumpet calls Barker from his slumber, Smith Two slips on a pair of jeans and a T-shirt. Then he puts

98

on his coveralls and laces up his boots. He glances quickly in the mirror to check: the civilian clothes are quite invisible.

*   *   *   *   *

Acting Lance Bombardier Green has been awake for some time. He is sitting up in bed, regarding with satisfaction his new accommodation, which he has now started to make his own. On the chest of drawers, a double photograph frame holds a picture of his mother in her wedding dress on one side and his father proudly wearing his Falklands medal on the other. No hint of academic work pollutes the surface of his desk, which is covered with the apparatus of tea making and boot polishing; however, the folder containing the three-week cadet programme is in one of the drawers, together with a clipboard, purloined from the quartermaster's stores. Best of all, the wardrobe door has been left ajar, and the uniforms within are arranged in such a way that the first thing he has seen this morning are the bright new chevrons on the right arms of his shirts and tunics. Sorrell had helped sew them on, but it had still taken a couple of hours. He hopes to goodness that they don't all have to be unpicked soon.

Just as Gunner Chadwick walks on to the parade ground, Green leans out of bed and flicks the switch on his electric kettle. Then he reaches for the drawer which contains the folder, takes it out, and begins to read.

*   *   *   *   *

Gunner Chadwick brings himself to attention in the middle of the parade ground. He grasps the trumpet firmly, and extends his right arm out in front of his body before bringing the instrument to his lips. Then he takes a deep breath. At six-thirty precisely, the first notes of the *Reveille* cut through the air. The arpeggios cascade from his instrument, echoing off the walls of the stables, the accommodation blocks and the gun park;

combining, the sounds create a magical polyphony, which then blends back into one great chord of nature. This is how the soldier salutes the morning; this is his ecstatic dawn *raga*, his paean to Phoebus Apollo. From windows around him come the first signs and sounds of activity. Finally, the last notes of the call form a cadence; already, as Chadwick hangs the trumpet back by his side, the echoes begin to fade.

As he marches away, the only applause is the sound of his boots on the parade ground and the occasional clash of spur against spur. But this does not matter; in some instinctive way, he knows that he has been part of that great act of re-creation, which is the beginning of every new day.

*   *   *   *   *

For Smith Two, the call has brought a temporary relief; routine takes the place of thought, and the rituals of the morning provide a refuge. To Green, the music triumphantly proclaims the first full day of his new status. To Ashley, now half awake, the sounding trumpet comes as an intrusion into a dream, bringing to life the dry bones of some unspecified body which he has been investigating. The bones begin to dance around him, then a pale, skeletal horse approaches, and the bones leap into the saddle...

Ashley's eyes open wide and he sits up; light penetrates the thin curtains and the sounds of outdoor activity leak through the open window. He looks at his bedside clock and realises that he has no reason to rise for another half hour. He returns to his pillow and soon recaptures his strange, dreaming state of semi-slumber.

*   *   *   *   *

As Chadwick had lingered at the edge of the riding track, Ashley's nephew Tom stood, blinking, under the telescreen in the ticket office at Exeter St. David's. After a while, his bleary eyes had become used to the electronic list of departures and he found his train. As Chadwick marched smartly across the parade ground, Tom made his distinctly less military progress towards Platform 5; equally at odds with the world of the Troop, an overhead tannoy blurted out its ugly message at the same time as Chadwick's sublime greeting to the day sounded across the barracks. Only by yawning are the two worlds joined: as Tom's jaw gapes, so a hundred gunners open their mouths to take in new air.

At twenty-five minutes to seven, the London train pulls into the station; one or two passengers alight, and about a dozen climb into carriages. Tom sinks into a seat and, like his uncle, tries to go back to sleep.

There is no such luck for the soldiers; their world has come to life. Most are occupied in the inevitable morning task of mucking out; others, with no horse to mind, sweep first the parade ground, then through the whole barracks. Acting Lance Bombardier Green, tea in hand, watches from his window, grinning even more widely than usual. Yesterday, he was down there, in his lace-up boots and ugly coveralls, like Scott, who has just emerged from a stable block, staggering behind a full wheelbarrow, his sweat visible even at this distance. Green waves to him cheerfully; Scott mouths an obscenity in reply, then smiles broadly.

*　　*　　*　　*　　*

Ashley's morning dreams are troubled by vaguely connected thoughts. A flashing sword, reflecting the sun like a mirror; mirror image, left hand, right hand, quick-witted, slow-witted; tea, foul and orange; undrunk tea; tea poured into a bucket; vomiting, hands bound, not vomit now but blood splashing out as Lang and Green hold onto headless shoulders…

Once again, Ashley wakes. He tries to connect these odd images and to make sense of them. Do they have meaning? Will they suddenly re-order themselves into a coherent picture?

101

*　*　*　*　*

At seven o'clock, Robin entered with tea. Raynham, Dutton and Fox were coffee drinkers, so Ashley had a whole pot to himself. Somehow, after his dreams, he expected to see blood gushing from the spout as Robin poured: a thought which he did his best to banish from his mind.

'Do you drink tea or coffee in the morning, Robin?'

'Tea, sir. Always have done.'

'Good – go and get yourself a cup or a mug: I need to chat about things.'

Robin disappeared. Hoping that he didn't look as bad as he felt, Ashley lifted himself up in bed so that he could just see his reflection in the looking glass opposite. The bronze Gunner was in the way, but what Ashley could see of himself wasn't as grim as it might have been. He smoothed out a patch of hair which was sticking up, then settled back and took a mouthful of tea. The door opened once more and Robin re-appeared, holding a mug with the Troop's crest on it.

'Pour yourself some tea and take a seat. Then tell me about the Smith twins – don't worry, I don't want to trick you into saying anything incriminating about them. I just want to know what they're like.'

Robin, who had momentarily looked suspicious, relaxed. 'They're quite different, sir, once you get to know them. At first, you think they're identical...'

'And then you discover they're mirror images?'

'That's right – and you start noticing all the contrasts. Some are obvious, like the right hand, left hand thing and the fact that Smith One is very bright and Two is – let's face it – pretty thick. On the other hand, Two is a brilliant horseman, probably because he and the horse have similar brainpower, but One is no better than I am. He tries to tries to do everything by the book when he rides. You can almost see him thinking, "Heels down, straight back, don't grip with the knees", and all that sort of thing, whereas his brother just leaves it to instinct and gets it

102

right naturally. They'll probably make him a riding instructor if they think they can get him through the written part of the course.'

Robin took a mouthful of tea, then continued: 'Then there are much smaller differences, which you only spot after you've known them a while. Smith One has a tiny mole on his left cheek and Two has it on his right, that sort of thing. They speak slightly differently as well – Two is slower and a bit deeper than One.'

'If you saw one of them, say, across the parade ground, could you tell which was which?'

Robin nodded, confidently. 'Yes, I could – and lots of others could as well. The CO got them distinguished from day one and most of the men in their section now know them well enough to be able to tell them apart instantly. Other sections probably can't – Cooper never could, either. Smith One sometimes used to pretend to be his brother and Cooper never saw through it. We used to laugh a lot about that in the NAAFI.'

Ashley took a notepad and pencil from his bedside table and jotted down some of Robin's observations. 'Did Cooper pick on them like he did some of the others?'

Robin shrugged: 'Not to any real extent, sir. He sometimes made fun of Two because he's dim and is an easy target, but he only did that when One wasn't around. I think he wanted to get on with One because they were neither of them much good on a horse, but One mainly avoided him – or, like I said, pretended to be his brother.'

'Good for him. Thanks, Robin, that's been helpful.'

'Shall I run your bath, sir?'

＊　＊　＊　＊　＊

As Ashley wallows and returns gradually to life, with his pot of tea on the table next to the bath, Tom also begins to revive. He has been to the buffet, and coffee and a bacon roll have started

103

to do their restorative work. The train, which had slowed down as he waited to be served, now pulls into Taunton. Tom gazes out of the window and wonders if he looks as dingy as the people on the platform: surely not?

It is time to take stock of things. Tom would like to turn his mind forwards to the days to come, but first he disciplines himself to look back. Once he has put the past in order, he can start to enjoy the future.

First of all, school: exam results so appalling that even the new system, which has done its best to eliminate failure, can only describe two of them as passes, and then, only just. This rather pleases Tom. The school has turned itself into an examination factory, obsessed with league tables and statistics, and Tom, who has no objection to scrambling his way to a bit of learning here and there, but who is basically a sportsman, loathes it. He hopes that his results have helped to bring the school down a few places in the league tables.

Mother: well, there were tears, recriminations and threats, before her approach settled down to one of silent martyrdom. At the moment, she is still insisting on his return for the Upper Sixth, but there have been one or two occasions when he has detected a weakening. These mainly begin with statements such as, 'If you don't get A-levels, you'll never be able to…' followed by a selection of careers that her son has no intention of following. Other sentences begin with references to his father's academic brilliance and the shame that he would have felt, had he been alive. This, Tom feels, is a bit much: he has only just managed to resist pointing out that, if his father had been that brilliant, then he, Tom, must have inherited his stupidity from his mother.

Tom has only a few memories of his father and most of these seem to involve his mother moaning or nagging to such an extent that Tom assumes his father must almost have embraced the bus that brought his existence to an end one icy morning. Tom is fond of his mother, in a dutiful sort of way, but he sometimes finds himself thinking that life would be a lot more fun if the bus had taken the other parent. Anyway she has let him go to London now – mainly because he hadn't given her the option of refusal – and, as a final gesture of reconciliation, has driven him to the station. So far, so good.

Now the future. Three weeks with Prince Albert's Troop sounds good fun. Tom has often thought that the army might suit him and cursed his school for abolishing its cadet force – too much time away from lessons, the Headmaster had argued. His riding experience is limited to a few plods around the lanes following the pony in front, so he hopes the other cadets are similarly inexperienced. He has seen Prince Albert's Troop in action once, when they came down to the Devon County Show, and their glamour and panache appealed to him enormously.

And then there is Uncle George's case. He has read about the killing of Bombardier Cooper (by some miracle, his mother has not) and loves the thought of helping on a murder enquiry, as long as it doesn't go wrong. Two crucial emails had arrived yesterday: one was from a Captain Raynham, telling him when to arrive (ten o'clock, or "ten hundred hours" as Tom now supposes he must call it) and what to bring (not much); the second was from Edward Radford, whom Tom knows vaguely as his uncle's assistant. Tom is to follow his course exactly as the other cadets, but he is to do his best to get to know the gunners and chat to them informally. The instructor, a Lance Bombardier Green, is in on the secret, but nobody else. In no circumstances is he to seek out, or acknowledge his uncle: if he finds out anything important, he should speak to the lance bombardier, who will pass on the information to the detective via Captain Raynham.

There is a pleasing cloak-and-dagger feel to this, although Edward's email has made it depressingly clear that the task is unlikely to involve danger of any kind. Tom has not the faintest idea how he will actually go about his work, especially if he is trying his best to get all his cadet duties right; still, opportunities will doubtless arise. Edward is meeting him at Paddington and will brief him fully on the way to the barracks.

Tom, having organised his thoughts as far as possible, looks out of the window. The train hurtles through Bruton; past the ancient school and the magnificent parish church and then, with a great whooshing sound, between the platforms of the tiny station. In a field, a solitary figure walks a black Labrador; otherwise, there is not a person to be seen. Maybe, Tom muses, Bruton is still in bed, or perhaps, quite simply, nothing ever happens there.

CHAPTER TWELVE

THE CADETS

It took about five minutes for Acting Lance Bombardier Green to be accorded the status of a hero by the five impressionable young men waiting outside the guardroom. Admittedly, the first stage in this transformation from unknown factor to demi-god was more due to the skill of Gunner Barker than to Green himself: as he made his way assertively across the parade ground, his boots gleamed and flashed in the sunlight, dazzling the cadets. This had been Barker's way of congratulating him on his promotion.

Alongside Green, and walking in step with him, was Gunner Carlton. Unlike Green, magnificent in service dress, Carlton was in his everyday riding kit; a distinction that further served to make the lance bombardier impressive in the overawed eyes of the five. By the time he reached them, they were resigned to three weeks of sheer terror; a well-timed grin persuaded them that the three weeks might also be enjoyable.

'Five cadets for work experience? Right lads, pick up your bags and follow me – we'll do the introductions once we're in your accommodation. You don't want to be hanging around here in civilian clothes any longer than necessary, do you?'

They certainly didn't now, whatever their thoughts might have been a few moments ago. Feeling strangely inadequate in their mixture of jackets and ties, rugby shirts and jeans, casual shoes and trainers, they followed Green round the parade ground and into an accommodation block. Two flights of stairs and a corridor brought them to a dormitory containing ten metal-framed army beds. The five on the window side each had a pile of blankets, sheets and pillowcases stacked in the middle of the mattress; two pillows were at the head end. Next to each bed was a small table and, beyond that, a large metal locker. It all seemed very Spartan, an effect which the polished vinyl floor did nothing to relieve.

A moment later, Tom found himself standing at the foot of his allotted bed, doing his best to give a convincing impression of standing at ease. His luggage sat on the mattress behind him, between the pillows and the bed linen. Along the dormitory, the other four cadets and their beds mirrored this pattern. In front of them, Gunner Carlton also stood at ease: it was his immaculate example of the position that they were doing their best to copy. Green walked along the row, correcting details: 'Chin up – no, not that much – stomach in, feet a bit closer...' Tom was relieved to note that his attempt was not noticeably worse than the others. After a while, Green was satisfied. He moved to the middle of the dormitory, alongside Carlton.

'All right, that's not bad for a first time; we'll improve on it over the next few days. In the army, you spend a good deal of your time standing at ease, or to attention, and you want to look really smart – when you look good, you'll feel good. We'll do the position of attention in a moment, but first, I'm going to show you how to stand easy, so that we can talk a bit about the course while you're in a more relaxed position. Gunner Carlton will now demonstrate...'

To the untrained eye, standing at ease and standing easy look exactly the same. To the soldier, there is a world of difference, as Tom quickly discovered. Holding his hands slightly higher behind his back made his shoulders relax, and his neck immediately felt less stiff. Green told them that once they were used to it, they would find standing at ease and even to attention quite comfortable, but Tom found this hard to believe.

'Firstly, welcome to Prince Albert's Troop. I am Acting Lance Bombardier Green, your instructor. At times of instruction and on similar occasions, you will address me as

"Lance Bombardier". Do not call me sir: I am not an officer – I work for my living. At less formal times, you can call me "Lance".'

Green's speech, complete with formal delivery, mangled English and unfunny joke, was of the type that army instructors have been making for generations. However, it was all brand new to the five cadets and they lapped it up. Green's seemingly effortless smartness, his military bearing and manner of speaking were casting the same spell over them that Ashley had felt on his tour of the barracks two days earlier. As Green delivered his brief outline of the course, Tom found himself half in love with the brave new world into which he had been brought by chance. At the end of three weeks, would he be able to carry himself like Green or even Carlton? Probably not, but he was going to get as close to it as possible. Green finished his summary, consulted his clipboard and continued:

'Right then, time for you to introduce yourselves to me, and to each other. Since you need to be at the position of attention to do that, Gunner Carlton will now demonstrate. Gunner!'

Carlton braced his body back into the at ease position.

'Gunner – shun!'

Carlton raised his left leg until his thigh was parallel to the ground, then brought it back down to the floor with a dull thud. At the same time, his hands came from behind his back and moved to his side, his lightly-clenched fists resting against the seams of his breeches. Green pointed out a few important features, then gave his famous grin.

'Easy, isn't it? So, let's give it a go. Listen in! Room! Room – shun!'

It was like the first attempt of an inept ballet class to perform a simple arabesque. Tom began lifting his right leg, then realised his mistake and nearly toppled over as he tried to correct himself in mid-air. A glance out of the corner of his eye reassured him that the others had done little better. The two cadets who wore trainers made magnificent squelching sounds of rubber on vinyl as they concluded the manoeuvre; at least

Tom's leather-soled shoes had produced the same reassuring thump as Carlton's riding boot.

After a few more tries, the cadets had improved their technique and timing. Once Tom had corrected the leg problem, Green pointed out to him that his arms were flying out sideways before coming to rest, then that he was holding the palms of his hands flat against his legs, rather than clenching his fists. Finally, after one attempt when the squelching and thudding had happened almost simultaneously, Green pronounced himself satisfied: 'For the moment.'

'Right, stand at ease, stand easy. From the right, and in order, you will bring yourselves to the position of attention. You will announce your name, prefixing it with your rank, which is cadet. You will then give your age and tell us where you come from. At the conclusion, you will stand at ease. Once again, Gunner Carlton will demonstrate.'

The cadets watched admiringly as Carlton's boot slammed against the floor and his arms took up their rigid position by his side. 'Gunner John Carlton. Nineteen years old. From Gillingham in Dorset.' Another immaculate drill movement brought him back to his original position.

'And now you know everything you need to know about Gunner Carlton, and probably more than you wanted. So – number one.'

Five young men in succession did their best to echo Carlton's movements and manner.

A puny thud: 'Cadet James Geary. Seventeen years old. From Amersham in Buckinghamshire.'

A squelch: 'Cadet Keith Vernon. Sixteen years old. North London.'

Two more thudders and a squelcher followed: Tom himself ('Cadet Tom Noad. Seventeen years old. From Chagford, in Devon.'); another Tom ('Cadet Tom Marsh, seventeen years old. From Chichester.'); and Dave Corner, the second squelcher, sixteen years old, from Basildon.

Tom had a brief vision of them all as the finalists in a

seaside beauty competition ('Tom is seventeen years old, and comes from a small town near Exeter. His hobbies include skiving work, smoking and auto-eroticism. If he wins the prize tonight, he says he will blow the money on alcohol'). The vision disappeared as Lance Bombardier Green began to speak again.

'Good. Your formal address: Cadet Geary, Cadet Vernon, Cadet Noad, Cadet Marsh, Cadet Corner.' Green indicated each one in turn with an outstretched hand. 'If I'm convinced that you've all earned it, I may be persuaded to drop the "cadet" and replace it with "gunner" – but only when you all deserve it. Informal address: James, Keith, Tom One, Tom Two, Dave.

'If you have any questions now, or at any other time, do not put your hand up like good little schoolboys and definitely do not call out. Bring yourself to the position of attention and then I shall know that you have something to ask. Got that? Right, any questions?'

There were none.

'Good. Now we have three treats for you before you sample the delights of a cookhouse lunch. There is a tour of the barracks and a visit to the quartermaster to draw kit. But first,' Green smiled wider than ever, 'We all have an appointment with the army barber.'

$$* \quad * \quad * \quad * \quad *$$

Ashley knew how Lady Jane Grey must have felt. He had caught his first glimpse of Tom from the window of his room in the mess as the five cadets, doing their best to walk in step with Carlton and Green, had headed past the gun park and out of sight. Now, their hairless bodies were brought back in solemn procession. Would their scalps be placed on poles at the entrance to the barracks as a warning to all?

Tipped off by Raynham that Horse Guards would be free of police for the first time since the murder, Ashley had spent the earlier part of the morning there, scrounging a lift in a Land Rover with two backroom boys; today's equivalent of the Smith twins. They were a cheerful pair, who clearly regarded themselves as having the best of the Horse Guards duties.

'All right, sir, we miss out on the glamour of being chatted up by all the pretty girls, but we don't have to spend hours on our uniforms and tack, and we're in the same kit all day. It gets a bit hectic at change-over times, but otherwise, it's a pleasant day with lots of free time. The two backroom boys who have to ride over and take part in the inspection are the ones who have the worst deal; they get both types of work and less of the fun. Here we are, sir.'

Ashley had thanked them for the lift and climbed out of the Land Rover. Apart from the canteen, in which he had been stuck for several hours last Wednesday, he had only the vaguest knowledge of the Horse Guards complex. He had wandered around at liberty while the old guard prepared for hand-over and departure, then watched the ceremonies when Bombardier Croft arrived with the new guard. For half an hour, there was activity of one sort or another: new sentries to be posted, horses to be untacked, stabled and looked after. Finally, six gunners and two NCOs were able to look after their own needs, after almost two hours in the saddle. Ashley watched the men moving around. He observed that one retreating figure in ceremonial uniform looked very much like another – but surely that wouldn't apply when you knew and worked with the people involved?

Bombardier Croft had given him a full tour and then he had travelled back to the barracks on the Underground. It occurred to Ashley, as he sat musing at the window, hoping that Tom wouldn't mourn the loss of his hair too much, that he was really no closer to solving the crime. Certainly, he now had a good working knowledge of the Troop's routines and customs and had come to know several of the officers and men quite well. Yesterday's walk-through had been useful in establishing some basic points, but he had been able to eliminate not a single suspect. Nor had any of the soldiers come forward with further information. Was that because there was none, or did the soldiers prefer solidarity and comradeship to relief from suspicion? On the whole, Ashley felt that he sympathised with them if they did.

He continued staring rather blankly out of the window. After a while, the cadets appeared again, staggering under mounds of freshly issued kit. They were too far away to see exactly what it all was, but Ashley recognised familiar shades of green and khaki and the swirling, disruptive patterns of combat clothing. On top of each pile, and kept in place by the cadets' chins, was a pair of riding boots; a pair of standard issue army boots hung by their laces, like spaniels' ears, around each neck. Finally, a service cap adorned each freshly-mown scalp.

It felt like a good time for gin. Ashley wandered down to the morning room where he discovered that Dutton had obviously felt the same need. He was lounging in the same way as yesterday, with his spurs removed and his boots, crossed at the ankle, resting on the coffee table. It was obviously a favourite pose. He raised an almost empty glass cheerfully.

'Found the killers yet?'

'Alas, that final detail eludes me – but I keep on trying.'

'What's your next move? If you're looking for gin, by the way, Robin will be back in a second.'

'Thanks. As always, one observes and listens. Sooner or later something will crop up: I'm positive that nobody can commit such a macabre crime without being affected by it somehow – eventually this has to show itself in the actions of one of the perpetrators.' In reality, Ashley wasn't at all sure that this would be the case, but he wasn't in a mood to confess his uncertainty to Dutton.

Robin entered with another drink for the officer, who surrendered it to Ashley and ordered a replacement. While he waited for it to arrive, Dutton continued his questioning: 'Did yesterday establish any timings for you?'

'Not the time of the murder itself, if that's what you mean, though some periods were eliminated. It couldn't possibly have happened during the change-over times, for example. And I managed to establish a fair bit about who was where at certain points, which is always useful. It's much easier for a person to recall what he was doing at a particular time when he's walking it through, than when he's simply being questioned by an inspector with a sergeant taking notes. For instance, how specific could you be if I put you on the spot now and asked your movements between two o'clock and four o'clock last Wednesday?'

Dutton's second gin arrived and he contemplated it for a while. 'I think I see what you mean: I could talk you through fairly vague times, but if I actually recreated my afternoon, I imagine I could be pretty exact about it.

'Let me see. Wednesday is always a fairly slack afternoon in the army: a lot of sport gets played and not that much work done. I think I was still here, I mean, literally in this seat where I am now, at two o'clock. I went upstairs at, say, about ten past, had a quick shower and changed into civilian clothes. Sometime around half past I left the barracks and went to Jermyn Street – I needed to buy a new pair of shoes.'

Ashley interrupted: 'Now there's an interesting point. Buying shoes, clothes and that sort of thing can be a rapid task, or it can take a whole day. Our questioning inspector would immediately ask you to break down your movements in more detail – and that can be tricky.'

Dutton sipped his drink and nodded. 'Well, I didn't rush the job. I pressed my nose against Lobb's window, of course – they've got lasts of my feet but, frankly, I'm rather hard up at the moment, so I didn't go in. After a bit more window shopping, I settled for a pair of Oxfords from Church's. I suppose the whole process took me until about four o'clock. Then I popped into the Military for a drink. Would that be too woolly for your hypothetical inspector?'

'Well, he'd probably want to know if you had any witnesses to support your story, but you've given more detail than many could. Another thing he might want to know…'

But Ashley had no chance to share professional techniques.

A worried-looking Robin had appeared at the door.

'I'm sorry to interrupt you, gentlemen. Mr Dutton, Inspector Cowan has just arrived with two other policemen. Major Benson and Captain Raynham are out riding, so he would like to speak to you.'

Dutton swore and left the room. Robin remained, hovering nervously.

'You look shaken, Robin. Do you know what the inspector wants?'

'He didn't tell me, of course, sir, but I overheard him talking to his sergeant – he wants another interview with Smith Two.'

CHAPTER THIRTEEN

THE MISSING GUNNER

Tom and his four comrades found it difficult to believe that they had been in the barracks only three hours. It seemed impossible that in that short space of time, the wary huddle outside the guardroom had metamorphosed into five smartly dressed soldiers. Lance Bombardier Green would be up in a minute, to give them a quick check-over before their meal; he wasn't going to have them appearing in public looking anything less than "gleaming", as he put it. Looking round at the others, Tom thought that Green would be satisfied.

They were dressed, as instructed, in riding kit: a freshly ironed khaki shirt with the sleeves rolled up past the elbow; khaki breeches with the cherry and green stable belt of the Troop, and boots which now gave off a powerful, rich smell of freshly applied layers of polish. As yet, they had no spurs. The rest of their military clothing hung neatly in their lockers; their civilian bags, discarded and forgotten, were shoved into compartments lower down. Their service caps rested on the pillows of newly made beds. Tom, hovering at the end of his bed, felt that he could simply fall back onto the mattress and sleep for hours.

Tom Two walked up the room to a full-length mirror at the far end and admired himself from every possible angle, including a strained attempt to obtain a rear view.

'You've got to admit it – it's a bloody good uniform.'

They were all happy to agree. Tom One joined Two at the mirror. His new haircut, which had felt so strange at first, looked right, now that he was in the clothes that went with it.

He ran a hand over the short, stubble-like hairs on the back of his head and enjoyed the sensation of stroking them against their natural lie. The barber had given them a "number two" around the back and sides but he had let them keep a little more on top. Tom One had a centre parting; Tom Two's hair came to a small tuft in front.

'Come on, you gorgeous pair, get by your beds – the lance bomber's on his way up and he's got an officer with him.' It was Gunner Carlton. The Toms scuttled to their positions and were standing easy just as Green entered with Mark Dawson. Carlton came to attention and then called, 'Room!'

They braced up: somehow, it seemed a completely natural movement, now they were in uniform.

'Room – shun!' Green, standing slightly behind Dawson, grinned at them as five boots struck the floor simultaneously.

'Thank you, Gunner Carlton. All right chaps, stand at ease, stand easy.'

Dawson, in comparison with Carlton and Green, came across as surprisingly unmilitary. He also looked, Tom One noted, as though he was feeling as nervous as the cadets.

'I'm here on behalf of the commanding officer to welcome you to Prince Albert's Troop. Normally, he'd be here himself, or would send the adjutant, but they're both unavoidably detained at the moment. What I have to say to you won't take long, but they've asked me to mention two important things. First, to thank you, and congratulate you, on being here at all. You will all know that a murder was committed a week ago – it's been on television and all over the newspapers, so there's no point in pretending to you that it hasn't happened. As a result, a number of cadets withdrew from this course, but you have all had the guts to go ahead with it. My hunch is that, with that sort of positive attitude, you're going to make a very good team – and I must say, you already look smarter than most cadets manage after a week here.

'The second thing I want to say is, that in spite of our present troubles, Prince Albert's Troop is the finest outfit there is in the British Army. I'm proud to belong to it and I don't think you'll meet a man here who wouldn't say the same. I hope, over the next three weeks, that you'll start to feel a similar pride in taking your part in the life of the unit. Does anybody have any questions?'

A commissioned officer – even a young and timorous one – was far too grand to trouble with questions. Tom and his companions just stared ahead, to the obvious relief of Dawson, who was anxious to be gone.

'No? Then thank you, and enjoy your time here. Carry on Lance Bombardier Green.'

The cadets and soldiers came to attention once more and Green saluted Dawson out of the room. Considering Dawson had had no more than two minutes' notice to make his speech, it had been quite good. Green was almost as pleased with his officer as he was with his cadets.

'Well done lads – I'm impressed. Your lockers are neat, your drill was tight and you look smart. My guess is that you're feeling pretty positive as well. Let's see if we can keep up the good work. Listen in! Room! Stand at – ease!'

It was as smart as the previous movement. Green looked very happy.

'Stand easy. Are there any questions before Gunner Carlton takes you off to sample the chef's hot cuisine?' Tom heard the sound of someone coming to attention. 'Yes, Cadet Geary?'

'Will we be given riding hats and spurs, Lance Bombardier?'

'You will be fitted for your riding hat in the harness room before your lesson. Gunners are presented with their spurs when they have passed their basic riding course – so if you want them, you'll have to join up properly. You can put yourself back at ease once you've asked your question, by the way. All right, lads, you've earned a good meal. Make sure that you walk in step with Gunner Carlton on your way over. I'll meet you outside the stable block at two o'clock – which in army terms, means that you will be there five minutes earlier. Get your caps on, and off you go.'

Adjusting their caps and chatting enthusiastically, they followed Carlton out of the dormitory and clattered down the stairs.

*   *   *   *   *

Luncheon had been delayed in the Officers' Mess. Dutton and Fox were gloomily killing time in the morning room when Dawson returned from the cadets' quarters. Robin had given up making individual drinks and had placed a large jug of gin and tonic on a sideboard; he poured one for Dawson.

'Thanks Robin. Any developments?'

Dutton answered: 'Still no sign of Smith Two. Cowan's fuming away with the CO, and Raynham and Ashley are looking after Smith One.'

'One looked worried sick,' contributed Fox. 'I don't think Two has ever been more than a hundred yards from him before. If he's not somewhere in the barracks – and I don't see how he can be, with half the unit searching for him – how did he sneak out of the gate?'

'What do they say in the guardroom?'

Dutton, who had been in charge of the affair before Benson and Raynham returned from their ride, answered: 'They haven't seen him come or go all morning and he hasn't been caught on any security cameras. If he has managed to abscond, it's by far the most intelligent thing he's ever done. Thanks for going to speak to the cadets, by the way – how were they?'

'They seemed a very good bunch – very well turned out, and they had a brave stab at some drill. Green's obviously enjoying himself – I think he'll do a decent job with them.'

'Let's hope so,' replied Dutton, 'We're going to need some decent recruits after this mess.'

*   *   *   *   *

Food in the cookhouse was of the lots-of-it and chips-with-everything variety. Most of the cadets were fiendishly hungry and piled their plates high.

'It's the haircut – it's sapped my strength,' observed Tom Two, shovelling on as much as possible.

'And you're going to need all the strength you can get, this afternoon,' Carlton grinned evilly, leading the way to a corner table. 'That's when the real work starts. Anyone ridden before?'

There was a lot of mumbling; the general answer seemed to be, 'a bit', except for Keith Vernon, who had never been near a horse. As far as Carlton was concerned, this was the right answer. 'Those who come here showing off about how much they've already done, nearly always have to be taken back to square one anyway. They've picked up so many bad habits, they're often more trouble than they're worth. Even the good ones have to get used to particular army ways of doing things, because that's what the horses expect.'

'Will you be riding with us, Gunner Carlton?'

'It's John, when we're not being formal – and no, Dave, I will not. I shall be up in the gallery enjoying the sight of your pathetic struggles, along with the lance bomber.'

'I thought he'd be teaching us,' suggested James.

'No – he's a good horseman, but he's not an instructor yet. To become an instructor, you have to spend the best part of a year up at Melton Mowbray, learning all about it. We've got about seven or eight fully-qualified ones here and a couple away on the course. You can tell them by the spur badge on their sleeves. There'll be a gunner riding with you as well, just to give a lead, but I'm not sure who it is.'

The conversation continued as the mounds of chips gradually seemed to deflate. Carlton enjoyed his temporary role as Fount of All Wisdom and answered questions in a good-natured way. He was also happy to encourage the activities of the Lance Bombardier Green Fan Club.

'Yes, he's a great chap – we were all really pleased that he got made up, even the two gunners who might have got it instead of him. Mind you, they know their turn will come. He's only acting lance bombardier at the moment – the CO isn't confirming any promotions until they've solved the murder.'

This, thought Tom, was his chance. However, he was pleased that James Geary made the first conversational move.

'Can you tell us about the murder – is it true about him having his head chopped off?'

The floodgates opened.

'I heard that they played football with it afterwards!'

'That'd be brilliant! Did you see the body?'

'Do they suspect anyone yet?'

And so it went on. Carlton held up his hand for silence: 'Yes, he did have his head sliced off – with his own sword, it seems. No, they did not, as far as I know, play football with his head afterwards. Yes, I did see the body and, before anybody asks, yes, there was blood all over the place. Finally, the police seem to suspect everybody who was there that afternoon, so you will be delighted to know that you are having lunch with somebody who is under suspicion of having committed murder.'

They were all suitably impressed.

'Now, I can answer as many questions as you like, but approaching our table with his scoff is the very gunner who found the body, so you might like to pick his brains as well. Mind you, don't pick too hard – he hasn't got that many.'

Sorrell, unaware of his celebrity status, smiled at one of the cadets and said, 'Hi, Keith, how's it going? Mind if I sit here, Carlton?'

'No problem – do you two know each other then?'

'Yes, for years. We were at – school together.'

The cadets shuffled about to make room for Sorrell. They were too interested in Sorrell's status as Finder of the Corpse to notice the slight hesitation in his speech. Carlton understood it and nodded; he knew that Sorrell had spent most of his boyhood in an institution. He resolved that Keith was going to enjoy his three weeks with the Troop.

'I was just telling the cadets that you discovered the body, Ben.'

Sorrell became aware of five pairs of eyes staring at him and five pairs of ears desperate for information. Tom Two's ears, which stuck out a long way, looked particularly agog.

'Well there's not that much to tell,' he lied, before embarking on a long and detailed description of the events leading up to the search for Cooper and then his discovery of the body. Five plates of chips grew cold, and gravy congealed in meat pies as Sorrell spoke of bound wrists, pools of blood and a head resting in straw, several yards away.

At first, Tom flattered himself that he was being a great detective; then it occurred to him that his Uncle George must already be aware of this sort of thing. Still, he was getting to know some of the people involved, and that was his brief. He watched Sorrell grow in confidence as the cadets, fascinated, egged him on. They would happily have listened all through lunchtime, had Sorrell not been interrupted.

Lang, looking anxious, entered the canteen and scanned the room for familiar faces. He spotted Carlton and Sorrell and came over to their table. Sorrell had paused in his story for a mouthful of food and had just lifted his fork, when Lang asked, 'What's this I hear about Smith Two going missing?'

If Lang was looking for information, he had come to the wrong place; it was quite clear that neither Carlton nor Sorrell had heard the news. While the rest of the canteen had buzzed with little else all through the meal, the two gunners had been busy entertaining their eager audience. Both of them were dumbstruck, but there was more, Tom thought, in Sorrell's face than mere surprise. He was aghast – no, it was something else.

He was scared.

*　　*　　*　　*　　*

In the Mess, the meal finally went ahead without the commanding officer. Cowan was now grilling Smith One, and

Benson had insisted on being present. Ashley and Raynham had joined the others and they sat round the table, picking at their food in a desultory manner.

Dutton broke the silence. He asked Ashley, 'Do you think Cowan will arrest Smith One?'

Ashley considered for a while, then replied: 'I hope not. If he does, I think he'll be making an idiot of himself. I'd quite like to see that, of course, but I don't want poor Smith One banged up just so that I could enjoy the egg on Cowan's face afterwards. The lad's upset enough as it is.'

'Do we know what brought Cowan here in the first place? Was he coming to arrest Smith Two?' Now that the subject of an arrest had been mentioned, it seemed impossible to avoid it. 'You dealt with him first, Dutton – do you know?'

Dutton looked at Fox, who had asked the question, and then around generally. 'No, I don't,' he answered. 'Cowan wouldn't tell me – he just said that there were more questions he wanted to ask Two and could I arrange it? I stuck him in Raynham's office and sent out runners. They were starting to come back with negatives when the Bulldog and Raynham showed up. That's all I know.'

'I think I can add a bit to that,' Raynham entered the conversation. 'He didn't seem to have any warrant for Smith Two's arrest, otherwise I'm sure he'd have presented it to the Bulldog. From what I could make out, he just wanted to give the poor lad another of his bullying question and answer sessions. On the other hand, he seems to regard the disappearance as some sort of proof of guilt...'

'Seems fair enough, I suppose,' said Dutton.

'And the CO had to work very hard to persuade him not to put out a national alert.' Raynham finished his sentence.

'How did the Bulldog manage that?' asked Dawson.

'Well, he played the old military police card again and then he argued that the best way to get Two back was to use Smith One, and that One wouldn't co-operate if he thought that his brother was going to be arrested the moment he reappeared.

That's why One's in there now, not that he knows anything. Ashley and I had a long session with him before Cowan could get his claws in. What do you think of it all, George?'

Ashley wondered how much he should say. He really wanted a private conversation with Edward, so that he could bounce ideas backwards and forwards. He trusted Raynham totally, but who knew whether one of the other officers might not, in an unguarded moment, let out something important? Also, there was Robin to consider. Robin was a useful and entertaining source of information, but Ashley guessed that no keyhole was safe if Robin was in the vicinity. He decided to say only as much as anyone might reasonably have guessed for himself.

'In the first place, I think Cowan saw Smith Two as a soft touch. The boy hasn't many brains, as you all know, and is easily confused. To a bully like Cowan, that represents an opportunity. He'd drawn a blank at Horse Guards, so came here hoping to have another go at his easiest target.

'The second thing is...' Ashley paused. Should he come out with this? Was it really as obvious as he thought? Raynham interpreted his hesitation.

'Don't tell us, George, if you feel you shouldn't.' The others nodded agreement. Ashley decided that he was being over-cautious; it was all very clear, after all.

'No, I'm sure it's all right. I'm going to say what I think is in Cowan's mind, not what I necessarily think actually happened. I'm pretty certain that Cowan suspected the twins from the start. You don't have to be a genius to work out that there were two people in this murder – even if Cowan couldn't get that far through his own brainwork, he had the doctor to tell him. What neater solution, than that it should have been done by twins? You don't have to find two separate motives for a start. The twins were backroom boys, so could have done the killing at any convenient time; they didn't even have to spend time smartening themselves up for the four o'clock inspection as Carlton and Watson did. Smith One has all the brains and could have done the planning, while Smith Two, the instinctive one, would do the actual beheading. If only Cowan could back up the theory with a solid motive and some hard evidence, he'd have a case. I think that's why he wanted to have another go at Two today.'

'In the circumstances, I don't think we should be in any doubt that Cowan will take Two's disappearance as an almost certain indication of guilt. He'll be itching to arrest One, but he'll be a fool if he does. There's still no real proof one way or the other – and if he wants it, he'd be much more sensible to release One and keep a close watch on him. So, that's the insight into Cowan's mind as I see it. Does anybody else have any thoughts?'

'I don't know about thoughts,' said Dawson, dryly. He had been staring out of the window for the last part of Ashley's speech. 'But I know what I can see. If you turn around, you'll see Smith One walking between two policemen – and they've got him handcuffed.'

Everyone turned towards the window, in time to see Smith One, his arms pinioned behind him and his face angry almost beyond control, thrust into the back of Cowan's car. Cowan, who glowered with an unnatural redness, lowered himself into the front passenger seat; the two uniformed policemen went round to the other side of the car and climbed in.

The car drove out of the barracks.

CHAPTER FOURTEEN

RIDING LESSONS

Six horses stood in line in the centre of the riding school. Their military saddles, resting on folded brown blankets, shone in the half-light, contrasting with the duller, civilian bridles round their heads. To the left of each horse, standing to attention and holding the reins in their right hands, were, successively, Gunner Gillham and Cadets Geary, Vernon, Noad, Marsh and Corner. Green and Carlton, smiling, looked down from a gallery above the entrance to the school. They were going to enjoy this.

Every mounted soldier remembers his first riding lesson: the unforgiving solidity of the military saddle; the sensation of tearing ligaments on mounting, coupled with the sudden realisation that a horse is considerably wider than a bicycle; the unnatural agony of keeping the toes pointing inwards and the overwhelming aching of the whole body by the end of the relentless hour. After a very few lessons, the body adapts itself to all these conditions and they are taken for granted; nonetheless, the memory remains, and it is always fun to watch the discomfort of new recruits as they go through the same experience.

Sergeant Miller, the instructor, looked both grand and frightening. There was a wide red stripe down each side of his blue breeches and his tunic displayed the spur badge of which Carlton had spoken. He moved along the line, checking girths and adjusting bridles. When he was satisfied, he moved to the front of the riders and began his lesson.

'We'll have a nice easy session to start with...'

The cadets looked relieved; the regular soldiers recognised the old lie at once and smirked inwardly. Sergeant Miller continued: 'And the first thing to teach you is how to mount your horse the army way. Those of you who have ridden in civilian life will have used a mounting block, or put your foot into the near side stirrup and bounced yourselves up. In the army, we only use a mounting block when we are in full ceremonial dress. At all other times, we vault on. Gunner Gillham will demonstrate.'

Gillham led his horse to the front, then turned to face its near side, so that he had his back to the cadets. As Sergeant Miller described the actions, Gillham carried them out.

'You will observe that the military saddle is raised at both the front and the rear. With the reins in the left hand, you grip both ends firmly. After a couple of preparatory jumps to give momentum, the body springs up, so that the arms are straight, the stomach resting on the near side of the saddle.'

Gillham made it look easy. He gave two small bounces, then lifted himself off the ground. His body seemed to defy gravity; still in the position of attention he hovered alongside his horse. Miller pointed out details: 'Note that the arms are locked and the body is leaning slightly forwards for balance. The legs are straight and together. In a moment I shall tell Gillham to complete the manoeuvre; he will lean forwards a bit more, swing his right leg over the horse's hindquarters and lower himself gently into the saddle.'

Maliciously, Miller waited until he could see sweat breaking out on Gillham's forehead before saying: 'All right, finish off, then back to your place.' Relieved, Gillham swung himself elegantly into position. Without looking down, he found the stirrups and placed his feet in them. Then he gathered up the reins and, without any obvious instruction to the horse, walked it round behind the five cadets into its original position.

Miller looked round at the cadets and smiled: 'Now your turn.'

Tom knew that it was going to be the first drill lesson all

over again, only with infinitely more opportunity for disaster.

'This means of mounting is known in the army as "quickest and best". Now, turn in to your horses; reins in the left hand; hands grasping the front and rear of the saddle. Listen in for the word of command. Prepare to mount! Quickest and best – mount!'

The chaos was splendid: Cadets Geary and Corner, unable to lock their arms in position, merely slithered back down the side of their horses at each attempt. Tom managed to spring up far enough to lock his arms but then felt the world move underneath him as his horse chose that moment to walk backwards. Unable to do anything except cling on, Tom froze in position while the horse wandered as it would. Tom Two, meanwhile, had sprung up with such force that his stomach was now flat on the saddle and he was kicking his legs frantically in an attempt to prevent himself sliding head first down the other side. Ironically, only Keith, who had no experience at all, got it right straight away.

Tom's horse turned through a hundred and eighty degrees, which allowed him to see Carlton and Green creased up with mirth in the gallery. He also saw Miller grab the seat of Tom Two's breeches just in time to save him from plunging to the ground.

'Now, get your balance; that's right, lock the arms, and – over! Well done. More muscle power required, second and sixth in line. If fourth in line would care to slide gracefully to the ground, he can lead his horse back to the ride and try again. You probably had the reins too tight.'

Tom did as instructed, then tried again. He was going to get it right this time. Reins firm, but not too short; grip on the saddle; one, two, THREE! Triumphantly, he locked his arms, swung his right leg over and...

'Ouch!' Instead of letting himself down gradually into the saddle, Tom had descended with full force. An electric agony shot through his whole body as he felt ball joints straining in pelvic sockets, thigh muscles ripping asunder and his backside splaying agonisingly about the high ridge of the hard saddle. Blinking through protruding and watery eyes, he saw that Tom Two was experiencing equal discomfort: when Geary and Corner finally completed their mounts, they also wore expressions suggesting the aftershocks of a jet-propelled and over-large enema. In positions one and three, Gillham and Vernon sat serenely.

'And now you are all up on your horses, you will have noticed that the military saddle has a ridge along the middle. This is designed to make it more comfortable for the horse.'

'Well, that's all right then,' thought Tom, sarcastically.

*   *   *   *   *

In the outdoor riding school a more advanced lesson was in progress, in preparation for Friday's competition. A series of small jumps had been set up and six gunners were being briefed for their tasks. First, the fences were to be taken in the normal jumping position; then the gunners were to allow the reins to fall and jump with their arms folded; finally, they were to take their feet out of the stirrups as well. Before any of that began, they were to warm their horses up by trotting and cantering round the school. Ashley leaned against a rough wooden fence, watching the scene. There was something soothing in the natural rhythm of horse and rider working together.

He had spent a long time talking to the commanding officer. Smith One had not, after all, been arrested for murder, but for assaulting Cowan. The inspector had made a goading reference to 'your thick brother' and, before Benson could intervene, Smith One had struck Cowan in the eye with his right fist and then seized his throat in his left hand. Smith One was muscular, even by army standards and it had taken the full strength of both uniformed policemen to tear him from Cowan. Raynham was now at the station, doing his best to sort out the mess.

The thought of Cowan covered in well-deserved bruises

was a pleasing one, but there was no doubt that Smith One was now in almost as much trouble as his brother. If they were innocent – and some gut instinct told Ashley that they were – the only way to clear them was to find the real killers: an objective that was still tantalisingly out of reach.

He turned his thoughts to Smith Two. Assuming he had not committed the crime, why had he disappeared? Was he trying to protect somebody, to draw the scent off? Or had he seen something? Ashley sighed; it was all so much useless speculation. There seemed to be nothing he could do except wait for something to happen of its own accord.

He decided to relax and enjoy the riding. The horses were warmed up and the riders had halted on one of the long sides, facing into the school. Gunner Lang was the first to go. He left his place in the ride, brought his horse to a graceful trot and began to canter in the next corner. Ashley remembered the sheer hard work of his own childhood lessons, desperately trying to force a lazy nag into anything faster than a plod. Lang seemed to be achieving his aims with no visible effort, his own motions flowing with those of his horse, glorious examples of balance and poise.

Lang looked towards the first fence, turned his horse and approached it. As the horse took off, he rose slightly out of the saddle, allowing his upper body and arms to fold forwards; the horse extended its neck, making use of the extra rein length that Lang's action had given it. For a second, the two were in magical flight together, then the horse's front legs touched ground and Lang sat up to prepare himself for the next fence. It was beautiful to watch; Lang and his horse, in harmony together, took the next four fences, then came back to a trot and down to a walk. The gunner allowed the reins to hang loosely round the horse's neck, folded his arms and repeated the exercise, guiding the horse's motion and speed entirely through instructions from his legs. Finally, and Ashley would have thought this impossible had he not seen it, Lang brought his horse to a halt, took his feet from the stirrups and crossed the irons and leathers over the front of his saddle. Then he folded his arms and set off again.

Ashley marvelled; only perfect balance would enable Lang to stay on his horse through this round. He remembered a jumping lesson, years ago, frantically thinking, 'Heels down, *heels down!*' as he had approached a tiny fence, secure in the knowledge that with the balls of his feet firmly in the stirrups, he would not fall off. But Lang had discarded this basic safety device: surely he must come flying out of the saddle at the first fence, landing painfully and ignominiously in the dust? Lang did not. Once more, he completed the jumps with no apparent effort at all. As he sat up from the last fence, the other gunners cheered approval and he allowed himself a broad smile. He brought his horse to a halt near Ashley, who said simply, 'Gunner Lang, that was stunning to watch.'

'Thank you, sir. There was a slightly dodgy moment before the third fence, but I hope it didn't show.'

'Not to me, at any rate.'

'That's good to know, sir – if you'll excuse me, I must rejoin the ride.' He trotted back to his place.

Gunner Scott moved out to take his turn.

* * * * *

Inside, Tom and his companions were beginning to get used to the sensation of sitting astride a rooftop. They were walking on a right rein around the school, working on their posture. Sergeant Miller stood in the middle, calling instructions and giving advice.

'Remember, it's not enough to be able to stay on top of the horse and point it in the right direction – you've got to *look good*. The crowds don't want to see you bouncing around like a sack of potatoes, they want to see you sitting proud, with a straight back and your head up. By the end of this lesson, I want you looking like the five most arrogant bastards in London – smart enough to make the crowds go wild with excitement. Number one file – turn back on the ride and show them your impression of an arrogant bastard.'

Gillham peeled off and rode back towards them as they continued on their way round. Tom could see what the instructor meant; with his head up, his perfectly balanced torso practically motionless, save for his rhythmic echoing of the movement of the horse, Gillham looked as though he ruled the world. Tom did his best to copy the posture – was he succeeding, or was he merely becoming a longer, thinner bag of potatoes?

'All right – time for your first individual exercise. In turn, you will each peel off as Gunner Gillham has done and join the back of the ride. As you pass your fellow cadets, they will be observing your posture. We've mentioned the head and the back. I also want your hands steady, your heels down and your toes pointing in. Got that? Right, number two file, off you go.'

Geary turned his horse with too violent a tug at the rein, losing what little balance he had. Then, once he had managed to point the animal in the right direction, it stopped and refused to budge. Vernon, who seemed to be a natural rider, kept the others going round the school.

'Come on, number two file! Give him a good kick!'

Geary did so, and his horse broke into a lumpy trot, which seemed to devote all its energy to moving up and down rather than to propelling horse and rider forwards. At length, he managed to steer it to the back of the ride, where, recognising the friendly backside of Gillham's horse, it settled back into a gentle walk and behaved itself perfectly.

'So, everybody, was number two file an arrogant bastard or a sack of potatoes?'

Tom Two ventured, 'I think he might have been a sack of potatoes, Sergeant Miller.'

'Come on then – I want to hear it from all of you!'

'A sack of potatoes, Sergeant!' There is something reassuring about friendly derision. Geary, who had been feeling wretched a moment before, cheered up and grinned.

'Number three file!'

Vernon, to his own astonishment and delight, was unanimously declared an arrogant bastard.

'Number four file!'

Tom unconsciously echoed his uncle's thoughts from twenty-five years ago, thinking to himself, 'Heels down, *heels down!*' as he turned back on the ride. He did his best to sit tall and to look straight ahead, knowing that all eyes were on him. The rear end of Vernon's horse was a welcome sight as he finished his individual torture and joined the back of the ride.

'A difficult one to judge, number four file,' declared Miller. 'Posture was not bad at all, but the look of acute concentration spoiled the effect. Most riders, having no brains, are unable to look so intense. Those who *do* have brains should do their best to conceal the fact. Arms out those who think that number four file is an arrogant bastard!'

They had been shown to extend their right arm in front of them, parallel to the ground and with the palm open, if they wanted to ask a question. Vernon and Tom Two charitably extended theirs now, leaving the treacherous Geary and Corner to vote against.

'A casting vote, Gunner Gillham?'

'I think, Sergeant, that we should compromise and declare number four file an Arrogant Sack of Potatoes.'

'Thank you, Gunner Gillham. All right, everybody, what was number four file?'

'An arrogant sack of potatoes, Sergeant!' They chorused, joyfully.

Like Geary before him, Tom felt strangely cheered.

*   *   *   *   *

Not all the riders in the outdoor school had been as impressive as Lang. Scott had looked distinctly wobbly in the final round, though by some miracle he had managed to stay on. Relieved, he rejoined the ride, where Lang patted him reassuringly on the back. The third rider, Gunner Watson, didn't even get as far as the third round of fences. He lost his balance in an upward transition to canter and simply flopped sideways off the slippery saddle and down to the ground. There was a whooping cheer from the other gunners, which continued as the unfortunate soldier picked himself up and chased after his horse, who was happily jumping the fences without him.

'Well, I don't know about you, Gunner Watson, but your horse's technique improved enormously once you left him to get on with it. Jump back on and rejoin the ride.'

There were three more to go. Barker was almost as impressive as Lang; Hall struggled to the very last fence before coming down and a final gunner, whom Ashley didn't recognise, jumped the fences but knocked down several poles. Chadwick, who was acting as course builder, ran across and repaired the jumps. The riders enjoyed the interlude in their exercise: Lang removed his hard hat and ran his fingers through his dishevelled blond hair; Watson and Hall compared bruises.

Ashley became aware of footsteps behind him, then of Lance Bombardier Green leaning against the fence next to him. Green spoke in an uncharacteristically soft voice.

'I thought you'd like to know, sir, he's doing very well.'

'I'm delighted to hear it – I wish I could say the same for myself.'

'Come up against a brick wall, sir?'

'Not only against the wall, the firing squad are loading and will shortly be taking aim. You know about the Smith twins?'

'One arrested and Two done a runner, sir? It's all over the barracks. I think most of the chaps are more upset by it than they were by the killing of Bombardier Cooper – after all, everyone disliked Cooper. The twins haven't got an enemy in the world – at least, not in the Troop.'

Ashley smiled for the first time in hours. 'I suppose it comes to the same thing, really, doesn't it?'

'Absolutely, sir.'

They watched the next phase of the lesson in silence.

Gunner Lang, his feet back in the stirrups, was now wearing a combat jacket. Arms folded as before, he established a canter, unfolded his arms and began to remove the jacket. He gave the impression of ignoring the fences completely and being solely concerned with the process of unbuttoning and withdrawing his arms, though even Ashley could see that he was helping the horse at every stage of the exercise. The jacket was removed exactly as his horse jumped the last fence; as it landed, Lang held the camouflage material aloft triumphantly. He then threw it to Scott as he cantered past him.

'Nice one, Blondie!' called Green, as Lang brought his horse to a walk and rejoined the ride.

'Is all this as difficult as it looks, Lance Bombardier Green?'

'Well, sir, there's a knack to most of these things, as you'll see if you watch the competition on Friday. Everyone who passes the normal rounds gets to do some of this fancy stuff. If your balance is good, you can do almost anything, but as soon as you lose your balance, you're in trouble – like Scotty now.'

Poor Scott, struggling with a button, forgot to maintain his momentum. His horse refused the first fence and his body jerked forwards, only just managing to stay in the saddle. Looking cross, he guided the horse back to the start and began again. Green continued; 'Blondie Lang is earmarked for the instructor's course next year. Probably only Smith Two among the gunners is better than him. Barker's good; his riding went through a bad patch for a while, but it seems to be picking up again now. We all have our rough days.'

'Like mine today, perhaps?'

Green gave a passable impression of Mr Micawber, of whom, Ashley thought, he had probably never heard. 'Don't worry, sir, something will turn up.'

'And if it doesn't – and the police charge Smiths One and Two with murder?'

Green paused for thought. Then he turned to look directly at Ashley: 'I'll tell you what, sir – even if they're charged and found guilty, I'll never believe it. Neither will anyone who knows them well.' For a moment, the two were locked in eye contact; then, as if embarrassed by his assertiveness, Green looked away. 'If you don't mind, sir, I'd better get back to my lads.'

Ashley watched Green head towards the procession of cadets and horses now leaving the indoor school. He trusted the young soldier's judgement. And Green hadn't just given him reassurance – he had given him an idea.

CHAPTER FIFTEEN

ASHLEY IN THE PARK

Grooming a horse after a lesson removes any sweat and dirt accumulated by the animal during its period of activity. That was what Sergeant Miller had said when Gunner Gillham had demonstrated the correct manner of picking out and oiling hoofs, brushing the horse down and cleaning the eyes and nostrils. What he *hadn't* said, Tom noted, was that during the process all that sweat and dirt is transferred to the rider. Tom, like all the cadets, now had dust in his throat, hair and eyes, and sweat everywhere. He smelled more of horse than the horse did.

Tom ached from the lesson, but it was worth it. They had all felt themselves improving as the hour went by, and then Miller had brought the session to an exhilarating end by showing them how to dismount by backwards somersault. It turned out to be a surprisingly simple manoeuvre, as Tom discovered, landing correctly on his feet and in the position of attention, rather than, as he had predicted, on his head and in a crumpled heap.

He stepped back to admire his horse. It positively sparkled – surely he could stop brushing now?

'Not bad,' observed Miller, crushingly. 'Keep going.' Tom gave an inner whimper, scraped the body brush against the curry comb for about the thousandth time and reapplied himself.

Gunners Gillham and Carlton wandered from stall to stall, correcting the cadets' technique and occasionally lending a helping hand when Miller wasn't looking. Lance Bombardier

137

Green supplemented their practical assistance with his own version of moral support.

'If you think that this is hard work, lads, remember, you've got the saddle and bridle still to polish. That's the hardest bit of all – you'll love it.'

It was when Tom was struggling with a rear hoof and a hoofpick that Green came quietly into his stall. Probably Tom hadn't picked up his horse's leg as neatly as the animal was used to; whatever the cause, it seemed to be leaning all its weight on his bent back. This, on top of the muscular work of the lesson, was almost too much to bear; Tom was sure that he would soon give way and be crushed to death by the weight of his falling horse.

'How's it going, Tom One?'

Tom gave a series of grunts, then managed a few disjointed words: 'Hang on, Lance – nearly done – just a bit more...' The clean hoof returned with a clatter to the floor and Tom straightened up to the sound of cracking vertebrae. He turned his dirty, wet face to Green and asked, 'Is it always this difficult, Lance?'

'Well, it's never going to be anything other than hard work, but you get used to the pain, after a year or so. Anyway, you're not doing a bad job for a first time.' Green lowered his voice to a whisper: 'How's the other job going?'

Tom, like the other cadets and the two gunners, had pulled on a pair of coveralls for the grooming. These had slits instead of pockets; Tom put his hand through one of these and pulled a folded sheet of paper from the pocket of his breeches. He passed it to Green, who tucked it into his service tunic.

'It's probably nothing, but you never know.'

'Good lad – here's hoping.' Green raised his voice back to its normal level: 'Just the other three hoofs to do now.' Then he grinned and moved on to the next stall.

*　*　*　*　*

Raynham and Ashley were drinking tea in the Mess. Raynham, who was exhausted, had sunk as low as possible in his armchair and was balancing his cup and saucer on his ribcage. He was drawing as much comfort as possible from obscenity and invective, which he muttered softly, like a priest mumbling a litany.

'Bloody, shit-bag Cowan, bloody pig-head Smith One – the uncooperative bastards bloody deserve each other. Bloody Cooper for being such an ass-hole and getting himself bloody murdered in the first place, bloody Smith Two for buggering off at the wrong bloody time, bloody…'

If he had paused for breath between clauses, Ashley could have sung an Amen to show solidarity, but Raynham flowed on until there was nobody left to curse. Then he said, 'Bloody, *Bloody*, BLOODY!' and fell silent.

'More tea, sir?' suggested Robin, helpfully.

'Bloody tea…,' responded the adjutant, with an air of finality. Then he changed his mind: 'Actually, I will. And sorry, Robin – that was uncalled for.' He sat up and held out his cup.

'That's all right, sir. Would you like me to take your jacket and hang it up? It's getting very creased in that chair.'

Raynham leaned forwards and removed the jacket, handing it to Robin.

'You know,' he said to Ashley, 'I hate civilian clothes – they always spell trouble. When you put on a uniform, you prepare yourself for a time of orderly, useful and enjoyable activity. Civilian clothes? Prepare yourself for chaotic, time-wasting buggeration. I don't know how you can bear it, day in, day out. Thanks, Robin – don't bother coming back when you've hung it up; we can pour our own tea.'

'Thank you, sir – just ring if there's anything else you need.' Robin departed with the jacket and shut the door.

'So you've had a grim afternoon?'

'*Grimissimo*. Fat chance of getting bail for Smith One; once that boy loses his temper, it stays lost for quite some time. In the end, I could only tell him to keep his mouth shut and refuse any interview unless he had me or the Bulldog with him.'

'Good advice. Cowan hasn't any real evidence, so he has to hope that the twins will incriminate themselves.'

'Well, let's hope One has the sense to do as he's told. Of course, this business means that I won't be able to go to the funeral tomorrow. Did I tell you, by the way, that the CO fixed it up for Scott to drive you over in a Land Rover? The Bulldog didn't fancy three of us in the back of his Jag all the way to Upminster – but I suppose that's all gone pear-shaped now. There'll be plenty of room in the car if I'm holding Smith One's hand at the police station.'

Ashley considered this information. 'Actually, if Major Benson doesn't mind travelling alone in the back, I'd rather rough it with Scott. I haven't had much chance to get to know him so far – it could be quite useful.'

'All right, I'll make sure it happens. And talking of useful time, what time is it now, George?'

'About half past four. Why do you ask?'

'Because I want to know if it's worth getting out of these stupid clothes, changing into my nice, reliable uniform and going for a ride in the park. I think it is, and I'll tell you what, George – you're coming with me.'

*   *   *   *   *

There was a pile of smouldering, dirty shirts and coveralls by the door of the harness room. The cadets had stripped down to the waist on the advice of Gunner Barker, whom they had found putting a spectacular shine on his own saddle. In spite of Lance Bombardier Green's prediction, the work of polishing the bridle and saddle was not as tough as the grooming; nonetheless, coming at the end of a long afternoon, it was still long, hard and hot work. To the dust and sweat on their bodies, they had now added liberal streaks of polish, which made them resemble primitive tribesmen prepared for war.

Still, what did it matter? In line, on the metal frame which ran down the centre of the room, were five sparkling saddles. Even Barker was impressed as he walked up and down, giving an impromptu inspection.

'You'd better not get much better than that, or you'll be taking away all my income.' He spotted a tiny blemish on Geary's saddle, breathed on it and rubbed vigorously. 'I think the lance bomber's going to be pretty pleased with you lot.'

Green was. He went up and down the line of saddles, beaming. 'You know how we describe this sort of polish in the army, lads?'

The cadets got in before he could: 'Shiny as an otter's turd, Lance Bombardier!'

'I see – Gunner Barker has been corrupting you already. Barker!'

'Yes, Lance?'

'Don't steal all my best lines. Now lads, I think you've earned yourselves a mug of tea.'

Five minutes later, the five were perched on work surfaces clutching mugs of Green's trademark tea. Barker had discreetly disappeared, leaving a second saddle on the frame to be cleaned later. Green swung himself onto it, put his feet in the stirrups and took a large slurp of steaming orange fluid.

'So, lads, how's it been?'

Tom Two spoke for all of them: 'Brilliant, Lance, just brilliant.'

'Good – you've not been so bad yourselves.' Green smiled broadly. 'Normally we find ourselves having to cope with one or two wet kids who hold back all the rest – they must have been the ones who were too scared to come this time. Anyone got any questions?'

It was too informal an occasion to leap to attention, but Tom instinctively extended his arm as they had been shown in the riding lesson.

'Yes, Tom One?'

'Lance, why did we ride with a civilian bridle? What's the difference between that and a military one?'

'Good question. A civilian bridle has only one rein, which you hold in both hands. A military bridle has a double rein and is controlled entirely by the left hand – the four strands of the reins fit between the fingers. This leaves the right hand free to carry a sword or lead another horse, or whatever you need to do. It takes a bit of getting used to, so you always start with the civilian one. We use civilian bridles for jumping lessons as well – it's more convenient. Dave?'

'Do you think we'll get to do any jumping while we're here, Lance?'

'If you keep going at your present rate, I don't see why not. We've got a small jumping competition coming up the day after tomorrow; I'll try to jiggle the programme a bit so that you can be the arena party – that's always fun, and you'll get to see the things our chaps do once they've made enough progress.'

Green drained his mug in a single gulp. 'Right – there's still a few things to be done. Let's get these mugs washed and your shirts back on. When we get back to your accommodation, you'll need to stick your dirty kit in the wash, then rub down your boots with soapy water and give them a good polish. Judging by the smell in here, you then all need a good shower yourselves. That will bring you up to supper time. I didn't see the end of your lesson today – did Sergeant Miller show you how to dismount the army way?'

They nodded. Green said, 'Here, grab this,' and passed his mug to Tom Two. Then he swung his left leg over the front of the saddle, so that he was sitting sideways. He gripped the raised front and rear of the saddle and executed a perfect backwards somersault.

'All right, lads – let's go.'

*   *   *   *   *

Raynham's instinct had been a sound one, Ashley decided, as they trotted along the riding track together. It was a good thing that Sergeant Miller and his cadets were nowhere near, otherwise Ashley, rising and falling awkwardly, would have been unanimously declared a sack of potatoes. Nonetheless, he was gradually recalling the techniques of his childhood and beginning to enjoy himself.

Raynham had raided the rooms of his brother officers and fitted Ashley into a pair of Dawson's boots and breeches and a rather baggy hacking jacket belonging to the commanding officer. He had offered Ashley one of the Bulldog's bowler hats as well, but Ashley decided that a proper riding hat was in order, so they borrowed Lang's, who tacked up their horses for them. Ashley noted with gratitude that Lang had thought to give him a civilian saddle as well as the bridle. Raynham, naturally, was uncompromisingly military, riding one-handed and looking every inch a Miller-approved 'arrogant bastard'. He spurned a hard hat and rode in his cap.

'Do you feel up to a canter?' They had come to a long stretch of deserted parkland.

'I'll give it a go,' Ashley replied, trying not to sound too nervous.

'Just stay behind me – I'll keep it steady. If anything feels uncomfortable, sit back, give a yell and I'll pull up.'

They set off together. Now that he was in the canter, Ashley remembered that it was a much more comfortable pace than the bouncy trot. He had a responsive horse who was looking after him well; keeping his heels firmly down and relaxing as much as possible, he hoped that he didn't look too much of an anticlimax in the wake of Raynham's stylish elegance.

After a while, Raynham slowed to a trot and then brought his charger down to a gentle walk. Ashley allowed his horse to follow suit and then drew up alongside.

'How was that?'

'Fine; I'm amazed at how well it's coming back – mind you, the horse is helping a lot.'

'Yes, she's a good girl that one. The previous CO used to ride her a lot, so I'm told. She's very reliable. I don't know about you, but this is making me feel a lot better.'

'I think you're right – I'd forgotten how therapeutic a good canter can be.'

'Let's have another one, then. Stay alongside this time, if you want – she won't race off with you.'

Once more, Ashley felt the wind in his face and the controlled power of the horse beneath him. To his amusement, he saw that Raynham was making imaginary sword strokes with his free right hand; he imagined the two of them charging lines of French infantry, creating havoc on their way, or else dying gloriously.

This canter lasted much longer than the previous one. It became much faster, too. Now that they rode as a pair, Raynham could see that Ashley was coping well, so continued until he felt that the horses need a rest. Afterwards, as they walked the horses on a long rein, Ashley decided to mention his idea to Raynham.

'Frank – Friday's competition – tell me how it works.'

'It's just a bit of fun really, according to the Bulldog, but he says the lads always enjoy it. It's organised so that sections compete against each other, though only in the vaguest way. Anyone can enter; the first round is for gunners who have been with us for six months or less, so the fences are very easy. Then they go up a bit for the second round, when all the chaps from the first round who went clear jump again, and gunners who have been in for between six and eighteen months join in – and so it goes on, until everybody has had a go and some of the younger lads have had a lot of good experience. Burdett keeps the scores – he's the only one who can understand the system. Then at the end, the dozen or so best riders compete in some fancy stuff – without stirrups and that sort of thing.'

'I saw some of that this afternoon – I'm glad I never had to do it.'

'Well, it's not too bad, once you get used to it. At the end, everyone still alive seems to get a prize and anyone who fell off has to buy lots of drinks in the bar. Apparently, the riding master came a cropper last time and had to buy drinks for the entire Sergeants' Mess – it cost him a fortune. He's a notoriously stingy Welshman, so it must have been very funny.'

Ashley smiled at the thought. 'Frank, this is a long shot, but you never know, it might work. Do you think we could add a surprise round to the end of the competition?' He began to outline his plan.

Raynham listened carefully. He saw some difficulties, but knew how they could be overcome. 'We'd need a double bridle like the one I'm using at the moment, and they'll only be using civilian ones for the jumping. But we can simply have a horse tacked up ready and make it part of the competition that they all ride the same horse – yes, that would work, I think. Now, I wonder if we have a lance anywhere?'

Discussing the scheme occupied them until their return to the barracks. At the gate, they were met by Green.

'Evening sir, evening Mr Ashley.' He saluted Raynham, then turned to Ashley: 'A note for you, sir. Tom says it's probably unimportant, but that you never know.'

Ashley leaned down from his horse to take the note. It was written on a page torn from a pad and then folded several times. Inside, he recognised his nephew's scrawl:

I think Sorrell knows something.

CHAPTER SIXTEEN

SORRELL'S SECRET

By half past six, most of the soldiers in Prince Albert's Troop had finished for the day. Members of Thursday's ceremonial guard were still putting the finishing touches to their uniforms and their tack, but the vast majority had changed into casual clothes and eaten their supper. Those with ready cash talked of visits to cinemas and clubs; others, less well off, stayed in barracks to enjoy the lower prices of their own NAAFI bar.

Toms One and Two, feeling distinctly odd to be back in ordinary clothes, peered tentatively round the door of the bar and, after some hesitation, ventured in. Somehow, they found the world of the off-duty soldier more intimidating than the daytime life of the barracks.

Gunner Gillham, whom they remembered from their riding lesson, was at the bar and made them feel much better by signalling them to join him.

'Had a good day, lads?'

'Yes, thanks – great. And thanks for giving me a hand with picking out the hoofs.' Tom Two had had as much trouble with this as Tom One.

'No problem – there's a knack to it and once you get it, it's easy. Well, if you're offering, thanks a lot – lager please.'

Gillham was not above scrounging drinks from underage cadets when he was hard up but he made up for it by making them feel welcome. They moved to a table near the dartboard, where Lang and Scott were playing for the next round of drinks. The Toms stared around them, taking in the strange atmosphere of this gunners' playground.

146

'It's a bit of a dump,' said Gillham, 'but the booze is very cheap. It gets quite full towards the end of the month, when everybody's out of cash. Where are your mates?'

'They'll be over when they've finished ironing their shirts and coveralls – we threw dice to see who got first go on the ironing board and I won,' said Tom One. 'So I ironed Two's stuff as well while he did my boots.'

'Sounds like Two had the better deal,' mused Gillham. 'Polishing's all right, but I hate ironing. Who was the lad riding number three this afternoon?'

'That was Keith,' said Two. 'He's never ridden at all before.'

'He's a natural. I've never seen anyone take to it so quickly since Smith Two.'

Tom One felt himself switch into detective mode. 'That's the one who's gone missing, isn't it?'

'Yes – and they've arrested his brother as well, it seems. It looks as if our murder case is about to be cleared up.'

Two asked the question that One had hoped for. 'Do you think they did it, then?'

Gillham drank deeply before replying: 'If you'd asked me that yesterday, I'd have said "not in a million years", but I must admit it looks bad at the moment. I'd like to know…'

There was a triumphant shout from Scott, as he scored his double to end the game of darts. Lang stomped off to the bar and Scott joined Gillham and the Toms. His single eyebrow formed itself into a triumphant arch. 'Did you see that? He was down to two and had four chances to win, but couldn't get the double one – I got the double eighteen first go.'

'You must forgive Shifty Scott's manners – he doesn't get much excitement in life. Mike, these are two of the new cadets, Toms One and Two.'

'Hi, there,' Scott shook hands with them both: 'And this is Blondie Lang coming over with my victory pint now.' More casual introductions followed, then Tom One steered the conversation back to its former path.

'You were saying about the Smiths.'

147

'Oh yes. I just don't see why Smith Two would go missing if he hadn't been involved in some way.' Gillham turned to Scott and Lang. 'What do you two think about it?'

'I just can't believe it of them,' said Lang. 'Smith One's the sort of person who can flare up, especially if he thinks his brother's being picked on, but this can't have been an incident like that. At least, not if that walk-through yesterday was accurate. That would all have taken careful planning, surely? What do you think, Shifty?'

Scott's brow was forming a furry rim around his pint glass: when he stopped drinking, flecks of froth stuck to the dark hairs. He wiped them off before answering. 'I hate to say this, but I think they must have done it. It all just seems to fit together. The only thing is – why would they want to do it?'

'Because he was a bastard, of course,' suggested Gillham. 'We all hated him, remember?'

'Sure,' Lang came back into the conversation, 'but it must take something more than that. It wasn't as if he picked on them much, like he used to with Green or Adam Barker.'

'And Chadwick,' added Scott. 'Perhaps he'd done something to them we don't know about.'

The speculations continued through two more rounds of drinks.

*　　*　　*　　*　　*

Smith Two, tired, dishevelled and hungry, is sitting on a bench watching the Thames flow past. He desperately wants to unlace his muddy boots, to let his aching feet breathe and to feel the fresh river air between his toes; but he knows how difficult it will be to get the boots back on again, so he sits and suffers. Fifteen minutes, and he will press on.

He has managed to hitch lifts for a few miles and he had a lucky break all the way to Windsor; for the rest, he has been walking, walking, walking. He has no map, but he knows that the small town he is heading for lies on the river, so he will now

148

simply follow its course until he gets there.

A few people are enjoying a stroll along the riverbank, but Smith Two is invisible to them. They do not want to see the dirt on his clothes and boots, or the hunger and misery on his face, so they look elsewhere. Two has done the same thing himself in London, walking straight past the tramps and asylum seekers, so he knows how the passers-by feel. He fumbles in his pocket for cigarettes: there are half a dozen remaining in the packet. One now, one before going to sleep, and the rest for tomorrow. If nothing else, they help to keep the hunger at bay. He lights up, then looks at his watch. Another ten minutes and he will start walking again…

*   *   *   *   *

Ashley finally found Sorrell in the gun park. Not wishing to socialise, the young soldier was taking refuge in work and was on his knees, polishing the brass fittings of one of the guns. He seemed cheerful enough when he looked up and saw Ashley walking towards him.

'Hello, sir. They got you up on a horse, did they?'

'Hello, Gunner Sorrell – yes, I've been in the park with Captain Raynham. We both needed to blow away a few cobwebs.'

'Best way, sir.' Sorrell looked Ashley up and down with a professional eye. 'Let me guess, sir – you're Mr Dawson from the waist down and the Bulldog from the waist up.'

'Ten out of ten – it's a strange combination, given that your commanding officer is a bit fatter than I am and Mr Dawson, alas, a little thinner, but they were the best fits that came to hand. They're comfortable enough. Why are you working so late? I should have thought you'd be in the bar by now with the others.'

Sorrell shrugged: 'This job needs doing, sir, and there won't be much time tomorrow, with all the practice for the competition going on. Besides, I'm a bit short of cash at the

149

moment. I lost a lot at cards to Gunner Boyd the other day.'

Ashley recalled the name from somewhere, but couldn't quite place it. Then he remembered. 'Of course – the gunner who paid Lang and Barker to do his kit for him.'

Sorrell grinned: 'That's right, sir. He's not much good at polishing, he doesn't have the patience, but he's always wanted to be a boxman, rather than one of the dismounted guard. It didn't do him any good, though – he came out of the stable and walked right into a pile of muck just before the inspection. You should have heard him swearing, sir! Everyone helped him clean up, of course, but it wasn't the same.'

Ashley gave the satisfied sigh which generally indicates the warm inner glow of *schadenfreude*. 'Poor Gunner Boyd – fifty quid down the drain and condemned to a day of foot-slogging. He must have been livid.'

'That's right, sir. They said, if the tourists had tried to take any pictures of him, his glare would have cracked the camera.' Sorrell gave a final caress to the hub on which he had been working and stood up to inspect his work. 'That'll just about do.'

It was good, thought Ashley, that their conversation had got off to this relaxed start. There was something about Sorrell, his youth, perhaps, or his history, which made Ashley feel protective towards him. He continued the gentle approach.

'It looks fantastic to me. Presumably, like Gunner Barker, you have an appropriate phrase to describe it?'

'"Glistening like a Life Guard's helmet", sir,' Sorrell grinned broadly. 'It's a cavalry expression, of course, but we borrowed it.'

'Well, it's one to pass on to my Aunt Lavinia – she does the candlesticks in her local church every week, and she has a very innocent mind.'

'Well I hope the vicar has too, sir, or there could be trouble.'

They both laughed. Then Ashley asked, 'Can you show me how it's done? I'd love to have a go.'

'No problem sir – you'll want to take off the major's jacket

150

and slip on a set of coveralls.' He retrieved a set from a hook on the wall and passed them to Ashley. 'There's no special knack to it like there is with the leather stuff – this is just thorough work with attention to detail.'

He stood by, offering hints and suggestions as Ashley applied liquid polish to a cloth and began working it in to the opposite hub. The conversation kept going; they talked about life in the troop, the forthcoming summer camp and the recent promotions. Anything, in fact, except the murder and the events resulting from it. When the hub was polished as brightly as Ashley could manage (slightly less brightly than Sorrell's) Ashley asked the gunner to demonstrate the workings of the gun. They spent a happy half hour staring down the barrel, opening the breech and discussing matters of range and the strength of recoil. Sorrell positioned Ashley in one of the cast iron seats and passed him dummy rounds to load and fire. Ashley was still in the seat when Sorrell, replacing the rounds in their case, said, 'And that's about it, sir, unless you have anything else you want to ask.'

The question could be put off no longer. Ashley gave a sigh, and looked Sorrell in the eye.

'I'm afraid there is, Gunner Sorrell. There's something that you're going to have to tell someone sooner or later – and my guess is that you'd rather tell me than the inspector. What is it that you know, and have been keeping back all this time?'

There was a long silence. Then Sorrell sighed as well and replied, 'I wondered if you'd come to ask me that sir,. I'm glad really – I knew I'd have to say something soon, but I don't think I could have come out with it by myself. And thanks, sir, for being so decent. I appreciate that.'

He paused, organising the words. Then he said: 'Smith Two left the canteen just before a quarter past three. He was gone about five minutes.'

So that was it: the case really was that simple. Cowan; bullying, surly, stupid Cowan, had been right all along. He would soon have his little fragment of solid evidence. It would be more than enough to justify a warrant, then a national alert, an arrest and a trial – and then the world of Smith Two, his brother, their friends and the whole Troop would be smashed to pieces.

Ashley folded his arms on the gunshield and rested his chin on his wrists.

'I'm an idiot,' he said. 'I'd hoped that you'd tell me something that would help to clear Smith. But of course, if it were that simple, you'd have come forward when he ran away.'

'I'm sorry, sir.' Looking miserable, Sorrell sat on the ammunition case, put his elbows on his knees and cradled his head in his hands. 'I didn't think anything of it at the time, of course – it was only at the re-enactment yesterday that I realised he hadn't said anything about going out. Also, I hadn't realised until then that the killing could have been done in that time. After we finished, you asked people to come forward if they remembered anything else; I wanted to say something then, but...'

'I know, nobody wants to incriminate a friend.'

'That's right, sir. And then, he disappeared. I knew I'd have to speak then but, well, to be honest, sir, I was frightened. I've just been in here all day, trying to avoid facing up to it. I almost felt like running away myself but that would have been just plain daft.'

'It would have been, but I know how you must have felt. I need to ask you some more questions, of course, but first of all, if you've been here all the time, you need to eat something. You must be starving.'

Sorrell was untroubled by the loss of a meal. 'That's not a problem, sir – I've got some chocolate in my room if I feel hungry later. A cup of tea wouldn't go amiss though – I can make some here if you like. We've got tea and some powdered milk in one of the ammunition boxes.'

Oh well, thought Ashley, you've got to suffer in the cause sometimes...

'That would be great, Gunner Sorrell.'

152

Lance Bombardier Green had too much common sense to order his cadets to bed. Instead, he arrived in the bar at a quarter past nine and announced, 'Evening, lads. Briefing at half past in the accommodation block. Don't be late.'

The Toms, on the whole, were rather relieved by this. They were both feeling tired and had been hugging the dregs of their third pint for ages, not wishing to risk a fourth. They drank up quickly and headed out of the bar. The other cadets, having arrived later, lingered for a few more minutes.

Skirting the parade ground in silence, Tom One felt a mild disappointment that his detection had achieved no brilliant result this evening. He had now met most of the soldiers connected to the case but, beyond discovering their opinions concerning the Smiths, he had nothing to report to his uncle. After the thrill of passing a secret note to Green this afternoon, this came as a major anticlimax.

These thoughts were dispelled by a long streak of light cutting across the parade ground. One of the doors to the gun park had opened and emerging from it were his uncle and Gunner Sorrell. Tom had to fight the urge to run across and ask how their conversation had gone. Instead, he forced himself to take no notice of them and continued on his way with Tom Two. Out of the corner of his eye, he saw Sorrell lean back inside and switch off the light. The parade ground became dark again – darker than before, it seemed – and Ashley and Sorrell walked off in separate directions. The realisation that his note must have been important enough to prompt his uncle to take action made Tom feel much better.

The Lance Bombardier's briefing was short, and to the point. He entered the dormitory at exactly half past nine and Tom Two, by pre-arrangement, called the cadets to attention. Green was visibly pleased.

'Less than ten hours here, and you're already thinking like soldiers. By the end of three weeks, you'll all be army barmy, just like the rest of us. In the meantime, relax. Sit on your beds if you like.

'First things first. You've had a good day today – I'm pleased and I know that Sergeant Miller is as well. He's got some fun planned for you tomorrow – you'll enjoy it. So keep up the good work.

'Tomorrow, you'll rise at six-thirty…' There was a collective groan. Green grinned and continued: 'And you need to be standing by your horses at six forty-five. The same ones that you rode today. Order of dress is lightweights, coveralls and lace-up boots – and service cap, of course. We muck out and feed the horses, then it's back here for a shower and change into riding kit. Breakfast at eight hundred hours and report to the stables at eight-thirty. You ride from nine hundred hours until ten-thirty and then, after grooming and tack cleaning, I'll brief you about Friday's competition. I've wangled it for you to be the arena party. Any questions?'

Now they were sitting on their beds, the cadets longed to climb into them and rest their aching bodies. The accumulated effects of an early start, solid, punishing hard work and three pints of lager had combined to create a state of collective narcolepsy. There were no questions.

'Good. If you take my advice, you'll get straight to bed and then you'll be all set up for tomorrow. No, don't get up, I can manage to find my way out for once without you all standing to attention.'

Then Green, who had more stamina than his cadets, returned to the bar.

*   *   *   *   *

It is becoming too dark to follow the river path, so Smith Two has turned away from the water and into a small copse, which stands on higher ground. The earth will be dry there. He sits and, at last, removes his boots, carefully unravelling the laces and easing the leathers round his ankles. Then he takes off his socks and enjoys the sensation of his feet breathing and his toes relaxing. Leaning his back against a tree, he lights himself the promised cigarette.

His brother will be worrying about him. They have never before been apart for as much as a day. But at least his brother will not be suffering from the sick anxiety which still troubles Smith Two. Tomorrow, or the day after – unless it is even further than he thinks – he will reach his destination. Then he can unburden himself. Then, one way or another, everything will be all right.

He takes a final draw on his cigarette and enjoys watching the end glow more intensely in the darkness. He extinguishes the butt and slides his body down until he is lying on his back. Using his hands as a pillow, he goes to sleep.

CHAPTER SEVENTEEN

FUNERAL PREPARATIONS

It is seven thirty on Thursday morning. The cadets, returning from mucking out and feeding, already feel as if they have been working the whole day. The steaming hot water of the shower cuts through their dirt and sweat, and they relish the feeling of the soap on their skins and the lather of shampoo in their short hair. Yesterday, they had self-consciously taken turns to use the shower; today, their inhibitions broken down by lack of time and the comradeship of almost a full day, they run in together, to get maximum time under the rejuvenating water.

*   *   *   *   *

Ashley is lingering over his tea in bed, alternating between contemplation of Cooper's funeral and recapitulating his conversation with Sorrell. He has one more crucial piece of information from the young gunner, which refuses to fit into any theory. On the bed and the floor around it, are scattered Ashley's notes concerning timings, his map of Horse Guards and transcripts of Cowan's interviews with the soldiers. Somewhere, he tells himself, the answer lies in these, if only he can navigate his way correctly through them.

*   *   *   *   *

Raynham descends the steps of the Mess and climbs into the Land Rover that Gunner Watson has brought round to the front of the building. The adjutant is dressed in the hated civilian suit and he looks enviously at the gunner in his combats and beret. Watson salutes him smartly, holding open the passenger door. Then he walks round to the driver's side, climbs in and turns the ignition.

'The police station please, Gunner Watson.'

'Very good, sir.'

*   *   *   *   *

Sorrell is cheerfully helping his roommate with his ceremonial uniform. With the burden of unwanted knowledge off his mind, and his morning's work in the gun park already done the previous evening, he is happy to lend a hand if it helps his friend become one of the boxmen. While his colleague brushes his busby for the hundredth time, Sorrell, his arm up to the shoulder in a riding boot, spits onto the leather and begins to work in a final layer of polish.

*   *   *   *   *

Smith Two has already been walking for over an hour. It is a beautiful morning on the river and he could almost enjoy the swans and ducks, the oarsmen and dog-walkers, were it not for his anxiety and his hunger. As it is, the gnawing emptiness of his stomach has become a physical reflection of his mental state. For the hundredth time, he curses himself for leaving his wallet in the barracks – the instinct which had told him to put on civilian clothes under his coveralls had not reminded him to provide himself with money.

For half the morning he had worked away as usual in the stables, but he had lingered in his stall after the others had gone to practise for the competition. All the time, he had been wondering what to do. Then, in the distance, he had seen the police car draw into the barracks and his mind had been made up. It had been the work of a moment to discard the coveralls and run behind the stable block, where the army vehicles were parked. He had climbed onto the roof of a four-ton truck and leapt the few feet to the barrack wall. He had been lucky; not a single person had witnessed his departure.

He had travelled half way across London before realising that his wallet was safely padlocked in the cupboard by his bed.

*　*　*　*　*

There was a knock at the door; it was Robin.

'Excuse me, sir, Lance Bombardier Green is hovering outside the back door of the Mess, wanting to see you. I told him that you were still in bed, but he says it might be important.'

'Is he allowed to come up? I'm not really in a fit state to come down at the moment.'

'Strictly speaking, sir, he shouldn't, but the CO isn't around yet and Captain Raynham's already gone out, so I should be able to bring him here without too much trouble. Mr Dutton and the others are so busy filling their faces with breakfast that they won't notice.'

Five minutes later, Green was sitting on Ashley's desk, his gleaming boots resting on the seat of the hard chair. He was drinking tea, which Robin had made to his careful specification, from the largest mug the Mess could provide. Ashley was studying three pages of his nephew's sprawling longhand.

'Well, good old Tom for being so thorough, though I'm not sure it gets us much further – none of the people he spoke to in the bar gave any useful information away.'

'He didn't think it would add up to anything, sir, but then we thought that you might see something in it that he'd missed.'

Ashley added the papers to his scattered collection. 'Well, of course, it's interesting to get the opinions of the gunners concerning the Smiths. Make sure you tell Tom to keep trying. Incidentally, how did he sneak away to write this little lot? It must have taken quite a while.'

Green laughed: 'He visited the loo three times sir – the other cadets think that the action of the saddle yesterday messed up his bowel movements. They're convinced he's going to have an accident in his lesson today – as in the old troop joke, "I used to think number twos was my second best uniform, until I rode on an army saddle".'

'Thank you, Lance Bombardier – I shall do my best to put that little military gem out of my mind at the earliest possible opportunity.'

'Sorry, sir.' Green showed no visible signs of repentance.

'Now, Green, while you're here, I want your opinion. Sorrell's information yesterday was the bombshell that he saw Smith Two leave the canteen last Wednesday at about a quarter past three. He was gone for about five minutes.'

Green became serious: 'That looks bad, sir, doesn't it?'

'Very bad. First of all I asked Sorrell if he was absolutely sure that it was Smith Two: he said that he was. You know that there was a cricket match on at the time?'

'Yes, sir – I'd had to go out on guard at a very exciting point in it.'

'That's right – most of the people involved in the change-over were quite anxious to get back to the television afterwards. But Sorrell isn't interested in cricket. He was in the canteen with everybody else, but he sat quite a way off from the television. He says that Smith Two came in at about the same time as the others and stood by the door. Then, when everyone was absorbed in the game, Two left the room. Nobody else seems to have noticed, and Sorrell didn't think anything of it until the walk-through on Tuesday.

'The next question I asked Sorrell was this: Was Smith One in the canteen at the time? If he wasn't, the case closes at once but according to Sorrell – and he seemed pretty sure of it – Smith One was right by the television. What do you make of that?'

Green took a mouthful of tea and swigged it around as he thought. Then he swallowed and said, 'Well, sir, I said yesterday that I'd never believe it of the Smith twins whatever the evidence, and I stand by that. But I'll tell you this for certain –

Smith Two wouldn't have done it without One. Even with somebody else to help him, I just don't think he could.'

'What if One was the brains behind it and had sent Two out according to orders?'

Green shook his head. 'They do absolutely everything together, sir – until Two ran away, that is. If Two had done it, One would have been there – I'd swear to it.'

Ashley nodded: 'I think you're right – which means that there is still hope for the pair. Thanks, Lance Bombardier, that's been very helpful.'

'Thank you, sir. I ought to get on now, sir – the cadets will be waiting for me.'

'Of course. By the way, Captain Raynham tells me that you and the cadets are the arena party tomorrow. Has he told you about…?'

'The extra round sir? So that was your idea, was it? Do you think it will work?'

'I don't know, Green, I really don't. But there's no harm in trying. Can you get it all organised?'

'No problem, sir; all the equipment is still in the stores. We'll have to get a couple of lances polished up a bit, but everything else is in good order. I'll keep my fingers crossed for you, sir.'

'I appreciate that – thanks, Lance Bombardier. And congratulations, by the way, on your promotion; I should have said that yesterday.'

Green shrugged: 'It's only Acting Lance Bombardier, sir. Nothing's settled yet.'

Ashley experienced one of those surges of optimism which keep us going when things are difficult. 'Well, who knows? If this experiment pays off, your appointment could be confirmed by the end of the week.'

Green smiled and leapt off the desk. 'Let's hope so, sir.' He headed to the door, paused and turned back to Ashley. 'It's the funeral today, sir, isn't it?'

'Yes – I suppose you're too busy with your cadets to attend.'

'We're specifically not invited, sir. We were given to understand that it would just be a family affair, though Chadwick says they keep changing their mind about whether they want the Last Post. I saw him having an early breakfast, but he still doesn't know whether he's playing or not, so he's gone to get into full dress just in case.'

'Well, let's hope his exertions aren't in vain.'

'I don't suppose he'd be too disappointed to be told he wasn't required, sir – he hated Cooper even more than the rest of us. I wouldn't be surprised if he tried to play "Happy days are here again" instead of the Last Post – only I don't suppose it fits on the trumpet. I gather Shifty Scott's taking you over, sir, and dumping you at the gates.'

'That's right – so that the family isn't offended by the sight of an army vehicle. He then drives off to sample the exotic joys of Upminster for an hour, while I hunt for clues at the crematorium.'

'Well, sir, I hope that you're in for less of a disappointment than Scotty is. Upminster's an armpit.'

*   *   *   *   *

Five to eight. The cadets, clean and fresh, have changed into their riding kit. Toms One and Two check each other over for smartness and the other cadets perform a three-way version of the same process. When they are sure that their appearance will be up to standard, they head out of the dormitory, make a leathery, metallic progress down the two flights of stairs and join the large number of soldiers heading steadily for the cookhouse. Sorrell and another gunner are just in front of them in the breakfast queue and Keith chats enthusiastically with them. Tom notes that Sorrell is looking much more cheerful this morning.

*   *   *   *   *

Using a duster, Gunner Chadwick carefully picks up his trumpet and places it in its case. He discards his coveralls and eases his long legs slowly into the tight-fitting trousers which form part of his dismounted dress uniform. The broad red stripe running all the way from his waist to his ankles serves to accentuate his height, so that when he stands upright he seems taller than ever. In his locker, next to his riding boots, is a shorter pair of George boots, the correct footwear to go with the trousers. Chadwick takes them out of the locker and holds them up to the window, where the mirrored surface of the leather and the brilliant metal of the spurs, riveted to the heels, deflect and radiate the sunlight. He smiles with satisfaction: they had been polished immediately after the last funeral – there is no need for any work on them now. He sits on the edge of his bed and slips his feet into them.

*　　*　　*　　*　　*

Ashley climbs into his bath; he has fresh tea and a copy of the regimental history to read. Before opening it, he turns his thoughts once more to the funeral. 'A family affair' was the phrase being used. What family did Cooper have? Did they know in what low esteem their relative was held by his fellow soldiers? And what positive remarks would the clergyman find for his sermon?

*　　*　　*　　*　　*

'So where were you last night? I thought we might have met up in the bar.'

Sorrell shrugged. 'Sorry, Keith – I was behind with my work. I'll meet you there tonight if you like. You'll lend me a tenner, won't you, Jeff?'

Sorrell's roommate spoke through a mouthful of sausage. 'If I get to be a boxman, I'll *give* you a tenner and think it cheap at the price.'

'It's a deal – I'll go and do your horse now and I'll see you at nine to help you with your kit. Catch you later, Keith.' Sorrell shoved a slice of bacon into some bread, crammed as much of it into his mouth as possible and scuttled off.

'He seems very chirpy this morning,' observed Keith.

The gunner agreed: 'Yes, I don't know what's happened to cheer him up. Still, I'm not complaining. When Sorrell puts his mind to grooming, he does it really well – he'll probably put lavender in the horse's feed to make its farts smell nicer. All right, lads, I'll be off too – lots of work to be done.'

They all wished him good luck for the inspection, and watched him depart.

'Do you think,' mused Tom Two, buttering another slice of toast, 'that the thrill of this way of life ever wears off? Does one reach a stage when smelling discreetly of horse is not the turn-on that it seems to us now, and when the endless grind of shovelling shit is no longer outweighed by the pleasure of looking God-like on a stallion?'

'We've only been here one day,' pointed out Geary, cynically. Then he grinned and added: 'But I reckon the thrill factor will see us through the next three weeks.'

'Providing our bums hold out on those saddles.' Dave had suffered badly: 'How are your bowels now, Tom One?'

Now it was Tom's turn to grin: 'Empty, so presumably safe. How long do you think it will take us to get used to riding on one of those things? I suppose there's no hope of it adapting to our shape rather than the other way around?'

'Fat chance – it's steel framed.' Tom Two popped a last morsel of toast into his mouth, chewed it quickly, and continued: 'Gunner Carlton told me that once you're used to it, a civilian saddle is just no fun anymore. He said, it's like sex without a good spanking first – but I think he was just joking.'

Carlton's *bon mot* brought the conversation to an end, so the cadets cleared their table and headed towards the stable block. At twenty-five past eight each cadet was standing easy by his horse's stall, waiting for the arrival of Lance Bombardier Green.

CHAPTER EIGHTEEN

THE UNWANTED PASSENGER

Just before nine o'clock, Ashley wandered down the front steps of the Mess. Chadwick stood waiting, in full dress, wearing an almost invisible black band on the upper right arm of his dark blue tunic. With the extra height lent to him by his busby, he towered over Ashley.

'Morning, sir – I don't suppose you know whether I'm needed or not, do you?'

'I'm afraid, Gunner Chadwick, that you can add that to the very long list of things about which I have no idea. I do, however, know that the undertakers promised to telephone, in case of a last-minute decision by Bombardier Cooper's family. You're looking very smart – I hope all your work hasn't been for nothing.'

Like all ceremonial soldiers, Chadwick took compliments in his stride: 'It didn't take that long, sir, and to be honest, I've no particular urge to do this funeral. Cooper and I weren't exactly on good terms – and I shouldn't imagine the show will be much fun.'

'Are they ever?' Ashley had never been to any funeral that might have been considered fun.

'Oh, yes, sir – the Old Boys always get a great send-off. About once a month we hear that some gunner from the Second World War has fired his last round and one of us goes off to do a Last Post and *Reveille*. All the veterans turn out in their medals and then get sloshed in the pub or British Legion bar afterwards. They always make a great fuss of any of us serving soldiers. Providing you don't mind listening to their stories of how they won the war single-handed – and actually, some of them are seriously impressive – they'll buy you drinks for as long as you can stand upright.'

Ashley suspected that, in Chadwick's case, that was probably quite a large amount: 'About ten pints?'

Chadwick grinned: 'I've never quite got that far, sir. At least, if I have, I don't remember it! I made the gallon a few funerals back when we buried a chap who'd got the Military Medal back in 1918. That was an amazing do. He was about a trillion years old, of course, and the whole town turned out to see him off – horse-drawn hearse, the mayor in all his robes, the local cadet force doing their best to march in step, and more Chelsea pensioners than you could shake a stick at. Somehow, I don't think today's affair is going to be like that.'

Ashley didn't think so either. He would have been happy to continue chatting, but at this point Robin emerged from the Mess.

'Sorry to interrupt, Mr Ashley – the undertakers have just called. The family left a message on their answering machine last night, Chadders – no trumpeter after all. They say sorry that they didn't get the message earlier, but they've passed it on straight away. The Bulldog says thanks for being on standby, but you're free now.' Robin disappeared back into the Mess.

Chadwick looked pleased. 'Well, then, if you'll excuse me, sir, I'll go and get out of my glad rags. I hope the funeral's not too grim.' Forgetting that Ashley was a civilian, Chadwick saluted him, realised his mistake, blushed and grinned awkwardly, before heading off in the direction of his quarters. Ashley watched the departing trumpeter until he turned a corner and disappeared. He had rather enjoyed the salute.

A moment later, the commanding officer's Jaguar pulled up. Gunner Hall left the engine running, and it purred away contentedly as the driver, dressed in an appallingly shiny suit from a cheap outfitter, climbed out of his seat and positioned himself by the rear passenger door. 'Morning, Mr Ashley – are you coming along as well?'

'Yes, but in a more lowly form of transport. It's very strange to see you out of uniform, Gunner Hall.'

'I know, sir.' Hall obviously shared Raynham's distaste for civilian clothes. 'I look as though my case has just come up in court, don't I? It's actually Carlton's suit, sir. He splashed out in Top Shop when his mother finally got married.'

Ashley was amused by the thought. 'I suppose it's too much to hope that the man she was marrying was Carlton's father?'

'I'm not sure, sir. He did once try to explain the complexities of the Carlton dynasty's matrimonial arrangements, but after three or four pints it all got a bit muddled. Anyway, Carlton bought the shiniest suit in the shop and we get to borrow it when we make our excursions into the real world. Apart from Chadwick, of course – he tried it on once for a laugh and there was a good six inches of hairy leg sticking out at the bottom, and the jacket only just met the trousers. The tie's all right though, isn't it, sir? It's Mr Dawson's.'

'That's kind of him.' Ashley was impressed by the young officer's thoughtfulness, until Hall disillusioned him.

'I don't think he knows, sir. None of the lads had a black tie, so Robin said he'd sneak one from the Mess. Rather a nice one, isn't it? A bit posher than Carlton's polyester spectacular. Excuse me, sir, here comes the Bulldog.'

Hall leapt to attention by the car door and the indestructible creases of the suit fell into rigid alignment. Benson, more expensively and tastefully dressed, but with a tie exactly matching Hall's, descended from the Mess. He exchanged a few words with Ashley, then seated himself in solitary splendour on the back seat of the Jaguar. Hall climbed back into the driver's seat, put the engine into gear and drove out of the barracks at a dignified speed.

Ashley began to feel that standing on the steps of the Officers' Mess was rather like dining in the *Café de Paris*: if only one stayed there long enough, the whole world would pass by. As soon as the Jaguar departed, with feline suavity, a Land

Rover juddered round a corner, came to a belching halt and throbbed noisily as Gunner Scott jumped out. Scott, befitting his vehicle, was dressed in combats and beret: he, after all, was going no nearer the crematorium than the gate. Ashley noticed that his single eyebrow ran parallel to the browband of his beret, giving the impression that a toy car had just skidded across his forehead.

'Morning, sir,' he said brightly. 'Lovely day for a funeral – hope you don't mind slumming it in this old crate. Captain Raynham pinched the nice new one to go to the police station.'

'Good morning, Gunner Scott. On the contrary, I shall enjoy pretending to be a real soldier, bouncing around in an army truck.'

'Whatever floats your boat, sir,' Scott grinned and his eyebrow merged with his beret. 'Are you ready to go, sir?'

Ashley was just climbing into the passenger seat when Dutton shot out of the Mess. Scott sprang to attention and saluted.

'Morning Ashley – glad I've caught you in time. You don't mind if I cadge a lift, do you?'

Ashley did mind. He had planned this journey carefully in order to speak to Scott, which would be quite impossible with Dutton in the way. Why had Dutton suddenly decided to go to the funeral? And why, in that case, couldn't he have travelled with Benson? Still, there seemed to be nothing that could be done about the situation. The only possible objection was raised by Scott, who also seemed annoyed by the alteration to the arrangements.

'There's not much room in the back, sir – it's full of kit. I could take it out, if you like, but it'll make us late starting.'

'That's all right, Gunner Scott, I'll squeeze in front – this is one of the old seats, so there's just about room for three. I'm sure Mr Ashley won't object.'

Once again, Ashley *did* object, but felt unable to say so. He fumed inwardly as the officer barged into the vehicle and shoved into him, while Scott slammed the door. Once Dutton was safely shut in, he relaxed back against the door and Ashley was able to put a tiny amount of space between himself and the lieutenant. As the Land Rover puffed its way out of the barrack gates, Dutton had the grace to give a sort of apology.

'God, this *is* a tight squeeze, isn't it? Sorry to do this to you, Ashley, but there was a bit of a last-minute panic. I was all dressed up to ride in the park when a chap from my time out in Osnabrück phoned. He's going to the funeral and suggested we meet and had lunch afterwards. I changed as quickly as I could, but I saw the Bulldog's car pulling off just as I was putting on my tie. Lucky I caught you.'

There were two types of luck, mused Ashley.

* * * * *

The cadets had graduated to a sitting trot. They were lolloping awkwardly around the riding school, following in the wake of Gunner Gillham, who somehow managed to make the gait look natural and comfortable. Even Vernon, who had done so well yesterday, was finding this one difficult.

'Try to go with the motion of the horse, Cadet Noad,' called Miller, as Tom was thrown onto the pommel of his saddle for what must have been the hundredth time. 'It can be very painful if you don't follow the natural rhythms of your mount.'

Tom had worked that much out for himself. On several occasions, he had had to blink away tears from his eyes, sit back in the saddle and try to recover his balance. Mercifully, the instructor decided it was time to give the cadets a temporary respite; 'Listen in! Ride – prepare to walk – and *walk!* This last instruction, loud and drawn out, spoke directly to the horses who, with no further instructions from the cadets, completed an instant downward transition. Tom's backside gave an unexpectedly large thud into the saddle and he too began to relax.

'Right, give your horses a long rein and listen in as you walk around the school. That wasn't at all bad for a first go. In the civilian world, you don't use sitting trot that much, only at times of transition, really. In the army, we use it all the time, so it's important to get the hang of it as soon as possible. Watch Gunner Gillham as he rides round the school – okay, Gillham, off you go.'

Miller provided a commentary as Gillham shortened his reins and squeezed his horse into the trot: 'See how Gunner Gillham is sitting well into the saddle and how his hands are perfectly steady. His heels are down, enabling him to balance and follow the motion of the horse. Note also, number four file, that his face is not screwed up into an expression of intellectual endeavour. On the contrary, Gillham displays that look of superior vacuity to which all gunners aspire.'

A few seconds later Gillham had caught up with the rear of the ride. He looked over to Miller for instructions.

'All right, Gillham, trot back to the front. First of all, we'll have another go as a ride, and then...' Miller paused, evilly, 'We'll do it as an Individual Exercise. *Trot on!*'

*   *   *   *   *

Dutton seemed to be oblivious to the fact that neither Ashley nor Scott was delighted to have his company. He kept up a running monologue, the only merit of which was that it required very little response. Ashley contributed the odd grunt and Scott mainly limited himself to grinding the gears whenever he felt particularly fed up; otherwise, the conversational field belonged to Dutton. He seemed positively excited.

'...of course, I hadn't intended coming at all. Although Cooper was out in Osnabrück at the same time as my posting, I hardly knew him – but when Jake rang this morning, I thought it was the least I could do. After all, he'd flown over specially. It'll be good to catch up on the Osnabrück gossip. I wonder if any of the other chaps will be there...'

Scott made one of his few contributions of the journey: 'If they are, sir, they'll be in mufti. Nothing military – that was the request of the family.' It was a remark so pointed that even Dutton paused. He looked down at his tie; the purple zigzags against a blue background could only have been a regimental design. Dutton was temporarily nonplussed.

'Oh – do you think I should have worn a black tie? Nobody wears a black tie these days, do they?'

'The major does, sir,' said Scott, grimly. He brought the conversation to a close with a particularly vicious gear change as the Land Rover approached a roundabout.

Dutton fell temporarily silent.

* * * * *

Green and Carlton, leering down from the gallery, had long known what the cadets were just discovering: that the words '"individual" and "exercise", used in combination, produced the most hateful expression in the entire English language.

Sergeant Miller had moved the lesson on a stage. Now, in turn, each cadet was trotting away from the rest of the group, riding a circle at the first end of the school, trotting up the opposite long side, making another circle at the second end and then rejoining the ride. Any cadet describing a less than perfect circle repeated the exercise immediately.

From the gallery, the two ends of the riding school looked like badly drawn mathematical diagrams. The hoof marks left by Gillham on his demonstration round could have been guided by a compass but around them were all sorts of wayward tracks, rivalling each other in eccentricity. Tom, who had just been round for the second time, contemplated his most recent attempts.

'Well, number four file, what do you think?'

There was no doubt about it; the first set of tracks was distinctly triangular. The second, more graceful in its curves, resembled a kidney bean.

'Sorry, Sergeant, the first one was a disaster – I lost balance. I don't think I used enough inside leg on the second one.'

'Spot on. When you ride the quarter of the circle which is away from the walls, your horse will naturally fall in, unless you use plenty of inside leg to keep her out. So, what are you going to do?'

Tom did his best to sound stoic: 'I'm going round again, Sergeant.'

'Good lad – off you go.'

Tom gritted his teeth and squeezed his horse back to a trot.

There was a sound of boots running up the wooden steps to the gallery: Green and Carlton, ready to leap to attention if an officer had decided to take a look, relaxed again when Chadwick's head popped above the stair rail.

'Hi, Chadders – not playing at the funeral after all then?'

'Hi, Lance. No – the family dithered until the last moment but finally decided that I was surplus to requirements.' Chadwick walked up the final few steps and joined them in the gallery. He was now dressed like Carlton, in the everyday riding uniform of the troop. Green was mildly surprised.

'I'd have thought, in the circumstances, you'd take the morning off.'

'I was going to, but I bumped into Blondie Lang. He suggested we put in some jumping practice for tomorrow, so I've been in the outdoor school for the last hour.'

Carlton joined the conversation: 'Good session?'

Chadwick looked a little sheepish: 'Well, it was very good – until I fell off.' He paused, then added, 'Twice.'

'Ah, well, we've all done it,' said Green cheerfully. 'You didn't land on those precious lips, I hope?'

'I did not, Lance,' Chadwick grinned. 'But this time tomorrow I shall have a spectacular bruise on a part of my body so intimate, that anybody who wants to see it will have to pay an entrance fee.'

Carlton pretended to rummage in his pockets: 'Hang on, I think I've got a penny here, somewhere.'

'Sod off, Carlton.'

Chadwick turned to look down into the riding school,

where Tom Two was trying to convince Sergeant Miller that the uneven parallelogram he had just ridden was really a perfect circle. 'How are they doing, Lance?'

'Brilliantly, all things considered. Miller's pushing them really hard today and the lesson's gone way over time, which is his way of showing he's pleased. They're pretty knackered now, so he'll probably stop soon.'

Chadwick nodded, remembering his own first trotting lessons. 'Do you think that you have to be an evil bastard before they select you to be a riding instructor, or is it part of the Melton Mowbray course?'

Green considered: 'Difficult to know, one way or the other – though in Miller's case, I should say the condition was definitely congenital. Still, he's a fantastic instructor.'

Down in the school, the horses were all back in walk. Tom was debating which of many unpleasant sensations was worst: was it the aching of every muscle in his body, or the revolting stickiness of the sweat-soaked shirt against his body? Probably beating these into equal second was the horrible stench that seemed to seep from his every pore. He hadn't been aware of this when trotting but now that he had a little time to take stock of things he was appalled by just how bad the smell was. Surely the lesson must finish soon?

Miller interrupted his thoughts: 'All right – we're nearly done. There's just one last exercise, if you're up to it, which will lift this from being a good lesson to a really excellent one. Do you want to have a go, or are you too tired? Number two file?'

The cadets fell for the instructor's cunning: they would rather have died than admit to being too tired. Beginning with Geary, and in succession, they pronounced themselves eager to complete one final exercise. Miller was pleased; he gave a wide smile, in which there was more than a hint of malice.

'Good chaps. Right then, we're going to do that last individual exercise again, but with one crucial difference.' The sergeant paused for effect.

'We're going to have our arms folded.'

CHAPTER NINETEEN

UPMINSTER CREMATORIUM

A group of reporters and photographers had assembled at the gates of the crematorium and Ashley cursed himself for not anticipating this. Scott sensibly drove on until the road turned a corner and they were out of sight. He pulled into the kerb and Dutton and Ashley alighted.

'What do you think, Mr Ashley – about an hour?'

'That sounds fine, Gunner Scott. Back here?'

'If the reporters have gone, sir, I'll be waiting a bit closer – otherwise, yes, back here. Did you say you were meeting a friend for lunch, Mr Dutton?'

'I did, Scott. Don't worry about me – I'll make my own way home.'

'Very good, sir.' Scott's expression was impassive but Ashley suspected that the gunner was as pleased as he was with the prospect of a return journey without Dutton. Scott managed not to grind the gears as he pulled off, and even gave a cheerful "parp" on the horn.

Dutton remained silent as they walked to the gates. Ashley guessed that the officer was putting himself into a funereal frame of mind and did nothing to encourage another outbreak of conversation. Cameras clicked as they walked past the press and a few reporters called out questions, which they ignored. Dutton was careful to place himself in such a way that his regimental tie was blocked from their view by Ashley's body.

Anxious to conceal the true nature of its function from the general public, the designers of the crematorium had placed it in the middle of a pleasant park. Ashley and Dutton walked for a quarter of a mile between well-maintained shrubs before they came to the building itself. Here, they found a sizeable group of elegant mourners, chatting to one another and admiring a large collection of wreaths. Dutton was surprised.

'I didn't think there would be this many people here – it's really rather a good turnout.'

Ashley smiled: 'Have you never been to a crematorium funeral before?'

'Actually, no – my family has a vault in the local church. Why do you ask?'

'Because these are clearly the mourners from the previous funeral. The crematorium business is like a conveyor belt; as soon as one funeral is over, the next one begins. At a guess, I'd say the present occupant of the incinerator was several social classes higher than Cooper, certainly considerably richer and – judging from the small huddle of men by that very large wreath – a freemason.'

Dutton was suitably impressed: 'I see what you mean, though I wouldn't have thought of it myself.'

'In contrast, that shabby-looking party heading over from the direction of the car park is quite likely to be a contingent of the clan Cooper. Shall we go in, so as to be sure of a seat at the back?'

They were not the first to arrive. There was a gathering of dingy-looking mourners near the front; Major Benson was seated alone a few pews behind them. At the end of an otherwise unoccupied pew was a character whom Ashley at first mistook for Gunner Hall; he had the same military haircut and was wearing a suit which must have come from a similar chain store.

To Ashley's surprise, Dutton said: 'Ah, there's Jake – I'll go and join him. See you later, Ashley.' He walked up to the young soldier and clapped him on the back. Jake turned and stood, revealing a wide smile, animated, bright eyes, and another zigzagging regimental tie. The two shook hands, sat down together and chatted in an enthusiastic but subdued manner.

Somehow, Ashley had imagined that Dutton's friend would be another officer but, after all, there was no particular reason why that should be the case. He gave a mental shrug and selected a pew very near the back of the chapel.

The interior of the crematorium was obviously intended to be soothing. The walls were an anaemic pastel shade and the windows contained swirls of coloured glass, vaguely suggestive of Chagall, only without the religious implications. The only hint of religion, indeed, was a cross hanging from a hook on the far wall. It was sufficiently low down that it could be removed with ease for non-Christian funerals. Ashley wondered what symbol, if any, had graced the wall for the previous service.

He sat back and allowed the inoffensive, piped music to wash over him. The small group they had seen approaching from the car park entered and sat just behind Dutton and the soldier called Jake, effectively blocking them from view. A few minutes later, Ashley became aware of a shuffling in the pew behind him. The new occupant knelt down, and he heard a soft, beer-smelling mumbling which he took to be a prayer. He shifted forwards in his seat, partly to give the praying figure some room and partly to escape the stale fumes. Then he realised that he, rather than God, was being addressed.

'I thought you'd be in the congregation, Mr Ashley.' Ashley swivelled round.

'Gillick, what are you doing here?' he whispered.

'Sheer curiosity, sir. I didn't have any duties today and it's only a short journey out on the District line, so I thought, why not? Charlie Hicks would have come as well, only he had to show some ambassador or other the Crown Jewels.'

'What do you expect to see? An open coffin with the head rolling around loose in it?'

'Well, I wondered about that, sir. Not the open coffin of course, but, well, what *do* you think they've done with the head? With Charles the First, they sewed it back on again. And then, the Duke of Monmouth…'

Whatever had happened to the Duke of Monmouth's head would have to wait for another time. An invisible hand turned up the volume of the characterless music and the funeral procession arrived. Gillick terminated his whispered anecdote, stood, and adopted a rigid pose, which he obviously considered appropriate to moments of solemnity.

It wasn't much of a procession: four undertakers carried the coffin, and three badly dressed, ugly individuals shuffled in its wake. The wrestler, Ashley decided, must be the mother, and the insignificant but shifty character next to her, the father. The third, a thug who looked as though he was on day release from prison, was presumably a brother, or perhaps a cousin. Ashley was rather enjoying his cynical musings on the Cooper family, when the mother turned to enter her pew. For the first time, Ashley noticed that she was crying. He was overcome by a sudden sensation of self-loathing: what right had he to intrude on the grief of these people, or to laugh at their clothes, class and character? Was he any better than them? Could he begin to understand how they must have suffered during the last week? The moment of shame passed, but Ashley was left feeling sombre.

A clergyman appeared, apparently from nowhere, pronounced a few platitudes and then gave out the first hymn. A wobbly pre-recorded organ introduction played the first two lines of *Crimond* and the tiny congregation had a dismal stab at *The Lord's my shepherd*. Half way through the first verse, they separated from the organ music, which, being recorded, could not adapt to them. It was an appropriately dreadful start to the service.

*   *   *   *   *

The grooming was agonising and apparently endless; cleaning and polishing the bridles and saddles was trance-like and robotic. When Green next saw the cadets, they had flopped onto their beds, too tired even to take off their sodden shirts or pull off their boots. Tom Two realised, as he hit the mattress, that he still had his service cap on his head. He flung it, like a Frisbee, to the end of the bed, where it hooked itself on the toe of his left boot. He let it hang there, limply symbolic of everything they were feeling.

'Don't even try to get up,' said the lance bombardier, cheerfully, as he entered the room. 'Even by our standards, you've had a punishing morning. But well done – Sergeant Miller thinks you're all wonderful.'

'He's got a very strange way of showing it, Lance,' groaned Tom Two. Several other grunts seconded this remark.

'Well, that's riding instructors for you. They push you as far as they think you can go, then just that bit further to see what happens. You were all fine. He'll get you trotting without stirrups tomorrow, or the day after.'

If this was meant to be encouraging, it failed. A chorus of wails rose from the beds. When they died down, Tom asked: 'Tell me, Lance, do we smell as badly as I think we do?'

Green sniffed the air and considered, in the manner of an expert *sommelier*. 'Let me see, I'm getting plenty of horse, naturally; and I think there's polish and saddle soap in there somewhere; a good dollop of soldier's armpit; and probably more than just a *soupçon* of cavalry crotch. If you could bottle it and sell it as *Eau de Gunner*, you'd make a fortune. Women would go wild for it.'

'That's a great comfort, Lance: I'll try to imagine that as I lie here and expire.'

'Well, it's good to know that you'll die with a smile on your face. Now, even if you lot can barely twitch, you can presumably listen. In the first place, seriously, well done. If you can survive that, you can survive anything. Second, we've got a bit of time before we eat, so Gunner Carlton has gone to sneak some beer from the Officers' Mess for you.'

There was a chorus of appreciative grunts. Geary was even moved to speech: 'Beer! The very word begins to revive me!'

'However, no beer for anyone until you're all showered.

Third, I've put back this afternoon's activity by an hour, so you can get a rest after you eat, if you want one. It's a good activity too, but I'll tell you about that when you're clean. Now, if you make a nice pile of all those sweaty togs, I dare say Gunner Carlton might be persuaded to take them down to the laundry for you while you get yourselves hosed down.'

Fifteen minutes later, wrapped up in their army issue green towels, they sat around drinking beer from bottles. Carlton returned from his trip to the laundry (a visit which had involved much swearing and obscene speculation on the causes of the various smells) and he, too, perched on a bed, taking large gulps from a bottle.

'I need the alcohol to disinfect myself after handling all your clobber,' he explained, bitterly.

'What's on this afternoon, Lance?' asked Vernon.

Green finished a mouthful of beer from his own bottle.

'Gun park,' he said, wiping his mouth. 'Bombardier Croft and Gunners Sorrell and Watson will tell you about the guns, show you how they work, and let you play with some dummy rounds. It's good fun: another time they'll get you on dismantling and cleaning and that's quite a slog, but today's easy. That's now at fifteen hundred hours, so I'll meet you outside the gun park five minutes before that. Order of dress is combats and beret, so that's what you'll get into in a minute. Any questions?'

Tom automatically extended his palm, then realised how silly it looked when he was only wearing a towel.

'So, we can just rest between eating and the gun park, Lance, is that right?'

'Well, there's a choice. Did any of you see that great giraffe-like figure visiting the gallery while you were riding? That was Gunner Chadwick, who is our top trumpeter. He said that anyone who is interested can pop up to his room after lunch and he'll show you the instruments and let you have a try. It's entirely optional. Anyone fancy it?'

Frankly, Tom thought he'd rather spend the time sleeping,

but he had a hunch that Green had him in mind when he had passed on Chadwick's offer.

'I'd quite like to have a go,' he said, and managed to sound as if he meant it.

'I'll join you,' added Tom Two. 'I used to have trumpet lessons at school.'

Green looked pleased; whether with Tom One or just generally was impossible to tell.

'Good – I'll tell him to expect the two of you.'

*   *   *   *   *

By the end of the second hymn, Ashley and Gillick had had enough. They sneaked out discreetly as the congregation trod the verge of Jordan, half a bar late. In the car park, they found Gunner Hall enjoying a smoke with the driver of the hearse.

'Hello, sir – have they finished already?' Hall was about to throw his cigarette away, but Ashley stopped him in time. 'No, you've got a while yet, so carry on smoking.'

'Thank you, sir. Will you have one yourself?' He offered the packet.

'No thanks, but if you're offering, I dare say Yeoman Warder Gillick here…'

'Of course, sir. Were you a relation of the bombardier, sir?'

Ashley answered for Gillick while the warder lit his cigarette from Hall's:

'The yeoman warder has a professional interest in decapitation – it seems to go with his job.'

Hall smiled broadly. 'Well, you've come into the right conversation then, Mr Gillick. I was just telling the undertaker here how we found the body and he was telling me what they had to do to get it ready for the funeral.'

Gillick's eyes glanced hungrily backwards and forwards from soldier to undertaker. Here was one man who had been at the very scene of a beheading and another who could tell him exactly how the corpse looked in the coffin. Uncertain as to

179

which of his hundred questions he should ask first, he remained pathetically silent, his eyes pleading for information.

The undertaker broke the silence: 'At our wits' end, we were, sir – and it's not as though we've got no experience of putting bodies back together. An arm or a leg, well, you can just shove them up the sleeve or in the trousers and nobody's the wiser. But the head, well, they want to see that, of course, when they come to the chapel of rest.

'We tried propping it between cushions, but that was no good – it flopped sideways every time we lifted the lid. When that happened, the mouth opened as well, and the cotton wool padding came out. Not nice.

'Then we experimented with various glues, but a head's just too heavy, sir, as you'll know if you've ever held one…'

Gillick looked as if he'd died and gone to heaven: 'You actually held it?' He extended his palms and cupped them around an imaginary head. 'In your hands?'

'Several times, sir. I had to, and it weighed a ton as well.'

Gillick hesitated before his next question. He struggled briefly with what was left of his conscience, but it was no good – it had to be asked: 'You didn't, I suppose, ever, well, *hold it aloft*, like at an execution, by any chance?' All inhibition gone, Gillick adopted his favourite Lady Jane pose.

The undertaker, Ashley was relieved to note, looked shocked.

'Absolutely not, sir. My father owns the firm and he would have had a fit if any of us had done that. He's very big on respect for the dead. We'd lose all our trade if folk thought we were doing that sort of thing.'

Gillick lowered his arm, disappointed. 'Ah, well, it was just a thought. Personally, I wouldn't have been able to resist it, but I dare say you're right. Anyway, how did you solve the problem in the end?'

The undertaker looked pleased with himself. 'It was my idea – a big fat splint going down the throat and up into the skull. That kept the body and the head together and then we stopped it swivelling with a hundred and twenty-four surgical staples. It did the job beautifully.'

'A head on a pole,' sighed Gillick, contentedly. 'Charlie Hicks is going to love this when I tell him. And now, young man…' He turned to Hall.

But Gillick had lingered too long over the undertaker's story. The small funeral party started to emerge from the chapel. Hall took a final drag on his cigarette, then threw it to the ground and extinguished it with his heel.

'It'll have to keep for another occasion, sir, I'm afraid. The CO will be out in a moment. It's time for me to go.'

Hall departed in the direction of the Jaguar. A thin column of smoke appeared from the chimney of the incinerator.

Apparently, it was time for Simon Cooper to go, too.

CHAPTER TWENTY

THE TRUMPETER

'Gunner Carlton, can you point us towards Gunner Chadwick's room?' Toms One and Two adjusted their berets as they left the canteen.

'Ah, Chadders' Regimental Museum! It's in that block over there. How are your legs?'

'Like jelly, still.'

'That's good, because Chadwick lives on the fourth floor. Up the first flight of stairs you come to, all the way to the top and then about halfway along the corridor. Have fun!'

They took the first set of stairs two at a time, but their thighs and calves rapidly began to wobble; they progressed ever more gingerly up the next three flights.

'He would be right at the top.' Tom One contemplated the final dozen steps. Tom Two whimpered agreement: 'We may have to crawl.'

Unsteadily, they crept up, then moved more easily along the corridor. It was easy to tell which room was Chadwick's, because the door was open and the sounds of trumpet music were coming from it. They knocked and went in.

'Hello, Gunner Chadwick, we've come to – wow!' Two stopped mid-sentence as Chadwick's room made its first impact. Tom One echoed his astonishment.

Almost every free space on the walls was covered with pictures of Prince Albert's Troop. Some had been cut out of magazines and newspapers, others downloaded from the internet. Many more were ordinary photographs. Round the whole room, as a sort of frieze, a series of about sixty enlarged pictures were stuck together, displaying the whole Troop in procession. Above Chadwick's bed was a poster-sized enlargement of six trumpeters sounding a fanfare; this was in a glass clipframe, as were other obvious favourites.

The Toms could now understand Carlton's remark. Their impression of being in a museum was enhanced by the other contents of the room: Chadwick had not yet put away his busby; his dress tunic and trousers hung on the door of his wardrobe and the George boots, fresh from another layer of polish, stood gleaming on a sheet of newspaper on the desk. Also on the desk were a bugle and Chadwick's long ceremonial cavalry trumpet. The gunner held a shorter trumpet in his hand, obviously the one he had just been playing.

'Do you like it?' Chadwick assumed an affirmative answer, which the Toms readily provided.

'It's fantastic!'

'Where did they all come from?'

Chadwick was more than happy to tell them. 'Various sources. It all started with this one.' He indicated a framed picture of two mounted figures, the first an officer, the second, Chadwick himself, in the middle of sounding a call. 'That was in *Soldier* magazine. I was trumpeter to Captain Johnson – that's the officer, he's out in Germany now. He was a good sort, so when he sent off to the magazine for a copy, he got one for me as well. Then I started collecting others. It's amazing – members of the public take photographs, have two sets developed and just send one lot to the guardroom here. Most of us have got quite a few, but I'm the only one daft enough to display them all. My brother did the big series at Trooping the Colour two years ago on an old camera: it took two rolls of film, so there's a slight break in it, but it turned out well, I think.'

It was clear that Chadwick could have gone on for hours, describing in detail the circumstances of every picture but the photograph of the fanfare trumpeters recalled the purpose of the cadets' visit to mind. He showed them the instruments.

'The long and short trumpet are just the same thing, really

– the short one has been coiled round more times, that's all. Here, have a go – only put these gloves on. I don't want to spend the afternoon wiping off fingerprints.'

Predictably, Tom One managed no more than a sort of strangulated raspberry. Chadwick tried to show him how to vibrate his lips but, somehow, as soon as he tried it with the mouthpiece, it all went wrong. Two, once he had got used to the idea of a trumpet with no valves, was really rather good. Chadwick spent a long time with him, playing calls on the shorter trumpet, which Two then played back on the long ceremonial instrument. Tom One gave himself over to studying the photographs while the lesson continued.

It was easy to spot Chadwick in the pictures; either standing or mounted, he towered over his brother soldiers. More challenging, and therefore more fun, was spotting other members of the Troop: Sergeant Miller, in a former incarnation as a bombardier, towards the head of the procession; further down, Green, Barker and Carlton as gunners on the same team. Other figures were more conjectural – was that Gillham just visible behind another gunner? And was that hint of blond hair sticking out below the back of a busby evidence of Lang?

On the desk, between Chadwick's George boots and busby, was a wallet full of more photographs. Tom sat on the hard chair in front of the desk and took out the pictures. At first, he just flipped through them casually; they were obviously recent shots from Horse Guards. There, in the first photograph, riding in formation, were nearly all the soldiers he knew; a later picture showed them waiting on the parade ground, and further ones were pictures of individual moments throughout the day. Tom was struck by two simultaneous realisations. The first was that the pictures, taken by a digital camera, displayed the date and the time of day in the bottom left-hand corner. The second was that the surly-looking bombardier, who appeared so uncomfortable on his horse, must be Cooper. Tom performed a quick calculation: the photographs had been taken eight days ago. The day of the murder.

Tom Two completed a piercing rendition of the call "Boots and Saddles". It was convincing enough for Chadwick to congratulate him and to look out of the window in case any gullible gunner was scuttling across the parade ground in response to the summons.

'That's pretty impressive. How are your lips holding out – do you want to try something else?'

Two was enjoying himself; he thought he could keep going for a bit longer, as long as there weren't any really high notes involved. Chadwick reassured him.

'No, the piece I'm thinking of is a fanfare for two trumpets. I'll take the first part, which has all the flashy stuff, you can take the second. Hang on a moment, it's in one of the drawers somewhere.' Chadwick leaned over Tom One, pulled open the top drawer of the desk and began to rummage through sheets of manuscript paper. Tom decided to take advantage of the lull in the music.

'Gunner Chadwick, these shots were taken on the day it all happened, over at Horse Guards, weren't they?'

Chadwick looked over One's shoulder.

'Must have been.' He seemed genuinely surprised. He took the pictures from Tom's hand and started to examine them. 'They only arrived in the guardroom this morning and I haven't looked at them yet.'

'So the bombardier there is...'

'Yeah, that's him all right. Ugly sod, isn't he?' Chadwick returned the pictures to Tom and went back to rummaging in the drawer.

Tom Two asked the next question: 'Was he as awful as everyone says?'

Perhaps Chadwick was off his guard. His mind, after all, was as much on his music as on Two's question. He had given up on the top drawer and pulled open a lower one: this forced him to lean further over Tom One and, for balance, he had placed a hand on the cadet's shoulder. With the other hand he still rummaged around in the drawer.

185

His reply made Tom One's whole body tighten under the trumpeter's grip.

'He was awful, and more. Everybody hated him and he got what was coming to him. He was a bullying, blackmailing bastard.'

* * * * *

Lunch in *The Gunner's Rest* was drawing to a close. Somehow, Gunner Scott had managed to shovel away an enormous portion of steak and kidney, with mountains of chips, followed immediately by a sponge pudding served in a bowl overflowing with thick custard. He would probably have washed this down with appropriate quantities of beer, had he not been driving. As it was, he stuck to cola.

Ashley, feeling an obligation to keep up with the gunner, now felt bloated. How did Scott manage it? Was he supporting a family of asylum-seeking tapeworms? Was his metabolism so fast that the journey from plate to lavatory took only an hour or so? Or did he have to eat that much to maintain his eyebrow? Scott spent a few minutes noisily scraping every last streak of custard from the bowl, then sat back and sighed contentedly.

'That was great, sir – thank you very much.'

They had passed a pleasant time since the funeral. There had still been a lingering pair of reporters at the crematorium gates, so Ashley had said goodbye to Gillick and walked to the bend in the road. Here he had found Scott, like Hall before him, enjoying a peaceful cigarette. Again, like Hall, Scott moved as if to stub it out, but Ashley told him to finish it off. They leaned against the Land Rover and chatted, while Scott blew smoke rings.

'So, did you explore the wicked world of Upminster, Gunner Scott?'

'Not likely, sir. It's the sort of place where you might catch a sexually-transmitted infection just by walking down the street. No, I went to see an old Patty who owns a pub near Ockenden.

It was Bombardier Burdett's idea – he runs the old comrades' website. When he heard I was coming out this way, he suggested I take a regimental plaque for the old boy to put up in the bar. Thrilled to bits, he was, sir – kept wanting to give me drinks, but I said I was driving, so he gave me a bottle of whisky to take home, and another for the bomber. Nice chap.'

'Is it a good pub?'

'Seems to be, sir – though it had only just started to come to life as I was leaving to pick you up. It's a free house, so he's got lots of good beer, and the food sounded all right as well.'

'In that case, let's have lunch together there – my treat, of course.'

'That's very kind of you, sir.'

Scott had finished his cigarette by this time, so he held open the passenger door for Ashley, then climbed into his own side and drove off in the direction of the pub.

Ex-Sergeant Pullman's army career may have been crowned with success and glory, or it may not. Whichever was the case, he now regarded it nostalgically as a time of unalloyed happiness. Delighted by the return of Scott, he pointed out the plaque, which had already been nailed to the wall. He had even changed into his regimental tie in honour of the occasion. He fussed around the young gunner, making sure that his portions of food were enormous, and sent complimentary drinks in Scott's direction every time his glass was empty. Ashley came in for some reflected glory and attention but Scott, smart in his boots and combats, with his beret rolled under the epaulette on his left shoulder, was undoubtedly the star of the show.

The retired soldier cleared their plates himself. 'Tea or coffee, gentlemen? On the house, of course.'

Ashley chose tea, Scott coffee. When Pullman returned, he had a second mug of coffee on his tray, as well as a plate of after-dinner mints. 'Would you mind if I joined you for a few minutes, gentlemen? It would be lovely to chat about the old days for a while – the best years of my life.'

It would have been churlish to object, so Ashley and Scott

listened politely to the memories of twenty years ago. Ashley sipped his tea gently and enjoyed the chance to relax after his huge meal: Scott worked his way systematically through the chocolate mints. Eventually, an involved and lengthy anecdote concerning a nosebag, the commanding officer's stirrups, and a pair of lady's stockings came to a long-awaited conclusion. Ashley smiled politely and Scott said, 'Good on you, Sarge.' This reference to his old rank pleased Pullman more than anything else could have done; he beamed all over.

'Well, Gunner Scott, you've made an old man very happy,' observed Ashley, as the Land Rover pulled out of the pub car park.

'It happens all the time, sir,' said Scott, giving a final wave to the retired soldier. 'A few years out of barracks and they forget all the hard work – the endless grooming and mucking out, or the polishing that has to be done all over again because some petty NCO says it isn't up to scratch. They just remember the times in the bar, or the big ceremonies with the glamorous uniforms, and all the available women who want to do it with a soldier...' He paused, philosophically: 'But then, I suppose I'll be like that as well, one day.'

This was Ashley's opening: 'And what will you remember, Gunner Scott? Will Bombardier Cooper be a happy memory that sticks in the mind, or an unhappy one that fades away?'

Scott paused for thought. 'I suppose, sir, it all depends on how it pans out – the whole murder thing will stick in the mind, of course. If, by some miracle, we could all be shown to be in the clear, I think I'd probably remember it as quite a jolly little episode, but that's not very likely, is it?'

'I don't see how it can be, Gunner Scott. Nothing would please me more than to discover that two crazed psychopaths had been lurking in the stable for days, awaiting their opportunity, but...'

'I know, sir. On the other hand, if the Smith twins go down for it, we'll all be really miserable. We're a close bunch – most of us are country lads, so we haven't got the hard edge that townies like Cooper had – and we stick together.'

'As the inspector discovered when he was trying to get information out of you.' Ashley could have added his own name to that sentence, but deliberately left it out.

Scott laughed: 'Well, sir, he isn't exactly the sort of person you'd want to confide in, is he? If I did know anything – which I don't – he'd be the last person I'd tell.'

Ashley paused, then said: 'And I suppose it would be foolish of me to hope that you'd tell me?'

Scott thought about that one for a bit as he negotiated a junction. 'To be honest, sir, you're right – I couldn't shop a friend. I wouldn't try to cover up for anyone, not for murder at any rate, but you'd have to do the finding out for yourself. Sorry sir.'

'Don't apologise. Professionally, of course, it's frustrating, but on a human level, I rather admire it. Just suppose, though, that the knowledge got too much to bear and you had to share it with someone. What would you do then?'

Again, Scott took time to think the idea through. 'If I could pluck up the courage, sir, I'd probably go straight to Major Benson. He scares the hell out of us, but he's a great commanding officer and he's on our side. If I couldn't face up to it...'

There was another junction and another pause. Ashley assumed that Scott was running through a list of the NCOs who might be more approachable than Benson. When the gunner continued, he took Ashley by surprise.

'I suppose I'd probably go to Father O'Brien over at our Lady and St Lazarus, sir.'

'Are you a Roman Catholic, Gunner Scott?' The religious life of the soldiers was something that Ashley hadn't remotely considered. Scott blushed slightly and grinned.

'Not a very good one, sir. My mother still thinks I go to Mass every week, but once every few months is more like it. There are a handful of us in the Troop – the Smith twins and Mr Dawson are the only ones you'd know. The local hospital has a big Catholic chapel in it and we go there every so often.'

'High days and holidays?'

'That's about it, sir. Mr Dawson takes it quite seriously; since he's been in the Troop, he's organised some of us to serve at the big festivals. Father O'Brien loves it, because soldiers are the only people with any discipline these days.'

Ashley couldn't help laughing at the thought of Scott and his friends robed as altar boys and acolytes. Scott laughed too.

'I know what you're thinking, sir. We look lovely in our lace, holding candles and swinging the incense. The four of us did the Assumption a couple of weeks back, but our dress rehearsal for Horse Guards had gone on so long that we had to run over, still in our uniforms. It wasn't until we knelt down in the sanctuary that we realised our spurs were sticking out from under our cassocks.'

'I hope they clanked merrily throughout the service?'

'We tried not to, sir, but it still happened quite a bit. Some of the old bags in the congregation were annoyed, but Father O'Brien thought it was wonderful.'

*   *   *   *   *

It was probably the tension in Tom's shoulder that made Chadwick realise what he had just said. He added quickly: 'At least, that's what I heard. Ah, here it is – have a look at this, Tom Two.' Chadwick released his grip and left One seated at the desk. Two, who had been leafing through a small volume containing all the trumpet and bugle calls and seemed oblivious to Chadwick's gaffe, took a sheet of manuscript from the trumpeter and made a few parping sounds by way of practising.

'Do you read music?'

'A bit.'

'Same here – we learn most of the stuff by rote. Look, I'll play your first phrase, and you play it back. Then, when you've got it, I'll add my part on top. That way we'll build up the music bit by bit. It's quite repetitive, so you'll soon get it.'

At any other time, Tom One would have enjoyed listening to them piecing together what was, after all, a spectacular fanfare. It had been written especially for Chadwick to play at some state event and the first trumpet part shot skywards on numerous occasions. But he couldn't get that word out of his mind.

Blackmail.

Blackmail turned ordinary people into killers.

The more Tom thought about it, the more convinced he became that he was in the company of a murderer.

CHAPTER TWENTY-ONE

THE GUN PARK

'Did you get anywhere?' Edward watched the Land Rover splutter out of the square before shutting the door of number 54 and heading back into the apartment.

'All the way to Upminster and back, which wasn't bad for that old wreck, I'd say.'

'Very funny. You know what I mean – how was the funeral? Did you learn anything?' They entered the sitting room and Edward moved instinctively towards the sideboard.

'Will gin jog your memory?'

'Well, I'm not sure it needs too much jogging, but it'll certainly help to oil it. Perhaps even to organise it.' Edward handed him a tumbler, which Ashley held up to the light. It was, alas, no substitute for a crystal ball. Ashley eased himself into an armchair; it seemed to fit more snugly than usual. Can one mix gin and indigestion pills, he asked himself? Probably not, better just stick to the gin.

'There were lots of little things,' he mused. 'Little nuances, little phrases, little mannerisms. The answer to so much that we do in our line of work lies in small details – but how do we know which detail is important? I saw and heard things today that fascinated me, but whether any of them is remotely important, I couldn't say.' He paused to sip his drink. 'Is it significant that everybody borrows Carlton's suit; that Scott and the Smith twins serve at Mass, or that Dutton appears not to own a black tie? What am I to make of a tower warder who is sufficiently bonkers that he takes a trip on the Tube to the funeral of a person he has never met; or of a young soldier who

192

has flown from Germany for the same event, when he almost certainly disliked Bombardier Cooper as much as everybody else?'

'So your jigsaw puzzle has lots of pieces but, as yet, no picture?'

'That's about it: all the ingredients but no recipe. As our military friends would say, all the gear but no idea.'

'Anything I can do to help?'

Ashley nodded. 'In the first place, there are some things I'd like you to look up on the internet for me. There's a website for old boys of Prince Albert's Troop, which I'd be interested to see – Bombardier Burdett's in charge of it, so my guess is that it's very well put together and maintained. Then I'd like you to browse around some Roman Catholic sites – try and find out if the hospital chapel of Our Lady and St Lazarus in North London has a page. Tomorrow afternoon, I'll need you at the barracks. You never know, my plan might work; even if it doesn't, you might spot something I've missed.'

Edward looked pleased. 'Do I get to dress up again? I rather enjoyed that.'

'As did the soldiers: but sorry, no. We shall be a pair of dull civilians, tagged on to the end of the pageant.'

'Like camp followers?'

'Speak for yourself, Edward.'

*　　*　　*　　*　　*

Tom was having a miserable afternoon. He sat, in exile, on a wooden crate, watching Tom Two and Keith Vernon operating the number three gun according to instructions given by Sorrell. Next to them, Gunner Watson was similarly guiding the other pair of cadets. Bombardier Croft wandered between the two teams, observing their progress and pausing every so often to glance in Tom's direction. Tom pretended not to notice, but blushed every time.

He couldn't get Chadwick out of his mind. He wanted to

because he liked Chadwick and his crazy room; even after his short time at the barracks, he could identify with the trumpeter's pride in Prince Albert's Troop. He had been impressed by the time and care Chadwick had devoted to Tom Two. He didn't want to have to think of him as…

Even in his mind, Tom tried desperately to find another word, but only one would fit; 'as a *murderer.*'

They had left Chadwick's room at the last possible moment and had made themselves run, despite their wobbling legs, as fast as possible down the stairs and over to the gun park in order to be on time. This had the advantage of concealing Tom One's agitation from his friend. In between panting, Two enthused about the lesson, the instruments, and about Chadwick himself.

'That was – fantastic! I never – thought playing – could be such – fun. No valves at all – my lips are still really buzzing – he's brilliant! Oh God – they're all waiting – for us. Faster!'

The moment the pair had arrived, Green had handed them over to Bombardier Croft and had disappeared. As Croft issued some preliminary instructions, Tom had watched in despair as the figure of the lance bombardier retreated across the parade ground.

This was a disaster. The only action that Tom had been able to determine on, as he sat in Chadwick's room, was that he had to find an opportunity to speak to Green as soon as possible. Would Green return? When? And, in the meantime, what would Chadwick do? Tom was positive that the trumpeter had felt and understood that tension in his body. Would the cadets come out of the gun park to find that Chadwick, like Smith Two before him, had disappeared? Was he, even now, consulting his accomplice?

Guns, like horses, require concentration. Tom had already been snapped at for inattention a couple of times when, in a moment of carelessness, he had almost lost a finger. There had been a shout from Croft, a rapid reaction from Sorrell: Tom's arm had been jerked back with such force that it still hurt half an hour later. There was a clash of metal against metal; the breech had slammed shut exactly where his finger had been.

Croft's Vesuvian eruption had been spectacular: like the soldier at Pompeii, Tom stood rigidly to attention while the world crashed to pieces around him. The bombardier began by spurting out a collection of red-hot expletives which, though limited in variety, had an accumulative effect through their constant repetition, so that Tom could almost feel the discarded abuse piling up around his ankles. Then came the steady, flowing lava of criticism. Tom now knew that he had none of the qualities necessary to be a soldier: particularly not a soldier in Prince Albert's Troop. He was Idle, Careless, Brainless and Gormless as well, apparently, as Deaf and Blind. If he wanted to add Maimed to all these other deficiencies, all he had to do was to go on behaving as he had done so far. But it damn well wasn't going to happen in Bombardier Croft's lesson.

And so, Tom sat in bleak solitude on his crate, watching his friends enjoy themselves. Croft, now calm, prepared the final exercise of the afternoon.

'Right, lads, we're going to put together everything that we've done this afternoon. With two guns, we will fire a dummy twenty-one gun salute. Gunners Sorrell and Watson will hand you the rounds and take them from you. You, the cadets, will load, fire and unload as you have been shown. There will be ten seconds between each round. Got that? Good.

'Listen in! Stand by your weapons!' The cadets and soldiers formed up behind the guns, their feet in the position of attention, their fists clasped and against their chests.

'Gunners – Ready!' The cadets sprang into position: Tom Two placed himself in the same metal seat that Ashley had occupied the previous evening. Watson and Sorrell, who would be doing the work of two soldiers, straddled the tails of the weapons.

'Load!' This was the command that had nearly cost Tom One his finger. Sorrell handed Two a dummy round while

Keith opened the breech. The round was thrust in and the breech slammed shut. Both guns were ready to fire, the cadets and soldiers alert, waiting for the word of command. Croft kept them in their positions for about half a minute, then:

'Number three gun – Fire!' Instantly: Tom Two, releasing the action; Keith, opening the breech and removing the old round; Sorrell, simultaneously receiving the old round from Keith and passing a new one to Two; the new round loaded and ready to be discharged.

'Number four gun – Fire!'

The exercise continued, the firing of each round slightly smoother than the previous. Even in his misery, Tom could not help being enthralled. The four cadets were showing all the concentration that he had so obviously lacked, so that never once was there a delay between the order to fire and the action. Every ten seconds the command came, and the rapid co-ordination of detailed tasks repeated itself, first on one gun, then the other.

Three and a half minutes later, the silent salute to the invisible dignitary was over. The bombardier, having counted off ten seconds for the last time, lowered his watch. He looked from gun to gun and from face to face.

'Well done – relax.' His congratulations were all the more effective for being said quietly. The cadets, Tom in particular, knew that Croft could speak with enormous power when he needed to; it was a surprise to discover that he had a softer side as well. This continued as he spoke to the two regular soldiers. 'Sorrell – how did you feel your two coped?'

'Pretty well, Bomber – the two dummy rounds were quite sweaty by the end, but even so there were no slips.'

'Good. Watson?'

'Same here, Bomber. Marked improvement throughout the afternoon.'

'I think so too. All right, you four, we're done. Early next week, we'll take you into the park to watch a full practice and you can see how it all happens on a larger scale. If there's time, we'll integrate you into the gun teams at the end of the session. In the meantime,' he consulted his watch once more, 'you're in good time to get out of uniform before the evening meal. Any questions?'

Vernon came to attention. 'Shall we clear up, Bombardier Croft?'

Croft looked around. 'It's only the four dummy rounds, really. If you each pick up one and put it in Gunner Sorrell's ammunition box as you go, that'll be fine. All right – off you go. See you next week.'

There was a slight hesitation before the four cadets left. Tom knew how to interpret it, especially when Two glanced in his direction. A strong sense of *camaraderie* had already developed among the group, and this was the first time that one of them had been in any kind of trouble. There was, however, nothing they could do. The awkward moment passed and Tom watched his friends leave, smiling and thanking the bombardier and his two assistants. Sorrell and Watson followed them out of the gun park. Outside, cheerful voices arranged a rendezvous in the bar.

Tom raised himself from his crate. When the bombardier turned to face him, he was standing to attention, looking straight ahead. He had been in trouble with his headmaster enough times to know that the best procedure was a straightforward apology: no excuses.

'I'm sorry, Bombardier Croft – I wasn't concentrating. It won't happen again.'

But bombardiers are not headmasters. Croft reached into the pocket of his combat trousers. His response to the apology took Tom utterly by surprise.

'Do you smoke?'

*   *   *   *   *

Smith Two is smoking as well, inhaling deeply, and holding in each lungful for as long as he can before breathing out. It eases his hunger and it makes the cigarette last longer.

His progress has been slower today: less than three miles an hour. Just after midday, he had counted out his steps. It had taken twenty-four minutes to walk the one thousand, seven hundred and sixty paces. Yesterday morning, it had only taken a quarter of an hour. Would he manage as much as forty miles today? Would he need to?

As his cigarette dies, Smith Two considers chucking the whole thing in. The next town will have a police station: he only has to go in and identify himself. There will be food, the chance to wash. An end to uncertainty.

But the vision of Cooper's bound wrists returns. He imagines his own arms fastened behind his back as he is led, helplessly – where?

He gets up from his bench and continues walking.

*   *   *   *   *

Tom remained alone in the gun park. Bombardier Croft's decency had been rather difficult to cope with. They had lit their cigarettes and smoked quietly for a few moments. Then the bombardier had started the conversation.

'Now, I know how you're feeling, because I've been there myself – we all have. What I want you to do, is to imagine how *I* felt when I saw a cadet in my charge nearly lose a finger. And you would have done – it would have been sliced right off. I've seen it happen.'

Tom had pictured the awful sequence of events – the blood, the ambulance, the operation. Then the inquiry, the apportioning of blame. In this context, the bombardier's outburst seemed restrained.

'I'm sorry, Bombardier Croft; it was really stupid of me.'

'Say "bomber"; we're not in a lesson now. And it's Tom, isn't it?'

'Thanks, Bomber. Yes, I'm Tom One.'

'Well, Tom, three things. First, if you're going to daydream, don't do it near a horse or a gun. Which means that in this place you need to have your wits about you most of the time. Second, over the weekend, I'll get Sorrell to spend half an hour with you, going through what you've missed. That way you won't get behind.'

'Thanks, Bomber, I appreciate that.'

'And third is, what's the matter? I can see there's something wrong. What is it?'

This was the second time that Croft had taken Tom by surprise. There was no time to think of a lie.

'I'm sorry, Bomber, I can't tell you – I would if I could. It's not the course, or anything like that. I – I really need to see Lance Bombardier Green as soon as possible.'

Croft deposited his cigarette butt in an old shell case. 'You've got a bit of a wait then, Tom. He's gone over to Windsor to see if he can sort out a polo lesson for you all next week. I shouldn't think he'll be back for a couple of hours or so. Are you sure there's nothing I can do?'

'Thanks, Bomber, but no, there's nothing.'

'Okay, I'll be off then. Finish your smoke – we use the shell case as an ashtray. Turn off the light when you go and flip the catch on the door. Look after yourself.'

'Thanks, Bomber.'

Tom returned to his crate to finish the cigarette, grateful to the bombardier for his kindness, and relieved to be alone at last. He needed to think things out.

Green was at Windsor.

Perhaps he should use the time to write everything down. But what could he write? He couldn't just jot down, "Chadwick is the killer", or something similar. Uncle George would want details.

The more he thought about it, the more Tom realised that he had to speak to his uncle. There was no other possible course of action. He jettisoned his cigarette butt and walked to the door of the gun park. After turning out the lights, he released the catch on the lock, as instructed. The parade ground was deserted; the soldiers were at supper. He wandered to the end of the gun park and turned a corner. The entrance to the Officers' Mess was opposite him, across the drive. A little further along, a sentry stood at the barrack gate: he might just as well have been standing in front of the door.

Perhaps Uncle George would come out?

Tom hovered, anxious and uncertain. Then, as he shifted his weight awkwardly from one foot to the other, he saw a passer-by ask the sentry for directions. For a moment, the sentry turned his back on the barracks.

In an instant, Tom was over the road and in the door of the Mess. He paused for a fraction of a second to get his bearings, then shot up the stairs.

'Tom – what the hell…?'

Tom gasped with relief when he saw Ashley emerge from a bathroom. It had suddenly occurred to him that he had no idea which room his uncle occupied. Instinct had brought him to the top of the stairs; now luck had thrown uncle and nephew together.

'Uncle George – I've got to speak to you!'

They heard the footsteps on the stairs at the same time. Ashley seized the cadet by his upper arm (it still hurt from Sorrell's wrenching) and flung him in the direction of the bedroom. With his free hand, Tom turned the handle and the pair swivelled round the door, slamming it shut.

They might just as well have continued talking in the passage.

In Ashley's room, Robin was laying out his dinner jacket.

CHAPTER TWENTY-TWO

UNCLE AND NEPHEW

Ashley swore, not as loudly as Bombardier Croft, but with just as much feeling. Robin, his face displaying surprise and curiosity in equal measure, looked at the tangled grouping of detective and cadet. Ashley groaned inwardly at the thought of having to place his trust in the orderly.

Tom felt his uncle's grip relax. A hand, firm, but not rough, propelled him towards the leather armchair. He sat and stared alternately at Ashley and Robin.

'This, Robin, is my nephew, Tom.'

'I knew it was Tom One, sir – but I didn't know he was your nephew.'

'Well, you know it now and I want you to forget it instantly. If anybody else finds out that we're related, or that he's been in my room, my chance of solving this blasted case will be reduced to zero. And if I don't solve it…'

'You don't have to tell me, sir, I know: the Smith twins will get clobbered for it. Don't worry, I won't let you or them down. Shall I go?'

'In a minute, and thanks, Robin. I think Tom and I are going to need…,' Ashley looked at his nephew questioningly: 'about a quarter of an hour?' Tom nodded. 'At the end of that time, I'm going to have to ask you to sneak him out of here. Is that possible?'

'It should be, sir. Most of the officers will be changing for dinner by then. Chef will be losing his temper in the kitchen and the others will be dodging saucepans. I'll sort it out, sir, don't you worry.'

'Thanks. In the meantime, I think Tom looks as though he could do with a drink – and I certainly know that I could.'

'No problem, sir. Gin for you, sir? And by the looks of things, brandy for Tom? Back in a second, sir.'

Robin left, rather more quietly than Ashley and Tom had arrived. The moment the door closed, Tom opened his mouth to begin blurting out all he knew, but Ashley motioned to him to remain silent. They listened to Robin's footsteps until Ashley guessed that the orderly had gone down the stairs. Then he opened the door and checked that the passage was clear. When he was satisfied, he shut the door again and turned to Tom. He spoke very softly, but urgently.

'Robin will be back in about a minute so don't tell me anything important until he's been and gone again. I think we can rely on him, because he's a good friend of the Smith twins, but keeping a secret doesn't come naturally to Robin. I want you to keep your voice right down, as I am: no one must realise I've got a visitor. When possible, communicate with nods and signals. Do you understand?'

Tom nodded.

'Good. Does Lance Bombardier Green know you're here? What about the other cadets? Did anybody see you come in?'

Tom shook his head to all of these, then added in a whisper, 'The lance bomber's gone to Windsor, otherwise I'd have spoken to him. I'm sorry, Uncle George – I didn't think about the risk I was taking – about the Smith twins and all that...'

Ashley's temper was similar to Bombardier Croft's. When he replied to his nephew, his tone was kind.

'That's all right – I can see it's important. Take your beret off and try to relax for a moment. No, don't say anything yet; just gather your thoughts together. They look as though they could do with it.'

Robin returned with a tray of drinks.

'So far, so good, sir. Nobody made any comments, so I presume nobody saw or heard anything. I'll give you a knock in a quarter of an hour, sir.'

'Thanks, Robin.' Ashley waited until Robin had gone before he handed the brandy to Tom. 'Take half a dozen sips, gently. When you've done that, you'll feel better and Robin will be out of earshot. Then begin.'

Tom nearly choked on his first taste of the spirit; it was hot on his tongue and burned his throat as he swallowed but, once it was down, he could see why Robin had suggested it. Over the next few sips, he found words for his story, so that when it came out, it was short and efficient. The whisper made it sound conspiratorial: if Tom hadn't been feeling so miserable, he might even have enjoyed it:

'Tom Two and I spent over an hour in Gunner Chadwick's room after lunch. There were photographs of the Troop there – including some taken on the day of the murder. I asked him about Bombardier Cooper, and he described him as a blackmailer. He must have been aware of my reaction, because he immediately tried to pass it off as something he had heard. But he was lying – I'm sure of it.'

Ashley listened in silence. When Tom had finished, he paced around the room, sipping his drink. After a while, he sat on the edge of the bed, facing Tom.

'It fits,' he said softly. 'It all fits.'

He lapsed back into silence.

'What happens now, Uncle George?' Tom envisaged police cars screaming into the barracks, dozens of uniformed policemen fighting to overpower the enormous trumpeter, a dramatic arrest...

Ashley punctured his vision.

'Nothing.'

Tom looked up, quizzically. He was surprised to see his uncle smiling.

'We've got the beginnings of a case, Tom, not the end of one. Describing a dead man as a blackmailer isn't the same as admitting to murder, though it's a valuable piece of evidence. If he is one of the killers, we've got to dig up some more information, and we've got to give him the chance to incriminate himself and his accomplice. Neither of those things is going to happen if we go in with all guns blazing now.

'Listen carefully. In a moment, Robin will be back to get you out of here. I want you to return to your accommodation and change into whatever kit all the other cadets are in. Join them for the rest of the evening. Don't bother with any more detecting for today – just stay with them, relax and enjoy yourself. Can you do that?'

'I'll try, Uncle George – I'll do my best.'

Ashley heard footsteps approaching the door. He looked at his watch.

'Good lad. This will be Robin. Off you go – and take care.'

A moment later, Tom was gone. Ashley stood at the window and stared out towards the parade ground; after a while, Tom came into view, crossed over towards his accommodation block and disappeared through the entrance. There was a tap on Ashley's door and Robin entered once more.

'All clear, sir. Nothing to worry about.'

'Thanks, Robin.'

'That's all right, sir – no trouble.'

'And, Robin…?'

'Yes, sir?'

Ashley was embarrassed to ask, but it had to be done: 'You really *will* keep all this to yourself, won't you?'

Robin grinned. 'I know, sir, I'm not exactly the soul of discretion, am I? But I do know the difference between a piece of gossip and something really important – you can trust me on this one. If you hear an explosion in the night, sir, it's me; bursting with the secret.'

*   *   *   *   *

The evening has set in. The other four cadets are in the bar. Sorrell and Watson have organised a pool competition and they are all gathered around the table, shouting encouragement to

204

each other, and laughing at bad shots. Gillham, watching them, clutches his empty glass, waiting for someone to buy a round of drinks. Across the room, Lang and Scott continue their vicious, friendly, vendetta at the dartboard. Near the bar, Hall is buying a pint of lager for Carlton, the rent for the loan of his suit, and describing in detail every aspect of the commanding officer's Jaguar. With one ear, Watson listens in eagerly, hoping he will soon get the chance to drive it. It would make a change from Land Rovers, horse boxes and four-ton trucks.

In the Mess, Ashley is taciturn, chewing his food slowly as he goes over his conversation with his nephew again and again. Raynham, after another tough day at the police station, is in no mood to chat, and the two subalterns, Dawson and Fox, have been cowed into silence. A place has been laid for Dutton, but he has not returned. Colin and John, the orderlies on duty, communicate with each other by means of raised eyebrows and furtive glances. They keep the wine glasses topped up, in the hope of bringing the evening to life.

On the top floor of the accommodation block, Chadwick is getting his kit ready for the next day. On his desk, leather and silver flash and reflect the light of his reading lamp. He has just the spur straps to polish now – five minutes' work, no more. He yawns and stretches; in doing so, his eye rests briefly on the scattered photographs of Cooper.

'Bastard!' He leafs casually through the pictures, then throws the whole collection into the bin. Why keep a reminder of that day?

*　　*　　*　　*　　*

Tom One, still in his uniform, is sitting on his bed, his knees crunched up to his chest, his back resting against the wall. His beret, rolled up, is clasped in his hands. He stares straight ahead. In spite of promising his uncle that he will rejoin the other cadets, he cannot face them. Not in the bar, at any rate, where all is cheerfulness.

Everything has gone wrong today. He has jeopardised his position and endangered the whole future of the case: if the Smith twins are charged with murder, it will be his fault. Almost as bad as this, he knows that he has been the first of the cadets to let the team down. His shame is made all the greater by his increasing awareness of a vocation to this military life. As well as wanting to help his uncle, he now desperately wants to make a success of his three weeks as a cadet.

Finally, he has betrayed Chadwick.

Tom had thought that helping to solve a murder would be fun. The secret accumulation of clues, the stealthy observation of suspects, the final unmasking of a villain – all of these were supposed to be thrilling, daring, exciting. It had never occurred to him that he might like and admire the person he was helping to ensnare; that the triumphant moment of accusation would bring about the destruction of a fellow human being.

'What's up, Tom One?'

Tom hadn't even noticed Lance Bombardier Green entering the dormitory. He recognised the voice, rather than the shadowy figure in front of him; Green was dressed in canvas trousers and a light cotton sweater – the first time that Tom had seen him looking even vaguely civilian. Receiving no reply, Green continued: 'I went to the bar to find you. They said you'd had a rotten afternoon – was it just Crofty, or is there something else?'

'No, Lance – it's not Bombardier Croft. He was quite right to yell at me. It's more than that.'

While Tom unburdened himself, Green sat on the end of the bed and made sympathetic noises. When he heard the word "blackmail", he whistled.

'Well, Tom, I'd believe anything of Cooper, and Chadwick hated his guts all right, but *blackmail* – that's in a different league.' He paused for thought, then added, 'The same league as murder, I suppose. What does your uncle say?'

'He says it all fits, but that it's only a start. He told me to rejoin the other cadets, not to do any more detecting today, but

I couldn't face it. I've just been sitting here.'

'I can see that, but your uncle's right – you should be with them. Tell you what, we'll go for a private drink first, if you like. There's a pub near the barracks. Get yourself out of that uniform and have a quick shower, then we'll head off.'

Tom was grateful: a pint with Green would make all the difference. He began to unlace his boots, but then remembered: 'I can't, Lance: I haven't done any of my kit for tomorrow.'

'A couple of pairs of boots and a bit of ironing? You go and have that shower – I'll make a start. Just don't tell any of the others, or they'll all expect it.'

For the first time in hours, Tom grinned. He finished unlacing his boots, pulled them off and removed the rest of his uniform. Grabbing a towel and his wash bag, he headed for the shower.

Green picked up one of the discarded boots: it only needed a quick layer of polish. He reached into the metal locker for the cleaning things, then spread Tom's discarded combat shirt over his knees and began to work the polish into the leather.

He was on the second boot when he heard footsteps. The door opened.

'That was a quick shower, Tom.' Green looked up, expecting to see the young cadet, wrapped in his army towel. Instead he saw Chadwick towering above him.

Chadwick was as surprised as the lance bombardier. 'Oh, hi, Lance – I didn't expect to see you here.'

'Well that makes two of us, doesn't it? Are you looking for someone?' Green was doing his best to sound natural, but he couldn't keep the hostile edge from his voice. Chadwick seemed sensitive to it, hesitating before replying.

'Sort of – I ran off a copy of a fanfare for that cadet, Tom. I was going to leave it for him.' Chadwick reached through his coveralls and pulled out a rolled-up sheet of manuscript paper.

'Was it Tom One or Tom Two?'

'Two, I think – the one with large ears.'

'That's his bed over there. I'll make sure he gets it.'

'Thanks, Lance – I'll be off then.'

'Okay – you're duty trumpeter again tomorrow, aren't you, Chadders?'

'That's right – the recital begins at six-thirty, same as usual. See you, Lance.'

Chadwick disappeared and Green paused in his polishing. With Tom's right boot still over his hand, he went to the window and waited there until he saw Chadwick return to his own accommodation block.

* * * * *

The arrival of Dutton, slightly drunk, at least served to enliven the Mess. Raynham scowled at his junior officer, but Dawson and Fox were clearly relieved by the distraction of his entrance.

'Hi, chaps – sorry to be late. You don't mind if I don't go up and get changed, do you? Any chance of some grub, Colin? A sandwich will do if there's nothing hot left.'

Colin scuttled off to the kitchen in search of food and gossip and Dutton flopped down in the place that had been laid for him. John brought him wine. Ashley thought he saw Raynham shoot a warning glance in the direction of the orderly: if his interpretation was correct, the young soldier failed to observe it.

'So you had a good lunch with Jake, then?' observed Ashley, dryly.

'Bloody good – we went to the River Café. Fantastic food. Ever eaten there? Then we took in a film and after that I gave Jake a tour of Horse Guards. Meant to get there in time for the inspection, but that didn't happen. How did it go, Mark?' Dawson, who was in mess dress rather than black tie, was the duty officer.

'Fine. No sign of Cowan or the press there today, so the lads were all much more relaxed. Gunner Horden claims to have been propositioned by a rich widow, but everyone else thinks she was chatting up the horse. The general opinion was that, since Horden has no brains and the horse has no balls, the poor woman is doomed to either intellectual or physical disappointment.'

Dutton laughed for rather longer than was necessary, and held out his glass for more wine. He continued his narration: 'Then we popped into the Military for a few drinks, and rather lost track of time. Thanks, Colin.' The orderly had returned and placed a plate of sandwiches in front of him. 'Any chance of some mustard?'

'I'll get it for you, sir,' volunteered John, who then disappeared for his own gossip with Robin and the chef.

*　　*　　*　　*　　*

Lance Bombardier Green pushed open the door of *The Loose Cannon* and headed for the bar. Tom was relieved to see that the pub was fairly empty.

'It gets packed out at weekends, but from Monday to Thursday it's usually all right for a quiet pint if you need one. What can I get you, Tom?'

'Lager will be great, thanks. It's a good name for a pub.'

Green laughed. 'That's fairly recent: it was called *The Ball and Tampion* for over a hundred years, until the wife of the last landlord kicked up a stink. Gunners kept calling it the "Bollock and Tampon" and she got all upset, for some reason.' Green paid for the drinks and glanced around. In a corner, sitting by himself, was Gunner Barker.

'There's Adam – I wonder why he's here tonight? We'll say hello, and then we'll go somewhere private.'

They moved over to where the gunner was sitting morosely, staring into the dregs of a pint glass.

'All right, Adam? Not in the NAAFI tonight?'

'Oh, hi, Lance, Tom. No, I put my head around the door, but didn't fancy it. What about you?'

Green looked uncertain, so Tom filled up the gap in the conversation.

'I got a blasting from Bombardier Croft today.'

'Bad luck – when Croft blasts, he creates dead ground for several miles around. It doesn't last long, though.'

'No – he was really decent afterwards. The lance bomber is giving me some tender loving care before I'm released back into the community.'

Green smiled. 'I'm being Uncle Lance for the evening; there'll be hot milk and a bedtime story later. Do you want another drink, Adam? Your glass is nearly empty.'

'No thanks – I'm going back to do a couple of saddles. The twins didn't get the chance to do their kit before – well, you know. I thought I'd polish them up ready for when they come back. Is there any news of them? It's really strange without Chris: I'm his roommate.'

This last remark was to Tom, who nodded sympathetically. Green replied: 'No news that I know of – he's not been to his parents. According to Robin, the police are convinced that Smith One knows where he is, but he's not saying.'

'Poor sods, both of them. I wish I could help them in some better way than just putting a bliff on their saddles. I'll be glad when all this is over.'

Barker drained the last of his beer and stood up. 'Anyway, see you both – have a good evening.'

Tom and the lance bombardier sat down at the table and watched Barker leave.

'He's taken it badly, hasn't he, Lance?'

'I think we all have, in our different ways, Tom. During the day, when there's work to be done, you can just get on with the job in hand, but in the evening, you start thinking it all over. Adam would probably be drinking with the twins now, if they were here – they're good friends. Anyway, cheers.'

'Cheers, Lance,' Tom raised his glass gratefully. 'And thanks.'

CHAPTER TWENTY-THREE

COMMUNION

Tom Two is the first out of bed. He leans against the window ledge and watches admiringly as Chadwick marches to the centre of the parade ground. When the trumpeter raises his instrument, Two opens the window in order to catch the full sonority of the morning call.

The other cadets are less appreciative. A dawn chorus of groans mingles with the phrases of Chadwick's call. Vernon and Corner plunge themselves under their blankets in the vain hope of delaying the start of the day. Geary takes refuge in gallows humour: 'I tell you what, Tom Two: since you're so keen, you can muck out my horse for me. After that, a cup of tea would be nice – five sugars, but don't stir it.' He emulates his friends and ducks back under the bedclothes.

Tom One joins Two at the window, catching the conclusion of the *Reveille*. If Chadwick is aware of any movements against him, it has not shown itself in his playing or in his bearing. One marvels at the way the trumpeter marches immaculately back to the guardroom. He must have cast iron nerves.

'Come on, One, let's get going.' Two moves to his locker and takes out his coveralls. Tom One lingers a little longer at the window. He is about to turn to his own locker, when something catches his eye.

Lance Bombardier Green, still wearing the civilian clothes of the previous evening, is sneaking around the perimeter of the parade ground. He reaches the door of his accommodation block and dives inside.

Fifteen minutes later, as the cadets are beginning their tasks of filling wheelbarrows with stagnant bedding and laying out fresh straw, Green joins them. His service dress, perfect in every detail, betrays no sign of having been put on in less than five minutes.

* * * * *

As sweat pours down the faces and bodies of the cadets, Smith Two takes stock of his own condition. Unwashed and unshaven for two days, he is greasy and odorous. His breath reeks of stale nicotine and his stomach contains nothing but air; when he belches to clear it, the smell is putrid.

But, thank God, he has arrived – or, at any rate, he has come across a milestone telling him that he has only a short way to go. If he had known which roads to travel by, or dared to ask directions, he would have seen signs long before. Along the river bank, they are rare; but there is the stone in front of him and ahead, not far off, is the small town. He uses the milestone as a seat, sinking on to it gratefully. He rewards himself with his final cigarette.

* * * * *

'Thanks, Lance Bombardier Green; I really appreciate what you've done. So would Tom, if he knew about it. I told him to stick with the other cadets, but he obviously didn't understand my warning.'

Green gave a mighty yawn, then drank deeply from his steaming mug. Stable duties were finished; the cadets were heading for the shower, and Green was sitting on Ashley's desk. It occurred to Ashley that he had never seen Green sit normally on a chair: he always had to be on something slightly higher. Perhaps the desk was a substitute horse?

Having taken in oxygen and tea, Green responded: 'That's all right, sir. It wasn't necessary, as it turned out, but Chadwick

212

coming up to the dormitory like that put the wind up me. I'd never have forgiven myself if something had happened in the night. I pinched a couple of pillows from one of the unoccupied rooms, so I wasn't too uncomfortable.'

Ashley pictured Green, dossing down in the corridor outside the cadets' room: the sheepdog guarding his flock. He repeated his thanks, then asked: 'Will you get the chance for some sleep later?'

'I can get forty winks in a minute, sir, while they change and have breakfast. If I still feel bad, I can pop off during their riding lesson as well. Chadwick's the duty trumpeter today, so he'll be fully occupied until Last Post. After that – well, as you say, we'll have to make sure Tom sticks with the others. I'll look after him, sir, don't you worry.' Green yawned again and looked at his watch. It was almost half past seven. 'And now, if you'll excuse me, sir, I'll go and get my head down.'

* * * * *

Half past seven. As Robin smuggles Green out of the Officers' Mess, Father Peter Rose is about to begin Mass in the tiny Catholic Church at Dorchester on Thames. On Fridays, he uses the Old Rite, so his congregation is larger than would normally turn out for a weekday service this early in the morning. With difficulty, he suppresses the pleasing vision of his bishop fuming at the popularity of the Latin. He joins his hands before his breast, saying softly, '*Introibo ad altare Dei*,' and hears his server respond, '*Ad Deum, qui laetificat juventutem meum*.'

* * * * *

Robin knocked on the door of the bathroom and brought in fresh tea. He poured a cup for Ashley and handed it to him in a conspiratorial manner.

'Lance Bomber Green safely delivered through the escape hatch, sir. I'm getting used to all this cloak-and-dagger stuff.'

213

Ashley drank his tea gratefully. 'And I, Robin, am slowly getting used to company while in the bath. Fortunately, as well as revitalising the muscles, the herbal bubbles preserve the modesty. Is that second cup on the tray just for ornamental purposes, or have you come for a gossip?' At the moment, Ashley felt, he would rather Robin prattled on to him than to his fellow soldiers.

'Well, sir, I thought you might like to hear about Mr Dutton's hangover – it's a beauty.' Robin produced a smile almost as wide as Lance Bombardier Green's. Ashley did his best to emulate it.

'Nothing would please me more – it serves him right for messing up my journey to the crematorium. Pour yourself a cup and tell me the worst.'

*   *   *   *   *

Tom, caught up in the routines of the day, felt much better. He sat on the edge of his bed, giving his riding boots a final rub with a cloth, simply because that was what the other cadets were doing. There was no real need: the lance bombardier had done a good job last night.

'So that's what you spent the whole evening doing.' Tom Two spoke with approval. He held up one of the boots, and ran a critical eye up and down the polished leather, doing his best to recreate the experienced, professional look that Barker had displayed in the harness room. 'How long did it take?'

'Oh, not too long,' said Tom, truthfully.

'I'll tell you what, if I do your ironing tonight, will you show me how you got them up that well? We could take them over to the harness room and bliff them up over a couple of cans of beer. The others are going to be playing more pool – but I'm really useless at that.'

Tom One was touched by this obvious overture of friendship, which was rather moving in its clumsiness; nonetheless, he was deeply apprehensive at the thought of being exposed as a fraud. Still, perhaps he could get a quick tutorial from one of the gunners after the riding competition. He decided to bluff it out.

'That'd be great. We could take a couple of extra cans in case Gunner Barker is there – he practically lives in the harness room.'

They stood up and performed the curious balancing act that pulling on a pair of tall boots requires. Then they took it in turns to stand to attention while the other carried out an inspection, adjusting a stable belt or the lie of a service cap. They formed a mutual admiration society and passed each other with flying colours.

'We look lovely: Lance Bombardier Green will be proud of us. Shall we hit breakfast, One?'

'All right, Two – let's go.'

*   *   *   *   *

'*Te igitur, clementissime Pater, per Jesum Christum…*'

Father Rose begins the canon of the Mass. As its ancient formula unfolds, he hears behind him the latch of the church door rise and fall. A latecomer, perhaps, or maybe a member of the congregation has to leave early. He brings his mind back to the prayer, which he has been saying automatically for the last few sentences, '…*quae tibi offerimus pro Ecclesia tua…*'

The rhythms of the ancient words flow as they have done for generations. The priest's voice falls to a cadence and the sanctuary bell rings. He bows his head down towards the elements and begins the next phrase, more slowly, more deeply.

'*Hanc igitur oblationem servitutis nostrae…*'

Now he is reaching the centre of the prayer. His voice is barely a whisper, yet audible through the church.

He genuflects. Rising, he takes the newly-consecrated host and holds it aloft. The sanctuary bell rings again.

At the back of the congregation, Smith Two raises his head.

Devotion comes naturally to the hungry and to the accused.

For a moment, Smith Two believes that he can see the wounds of the nails; that he can reach out and place his finger in the side penetrated by the lance. Like the rest of the congregation, he echoes the words of St Thomas:

'*Dominus meus et Deus meus.*'

Then he bows his head.

* * * * *

'You're still alive then, Tom One?'

'Oh, hi, Gunner Sorrell. Actually, the bomber was all right – I thought he was going to rip me to pieces. He said – and I hope it's okay – that he'd get you to run through things with me over the weekend.'

'No problem – I'm going to be around, anyway. I'd show you today, but it's the competition.' Sorrell moved to a table: 'Shall we sit here? There's plenty of room for the others when they come down.'

They sat down and began to wade through sausages and bacon. Coming up for air, Tom Two asked Sorrell about the competition: 'Apparently, we're the arena party, but we don't really know anything about it yet.'

'I'm not sure I can tell you much either – it's my first one. Those of us who have only been in the Troop for six months jump in the first round, when the fences are all of nine inches high. If we jump clear, we go through to the second round, and so on, until we die horribly. Everybody says it's good fun. You'll have your work cut out rebuilding fences, because practically the whole Troop will be having a go – as you can see.'

The Toms looked around the canteen. Instead of the usual mixture of soldiers variously kitted out in coveralls, combats or riding clothes, virtually everyone was in breeches, boots and spurs. Sorrell himself, whom they had so far only seen dressed for the gun park, was in his equestrian uniform, ready for a last jumping lesson before the afternoon's event. Tom Two paused in the contemplation of a sausage.

'Tell us, Gunner Sorrell, is a pair of spurs really the most desirable piece of kit on the planet; or is it just the fact that we aren't issued them that makes them appear so attractive?'

Sorrell gave a grin full of bacon, and clicked his heels metallically beneath the table.

'They're fun until you go flying arse over apex when you're trying to run downstairs in them. I'll bet you anything that one of us juniors will forget we've got them on at some point today, and get tangled up. They're brilliant for riding, though. Not because you need them on the horse very often, but because they force you to keep your toes in. That makes a big difference. Hi Keith, hi chaps.'

The other cadets placed their heavily-laden trays on the table and sat down.

'Hi Gunner Sorrell – are you up for more pool tonight?'

'Sure, if I can scrounge another tenner from Jeff when he gets back from Horse Guards. According to Robin, a rich lady slipped her telephone number in his boot while he was on duty, so I reckon he owes me a favour. If he hadn't been on a horse, she'd have noticed that he's practically a pygmy. Watson's really jealous – he only ever gets notes from dirty old men.' Sorrell had addressed this last remark to the gunner himself, as he approached with his breakfast. Watson shot him a mock glare, then grinned.

'Right! And if I'd wanted that sort of attention, I'd have joined the Household Cavalry. But I can't help my rugged good looks, can I? If a couple of you budge up a bit, I'll grab a chair and join you.'

The cadets made room. Watson put his tray between them and turned to look for a chair. In the process, one of his spurs caught on the other and he went into a spectacular dive. Sorrell contemplated his crumpled friend and smiled happily at the Toms.

'Told you so.'

* * * * *

Twenty-five past eight. Breakfast over, the cadets are standing by their horses, waiting for the order to tack up. In Dorchester, Father Rose, having finished Mass and retired to the sacristy, removes his vestments. He leaves his server and the sacristan to clear up and returns to the church, now empty except for one person praying in a back pew. The priest walks along the aisle, sits next to the kneeling figure and rests his hand on the quivering shoulders.

'Why have you come here, Christopher?'

Kindness is always disarming. Like Barker, four days before, Smith Two, still kneeling, buries his face in his hands and begins to sob.

CHAPTER TWENTY-FOUR

POST COMMUNION

Ashley had no intention of putting Chadwick on his guard by questioning him; he had nothing to do, therefore, except wait for the afternoon competition. It would have been pleasant to ride out in the park again, but Raynham was at the police station once more and Ashley hesitated to take another officer or soldier from his duties. He certainly didn't feel ready to ride out by himself. He watched the inspection and departure of the new guard, and then decided to climb up to the gallery of the indoor riding school and see Tom being put through his paces.

Carlton and Green were already there. Below them, the five cadets had been fooled into thinking their lesson was finishing early. They had somersaulted off their horses and were standing to attention along the centre of the riding school. However, once again, they had been outmanoeuvred by the instructor's cunning and had assured him that they were not too tired for more.

'Hello, sir, you're just in time for the fun! Sergeant Miller's about to begin his favourite acrobatic competition.'

'Right then!' Miller's voice rang around the riding school. 'We'll have some revision of mounting and dismounting. They've not been bad so far, but they need to be smoother, and they've got to look effortless. Let's see if you can manage that today. This time, we will split the mount into two stages. On receiving the word of command, "Quickest and best, mount – One!" you will spring up and lock your arms as you saw Gunner Gillham do on Wednesday. You will hold that position until I say, "Two!" and then you will complete the manoeuvre. Can you all see Gunner Gillham over the top of your saddles?'

They could.

'Good. Gunner Gillham, prepare to mount. Quickest and best, mount – One!'

As he had done on their first day, Gillham gave two small jumps, then launched himself up, until he appeared to be standing at attention several feet off the ground. Once again, Miller left him hanging there.

'Now everybody else. Listen in!' Miller went through the command sequence a second time. Tom gripped the saddle, made his initial bounces, then sprang up. Three lessons on, it was a much easier process. True, Geary needed two attempts before he could lock his arms, and none of them looked as smart and well balanced as Gillham, but there were no disasters and they were all in position. Miller strolled along the line – deliberately slowly, Tom thought – correcting their positions.

'Much better than yesterday. Are you all comfortable?'

They replied through gritted teeth: 'Yes, Sergeant!'

'Good, I thought you might be. Okay, the next stage – including you, Gunner Gillham. Quickest and best – Two!'

With relief, Tom leaned forward and swung his right leg over. He remembered to let himself down gently this time, so that although the saddle wasn't exactly welcoming, it felt a lot better than it had on Wednesday. It was easier to find the stirrups without looking, too.

Miller gave a satisfied look along the line. 'Right, now we're going to have some fun.' Tom groaned inwardly: he had only experienced a few lessons but already he knew that Miller's remark meant that the sergeant was going to have the fun, while the cadets had the back-breaking work, probably mixed up with a good dollop of sheer terror. Miller's next speech did nothing to dispel this thought.

'We need to be able to take the mounting and dismounting for granted, so now we're going to do a little exercise to practise them. You're going to dismount by backward somersault, run under your horse and mount the next one. You will show that you have completed the mount by folding your arms, then I will give the command for the next dismount. Any questions?'

'Won't we die?' was the question Tom wanted to ask. He had visions of running a gauntlet of kicking hoofs, not to mention the risk of breaking his neck on one of the dismounts. He had got it right so far, but who knew if that was just beginner's luck?

Ashley enjoyed the look of apprehension on the faces of the cadets. More enjoyable, though, was the exercise itself; it really *was* fun, as the cadets quickly discovered. As they progressed along the line, dismounting, diving underneath the horses and remounting in sequence, their actions developed a natural rhythm. Judging the leap became easy; locking the arms was no longer a problem. To their amazement, not one of the horses moved or kicked. Unlike the cadets, they had done this exercise many times before.

Tom found himself at the head of the line, on Gillham's horse. Like Gillham and the two cadets between them, he dismounted and ran round behind the horses to the far end. Another three times and he was back on his own mare, feet in the stirrups and arms folded. Ashley admired the straightness of his nephew's back, the natural riding position of his leg and the way he held his head well up, looking superior to all the world.

'Arrogant bastard,' he thought, smiling. Had he known it, they were the two words Tom most wanted to hear.

Sergeant Miller moved the exercise to its next phase. 'Now,' he leered cruelly, 'we do all that as an individual exercise.'

* * * * *

Father Rose was a practical man. He had let Smith Two cry himself out, then walked him across the road to the presbytery, his arm around the young man's shoulder. In the kitchen, he put Two into a chair and poured him a brandy.

'Take this, it'll make you feel better. No, don't say anything yet, just drink. I'm going to put the kettle on and then run you a hot bath. By the time you've finished washing, I'll have some breakfast for you, and when you've eaten we can talk. If you try to say anything now, it'll just be nonsense, so don't even attempt it.'

Even the most tired, hungry and miserable person feels better for a hot bath. Two lay soaking for what felt like ages until the smell of sausages crept upstairs and caused his stomach to ache more furiously than before: Father Rose must have decided that the soldier's immediate needs were more important than observing the Friday fast. Quickly, he soaped his body, blasted his hair with the shower attachment and climbed out of the bath. Father Rose had left a disposable razor by the wash basin, a clean towel on a rail and a spare dressing gown hanging from a hook on the door. Smith Two made good use of all of these and returned to the kitchen, feeling much better. He still had a load on his mind, but he now felt secure that it was going to be all right.

The priest watched him begin his meal, then returned upstairs. In a spare bedroom, he rummaged through the wardrobe of cast-off clothes, which were clean, ironed and ready to go off to the Society of St. Vincent. He found a white shirt and a pair of chinos which seemed to be the right sort of size for the soldier. In his own room, he found new pairs of socks and underpants. They certainly weren't the right size, but at least they had never been worn before.

Twenty minutes later – at about the same time as the cadets were practising their mounting and dismounting – Father Rose and Smith Two rested in easy chairs in the sitting room, large mugs of tea in their hands.

'And now, Christopher, if you feel ready, we can talk.'

Smith Two hesitated. During all the time he had spent walking, and during the last hour of silence, he had given no thought to how he should begin. The priest interpreted his hesitation and asked, 'Would it help if I asked you a few questions?'

Smith Two nodded. Father Rose paused to organise his words, then began.

'Where is your brother?'

'Back at the barracks.' Two had no idea that his brother was in a cell, resisting every attempt by Cowan to make him incriminate himself. 'He doesn't know I'm here.'

'How did you know where to find me?'

'It was in a letter our mother wrote – she said that you had moved to Dorchester on Thames. I didn't really know how to find it, so I just walked along the river until I got here. I had to get away and speak to somebody I could trust. Not my brother because – well, because I didn't want to put him through what I've been through. Besides, it had to be somebody away from the barracks.'

'I understand. There's been a murder, hasn't there? I read about it in the newspapers.'

Smith nodded. Father Rose sighed inwardly. The next questions were going to be difficult.

'Is the murder the reason why you're here now?'

Another nod.

'Remember, Christopher, I am a priest. This conversation is under the seal of confession and I will never break that seal unless you tell me that I may do so. In return, you must tell me the exact truth. Do you understand?'

This time, Smith answered: 'Yes, Father, I do.'

'Good. Christopher, did you kill that man?'

Smith Two lifted his head and looked into the older man's eyes. It was strangely chilling to be asked the question so directly.

There was a long silence.

*　　*　　*　　*　　*

One moment, Tom is admiring Keith's mounting and dismounting technique, the next, he hears Sergeant Miller's command, 'Number four – Go!' and he runs towards the line of horses. No need to do preparatory jumps the first time; the impulsion of his running helps lift him into the air and he is in the saddle in a second, feet in stirrups, arms folded. Now, the dismount – left leg high over the horse's neck – grip the saddle – slide down a little – lean back, spine across the saddle – knees to chest – and roll. He lets go of the saddle. His body leaves the horse and curves gracefully through three-quarters of a circle before his feet touch the ground. For a second he stands to attention, then ducks under the horse and runs to the next.

Ashley experiences a new emotion as he watches his nephew complete his individual exercise: he is proud of him. Through his new-found sense of self-discipline, Tom is acquiring skills, confidence and a feeling of worth. After years of rebelliousness, it seems that he has found his niche. Carlton has moved to the other end of the gallery, so Ashley risks a murmur to Green:

'He's doing all right, isn't he?'

'I'll tell you what, sir, we'll get him signed up before the three weeks is out – and a couple of the others.'

As Ashley contemplates this thought, Tom whirls through a final somersault and lands triumphantly. As he turns to walk back to the group, he hears Miller call, 'Number five in line – Go!' and sees Tom Two leap up onto the first horse. He also looks up to the gallery and notices his uncle for the first time. For a second their eyes meet; they both grin; then Tom looks away and heads towards the other cadets.

Ashley turns towards Green. 'I hope you do get him – but my sister, to borrow your disgusting phrase, will discover that "number twos" is not just an order of dress.'

*   *   *   *   *

At last, Smith Two broke the silence.

'No, Father, I didn't kill him – but the police think I did.'

Father Rose sighed with relief. He had never thought of Christopher as a possible killer, but a priest knows that there is no limit to human weakness. Who knew what temptation or mischance might have turned an ordinary, simple boy into a murderer?

'It is the job of the police to suspect, Christopher. If you know yourself to be guiltless, you have nothing to fear. Even if you were to be wrongly thrown into prison, your knowledge of your innocence would sustain you.'

'No, Father, it's not that...'

'Is it your brother that you are worrying about?'

Smith Two shook his head.

'Then try to tell me what it is that troubles you.'

There was another long pause, while the soldier struggled to find the right words. Eventually, he managed: 'Father, I know who the killer is – and the only way I can save my brother and myself from suspicion is to betray my friend.'

CHAPTER TWENTY-FIVE

THE COMPETITION

Lance Bombardier Green leaned back against the heavy wooden fence of the outdoor riding school, put the heel of his right boot on the bottom rail and raised himself up to sit on the top. He looked round at the carefully constructed jumping course and said, 'I think we're done, lads. The riding master will be along in a moment to check it through and then we can take a bit of a break.'

The cadets had had a heavy morning. After the fun of mounting and dismounting, the lesson had continued with another half hour of trotting and their calves, thighs and backs ached from the constant, relentless exercise. When grooming and cleaning tack had been completed, they were granted a blissful fifteen-minute shower break. Green was waiting for them in the dormitory when they emerged, five rugby shirts folded over his arm.

'Standard arena party order of dress,' he said, flinging a shirt to each of them. 'One size fits all. Combat trousers and lace-up boots from the waist downwards, these from the waist up. Don't tuck them into your trousers. No head dress required. I got these out of the stores when the quartermaster wasn't around, so with any luck you'll get to keep them when your time here ends. See you down in the outdoor school in ten minutes.'

So there they were now, tired after building the course, but looking relaxed in their curious half-uniform. The rugby shirts were quartered in the green and cherry colours of the troop, which went well with the disruptive pattern of their combat trousers. They were also pleasantly cool to wear.

There were eight fences to the course, arranged according to the riding master's plan, ensuring a variety of approaches and hazards for the horses and their riders. At the moment, they were set ridiculously low, two poles crossed, so that the centre was under a foot high. This, as Sorrell had told them at breakfast, was the course for those gunners who had been with the unit for less than six months. The fences would gradually be raised for successive rounds. In addition to the course, the cadets had set up some staging beyond the fence, with a large desk for the scorer and judge and a set of chairs for the officers. Some technically minded soldiers had set up a couple of loud speakers.

'Look up, lads, here comes the captain.'

Green dismounted from the fence, landing in the position of attention. The cadets braced their bodies and Green saluted. 'Good morning, sir – the course is ready for inspection.'

Captain Shaw walked through the course with Green, carefully pacing between each fence to calculate the number of strides. The second part of a double jump needed moving out by a couple of inches, which the cadets saw to straight away; otherwise everything was fine.

'And the adjutant asked me to check that you'd organised what he calls "the extras", Lance Bombardier. Does that mean anything to you?'

'Yes sir, they're all sorted. I've tucked the stuff up in the gallery of the indoor school, so that the men don't get to see it until the round starts.'

The riding master seemed peeved at not being in on the secret, but since the commanding officer had authorised it, there was nothing to be done.

'Well, then, I think that's everything. The first round begins at one-thirty, so we'll come out of the Mess at about twenty-five past.'

'You'll find everything ready, sir.' Green saluted again and the captain headed back to his office. Everyone became more visibly relaxed once he had gone.

'Right, lads, I reckon you've earned a beer. I've got some chilling in the cookhouse fridge. Tom One, come and give me a hand fetching it, the rest of you, harness room in five minutes.'

The two groups walked out of the riding school and towards the parade ground before heading in their different directions. Once the other cadets were out of earshot, Tom whispered: 'Thanks for looking after me last night, Lance.'

'No problem, Tom – how are you feeling today?'

'Much better, thanks. It was a good lesson this morning, wasn't it?'

'It certainly impressed your uncle. He's probably practising backward somersaults in the privacy of his own room at this very moment.'

They reached the back door of the cookhouse. Green left Tom at the door and re-emerged a moment later with six ice-cold bottles of beer. These he gave to Tom to carry. Their chilly wetness seeped through Tom's rugby shirt and the sudden cold sensation against his hot chest was blissful.

Green carried on talking: 'Now, this afternoon. Most of the time, we really only need four of you in an arena party, so I'm going to keep you next to me as a runner, a sort of messenger boy. In fact, your job is to observe as much as possible. Sometimes we'll have to join in with the other cadets but, whenever possible, we'll mingle with the gunners. You keep your eyes and ears open – and stick by me. Got that?'

Tom had. They entered the harness room and Green tossed a bottle to each cadet. There was a chorus of thanks.

'That's a pleasure, lads. Now, Cadet Vernon, if you'd like to get your bum out of that saddle, which is *my* perch, and rummage around in that tool drawer, you'll find a bottle opener. That's the one – pass it round.'

Green made sure they had all opened their bottles before prising the cap from his own. He raised his bottle.

'Cheers, lads – you're doing really well. No, forget that. Cheers – *Gunners*.'

They all smiled broadly and raised their own bottles to Green.

'Cheers, Lance.'

And six throats opened to welcome the refreshing beer.

* * * * *

Smith Two and Father Rose talked for a long time – about the murder, of course, but not only about that. They discussed Smith Two's parents and his brother, his life as a soldier – any subject, in fact, that came along. Like Sorrell, Smith began to brighten once he had unburdened himself. Gradually, however, his lack of sleep began to tell. His voice grew low, and he began to mumble. Father Rose took charge again.

'And now, Christopher, you're going to bed for a couple of hours. I'll show you where the spare room is. Just come down when you want to and I'll have some food ready. And then...'

He paused. Smith Two filled the gap.

'And then, I'll have to go back, Father, won't I?'

'Yes, Christopher. For all sorts of reasons, you have to go back.'

But Smith Two felt he could face it now. He knew that he would be in trouble with both the army and the police for his disappearance, but he realised that facing up to those two organisations would be easy compared with facing up to the truth.

* * * * *

By twenty-five past one, when the officers came out of the Mess, the barracks was seething with activity. Although it was not compulsory, nearly all the soldiers had signed up for the competition. Those in the very first round were already warming up in the indoor school, where Gunner Carlton was acting as a one-man arena party, reconstructing the single jump after almost every attempt. Other soldiers ran backwards and forwards from the harness room to the stables and yet more, those not jumping until the higher rounds, were arranged around three sides of the arena, eagerly awaiting the downfall of their junior colleagues. Robin had set up a vast tea urn in the forge, so many of the riders, including one or two already mounted, clutched paper cups.

Captain Shaw leapt up to the stage, where Bombardier Burdett and one of the brighter-looking gunners were already busying themselves with score sheets and pocket calculators. Major Benson ignored the seat that had been put out for him and leaned against the vacant side of the fence, just as the gunners were doing. The remaining officers followed his example, as did Ashley and Edward, Ashley squeezing himself between Dutton and Dawson. Shaw seized a microphone and his voice bellowed over the barracks:

'Commanding Officer, distinguished guests...'

'Is that us?' whispered Edward.

'Yes – and shut up!' replied Ashley.

'Officers, non-commissioned officers and men of Prince Albert's Troop Royal Horse Artillery: welcome to our Summer Inter-Section Jumping Competition.'

Shaw paused for the wild cheering which rang around the area.

'The rules are simple and have been circulated to notice boards so all those of you who are able to read have had a chance to digest them. You have also had an opportunity to walk the course. If you missed out on that, there is a plan of it on the door of the forge. The first round is for those gunners who have been with us for less than six months. First to jump – Gunner Armstrong!'

An extremely nervous boy rode into the arena to rapturous applause. Blushing brightly, he saluted the judges. The crowd calmed down to give him a fair chance, a bell rang, and he put his horse into a trot and then a canter. There was a communal intake of breath as his horse clipped the first fence but the pole stayed in place and, seven fences later, the boy's blush was replaced by a triumphant smile. The soldiers whooped noisily as he left the arena and was replaced immediately by the next rider. Tom Two and James dashed to the first fence to make sure that the pole was still correctly in position, then returned to their place at the side.

'Congratulations to Gunner Armstrong, who goes through to the next round. Next to jump – Gunner Brown!'

The competition progressed. In round one, only Armstrong and Sorrell jumped clear. They remained mounted, while their less fortunate colleagues returned their horses to their stalls and untacked them, before returning to watch the rest of the competition. The arena party raised the fences for the second round.

There were the usual triumphs and disasters throughout the afternoon. Armstrong, his head turned by the success of his first round, did a demolition job on his second appearance, bringing down four poles and a complete fence. Even Tom One and Green had to enter the arena to sort that one out. In a later round, Gunner Scott's horse played up and he sprang around the course like a bouncing bomb. Amazingly, he jumped clear, to well-deserved applause. Sorrell surprised himself by jumping all the way to the fourth round, then his horse refused a fence and he flew gracefully over it on his own.

Finally, a dozen expert riders were left without a fence down. Ashley didn't know all of them but, as the names were called out by Shaw, he recognised among them Lang, Gillham, Barker, Watson and Hall.

The rounds euphemistically entitled, "Traditional Skills" followed. Just as Ashley had seen the day before, the soldiers jumped with their arms folded, then with their feet out of the stirrups, and finally removed a jacket at the same time as jumping. Each round, successful or otherwise, was greeted with cheers and applause. When Hall brought this part of the competition to a close with a spectacular, but entirely unintentional backward somersault, the enthusiasm of the audience was immense.

Shaw grabbed the microphone once more.

'And that brings the formal part of this competition to a conclusion. While Acting Bombardier Burdett works out his scores and averages, we have an extra round of traditional skills for your entertainment. All twelve jumpers from the last round are automatically qualified for it – that is, assuming that the arena party can reassemble Gunner Hall. Although this round will not score towards the overall competition, there is a separate cup, which the commanding officer will present to the most successful competitor. I now hand you over to Captain Raynham, who will introduce this part of the proceedings.'

All through Shaw's speech, there had been an interested murmur from the spectators. The final dozen, still mounted, also talked among themselves. This buzz of conversation became louder as the cadets (fresh from carrying off Hall) began to dismantle the fences, dumping the poles and supports down one of the long sides of the arena.

Raynham took the microphone from Shaw.

'Thank you, Captain Shaw. As you can see, Acting Lance Bombardier Green, and the cadets who make up his arena party, are hard at work dismantling the course. The cadets have only joined us this week, by the way, so let's give them a round of applause...'

On cue, the audience cheered and whistled.

'A big thank-you to Cadets Geary, Corner, Noad, Marsh and Vernon. As they finish carrying off the poles and uprights, you will observe Gunner Carlton on his way towards the arena with the favourite charger of the previous commanding officer – she's attractively named Clytemnestra, and is known as "Clammy" for short.'

It was not clear whether the applause that followed was for the mare or for Gunner Carlton; the audience seemed past caring about such niceties. Ashley recognised the horse he had ridden when he went out with Raynham. She was now tacked up in full military kit.

'As you can see, Clammy is modelling a natty little double

bridle, which leaves her rider free to handle a weapon in his right hand. The two exercises which you are about to witness were once common equestrian skills which would have been practised by all gunners. If today's performance by our top riders goes well, they may be introduced back into our programme. In the old days, they were called "tent-pegging" and "cleaving the Turk", though my guess is that we'll have to find a more politically correct way of describing the second task.'

The cadets, having cleared away the fences, had run to the gallery of the indoor school and now brought into the arena the equipment for this new round: a lance (and a spare), various slivers of wood, spiked poles with weighted bases, a sword and, of all things, a sack of root vegetables.

The crowd roared.

'Yes, we thought you'd find it amusing, but these, believe it or not, are the materials required for these fine old traditional exercises. You'll see that on one side of the arena, two tent-pegs are being planted in the ground. On the other side, three poles, each topped by a turnip, are being placed in position. Our competitors, in turn, will enter the arena, take a lance from – I think it's Cadet Marsh – and canter down the course, attempting to spear one of the pegs. We've put down two to give them a second chance if they miss the first.'

'At the far end of the arena, they will hand their lance to Cadet Vernon and take the sword from Cadet Geary. They will then canter up the other side of the arena and attempt to slice the turnips in half. So, if the finalists would like to dismount from their own horses, we can begin. Gentlemen of Prince Albert's Troop, I give you – Gunner Lang!'

Lang walked into the arena to a rapturous ovation. He mounted the mare and gathered up the reins in his left hand. Tom Two handed him a lance, which he stared at for a while, then tried its balance in his arm. Still looking rather confused, he set off down the arena.

He had a pretty good go. His lance struck the first tent peg,

233

but failed to spear it properly. He regained his balance, but not sufficiently to attempt the second peg. He kept the lance upright and handed it to Vernon, who ran with it back to Tom Two. Now Lang had the sword in his hand – at least this was a familiar weapon. He cantered down the arena, in the direction of Ashley and the officers, and swung out at the first "Turk". His sword missed, striking the wooden pole instead, and Lang felt a great rush of pain up his right arm. He was too busy collecting himself together to try for the second target, but he had a go at the third and managed to give it a shallow scar. There was sympathetic applause from the audience. Dutton turned to Ashley and said, 'If anybody manages to do better than that on a first go, I'll be surprised.'

For a while, it seemed that nobody would. A gunner whom Ashley didn't recognise both speared and slashed at the air and retired to tepid applause. Gillham managed to spear the first peg, but as he held it aloft, it fell from his lance: annoyed, he made a wild cut to the first turnip, hit the pole, as Lang had done, and recoiled in agony. The sword flew from his hand and landed several feet away. Somehow, Gillham managed to dismount without using his right hand and rejoined the other finalists, nursing his wrist.

'This is going to be a fiasco,' muttered Dutton to Ashley. 'Whose idea was it to try this without any previous practice?'

Ashley shrugged and turned to watch the fourth finalist attempt the tasks.

This time, it wasn't a fiasco.

Admittedly, the rider missed the tent pegs. But he more than made up for that. He seized the sword and threw himself and the horse towards the first Turk. Keeping his eye on it all the time, he slashed – and the top half flew across the arena. He might easily have been put off by the roar of approval from the crowd, but a second later the next Turk was sliced across, and then the third. The crowd was jubilant; cheers, whistles and whoops rang around the arena and echoed through the barracks. The rider stood up in the saddle as he cantered round, holding his sword aloft in acknowledgement of the applause of his audience.

Naturally, he looked over to where the officers stood and for a second, he caught Ashley's eye.

And Ashley smiled.

The rider hesitated; the mare slowed and halted.

Ashley watched the expression on Gunner Barker's face change from triumph to apprehension, and from apprehension to fear.

CHAPTER TWENTY-SIX

FIRST AND SECOND MURDERERS

Barker recovered enough to dismount and leave the arena before most of the soldiers had noticed anything, but it was impossible for the officers, who had been directly facing him, not to realise that something was up. Dawson wondered aloud why the gunner had suddenly looked as though he had seen a ghost, while Dutton whispered, 'Bloody hell, Ashley – you've got him.'

'I think so,' Ashley replied softly. He paid little attention to Dutton, so intent was he on studying the other gunners. Surely there must be a reaction on the face of one of them?

Raynham introduced another candidate, then leapt down from the stage to join Ashley. He hissed in his ear.

'George, he's getting away!' Barker was already out of sight. He had walked straight past the group of finalists and round a corner towards the parade ground, leaving Lang stranded, holding on to both his own horse and Barker's. Again, Ashley only half heard the adjutant. He was watching Lang's expression; but the gunner merely shrugged and looked mildly curious. Raynham, getting no reaction from Ashley, whispered to Dutton, 'Follow him,' then leapt back onto the stage, just in time to announce the next rider.

Ashley gave up trying to read anything in Lang's face and registered what Raynham had said.

'No, there's no need to follow...' but Dutton had already gone. Ashley turned back to study the other gunners. Across the arena, he saw Tom doing the same thing, staring intently at Chadwick.

Sorrell, looking relaxed, one foot on the lower rail of the fence, chatting casually to his roommate.

Carlton, dressed in the same easy outfit as the cadets, taking the horse back from the fifth, unsuccessful, rider, holding her steady for the dismount.

Watson, walking into the arena and vaulting up into the saddle, easily and naturally; Chadwick, waiting by the gate, his trumpet hanging behind his back, oblivious to Tom's stare.

Gillham and Hall, holding their horses' reins and drinking tea.

Scott, just visible in the crowd, joining in the cheer when Watson becomes the first to spear a tent peg.

Nothing. Eight normal, cheerful faces, expressing no more than the emotions of the moment.

That left the Smiths. Smith One and Barker? Smith Two and Barker? Burdett and Barker, maybe?

Ashley watched the next three rounds with unfocussed eyes as he wrestled with theories and possibilities.

Then, suddenly, he realised.

*   *   *   *   *

Green sees Ashley and Edward move away from the officers. From across the arena, his instinct picks up the detective's sense of urgency. He nudges Tom, whispers, 'We're on,' and starts to work his way through the crowd. Tom follows behind him, squeezing between the same soldiers as the lance bombardier. The soldiers take no notice – they are cheering Hall, who has managed the first accurate slice since Barker.

As soon as they break free of the crowd, Green and Tom run to catch up. Ashley sees them and calls, 'Where's his accommodation?'

'Try the harness room first, sir – it's closer.'

Between stable blocks, over the riding track, then cutting the corner of the parade ground to get to the harness room. Green has overtaken Ashley and leaps the three steps up to the door in one bound. He enters the room, closely followed by Tom, but immediately turns and thrusts the cadet back out of the door. Ashley yells to Edward to stay at the foot of the steps, then joins Green.

They were right to come to the harness room first.

A bridle hangs from a hook.

Barker's eyes bulge from their sockets; a purple tongue protrudes from puffed lips.

The draught of their sudden entrance causes the body to swing slightly and the leather cuts more deeply into the raw throat.

'Oh God, sir – he's killed himself.' Green is pale and trembling. Ashley trembles too, but with rage – rage for this unnecessary, revolting death – rage at himself for not being in time to prevent it, and most of all, rage because...

Ashley turns to Green. The soldier is shocked by the detective's face, livid with anger, his fists, clenching and unclenching, his breathing, short and heavy. The words come out with effort.

'He hasn't killed himself – he's been murdered.'

*   *   *   *   *

And now three of them are running again, Ashley and Green across the parade ground, Tom back to the outdoor school to alert Benson, Raynham and the medical team. Edward stands guard outside the harness room door.

Over the riding track again and towards the main gates. A sharp turn to the left and in through a door. Ashley telling Green to wait until called for. Then Ashley alone, taking the stairs two at a time – his feet, pounding along a corridor – his hand, resting on a doorknob.

Entering the room.

*   *   *   *   *

Dutton is sitting, his eyes staring ahead. His hands, scratched and bleeding, grip the arms of his chair. He barely registers Ashley's presence.

A second ago, Ashley had wanted to kill him – to throw himself upon him and lash out until Dutton's bloody, battered face lost its humanity and Ashley's great anger wore itself out in violence. That was a second ago. Now, seeing Dutton paralysed with shock, Ashley's anger starts to dissolve.

He cannot feel sorry for the officer. But he no longer wishes to kill him.

Ashley breaks the silence with a single word.

'Why?'

As if in a trance, slow and monotone, the reply unfolds.

'He was going to give himself up. He'd wanted to since your experiment on Monday, but I forced him to keep going. After your trap, he wouldn't listen to me anymore. He said that I could clear out and run if I wished, but that he was going to Raynham the moment the show was over. Then he turned his back on me, and – and I lost control.

'I strangled him with a stirrup leather. He struggled a lot...' Dutton holds up the backs of his hands to look at the scars left by the desperate tearing of Barker's nails: 'He didn't want to die...

'I persuaded him to help me kill Cooper. Out in Germany, I'd done something stupid. Not something that would matter in civilian life, but it would have ruined my career in the army if it ever got out.'

It is easy to guess. Ashley simply asks, 'Jake?' and Dutton nods.

'God knows how Cooper found out, but he did. At first, he just goaded me privately, but soon he realised that he could use it to make money.'

'After six months of torment, I'd had enough. I applied for a transfer here and thought I'd escaped from him. That was stupid as well; I was too good a source of income for him to let me go. He followed me over.'

'Then, about a month ago, I saw him coming out of the harness room with that same evil, satisfied look that he always wore when I'd given him money. I went in and found Barker. I don't know why he was blackmailing him; I didn't ask.'

'We hatched a plan together: somehow, having two of us, it seemed right – an execution, not a murder, just as you said the other day. I went to Horse Guards in the morning, mingling with the crowd, to check which duty Barker was on. Just after three, when the coast was clear, Barker let me in the back entrance. I'd taken a copy of the key from the one in our guardroom and I hid in the stable, in the area beyond the stalls. Barker had told Cooper that he had more money for him and that he would hand it over there when the rest had gone into the canteen.

'Cooper fell for it completely. The killing was exactly as you reconstructed it. I shoved the cloth in his mouth while Barker held his wrists, then I bound them and kicked him down. Barker did the actual beheading, as you guessed this afternoon.'

Dutton pauses, his arms trembling as he grips the chair more firmly. It is as if Cooper's torso is in front of them, spewing out blood on the vinyl floor.

Ashley interrupts.

'And you kicked his head across the stable?'

Dutton nods again.

'It wasn't part of the plan. As soon as he was dead, we were going to get out of our coveralls and away as quickly as possible, but, somehow, at the sight of his head, lying there, I just had to pick it up. And then, as I looked into his stupid face, with the eyes still blinking at me, well, I lost it again. I drop-kicked it, as hard as I could. Got blood all over my shoe.'

He pauses for a wry smile. 'That's why I had to buy a new pair that afternoon.

'Barker let me out again and then substituted his sword for Cooper's. He joined the others in the canteen, I went to buy my shoes and then headed to the Military for a drink.

'I didn't feel any remorse – I still don't, as far as Cooper's concerned. But Barker was different. He was having dreams – and then, after Monday, they got worse.

'I should have let him give himself up then. I should have come with him. Even as I killed him, I knew that I was finished, but I'd lost all control – just kept pulling the strap tighter and tighter. The bridle was already hanging there. It was easy to wrap it round his neck and then pull up one of the leathers until his body was just off the ground. I kicked over a bucket, to make it look as though he'd done it himself.

'But then I stood back and looked at him…'

And now, Dutton's voice loses its even flow. He speaks more quickly and at a higher pitch.

'And I saw what I'd done to him. It wasn't like seeing Cooper dead – it wasn't fascinating, it was dreadful. I'd killed him – killed him because I was too cowardly to face up to reality. And then I wished that I was hanging in that bridle instead of him. I wished the life had been squeezed out of me instead of out of that poor boy.'

He raises his damaged hands to his face.

'That's what I wish now – I wish I could die too.'

Ashley said quietly:

'No one is going to stop you.'

$$* \quad * \quad * \quad * \quad *$$

There is a proper guard on the harness room door now. Barker's body has been lifted down and stretched out on a work surface. The attempts of the medics to revive him were hopeless. Soldiers mill around despondently, holding mumbled conversations. Carlton has herded the cadets into the gun park. Both military and civil police have been summoned.

The guard on the gate must think it strange to see Dutton, dressed in civilian clothes, walking out of the barracks. It is particularly odd that he is wearing gloves. But the guard has been given no orders concerning the movement of officers, so he simply comes to attention and presents arms. Dutton does

241

not respond: it is the first time in his career that he has ignored a salute.

It is a short walk to the Underground. Dutton buys the cheapest ticket from a machine, passes through the barrier and travels down the escalator.

He stands at the very end of the platform and feels the rush of the first train passing him. The force of the air against his body is exhilarating, almost pleasurable. He allows another train to hurtle by and then a third.

One more will be cowardice.

As the next train shoots out of the tunnel, he launches himself from the platform.

It will take a post-mortem to establish the exact cause of death. It may be that Dutton was killed instantly by the train smashing into his body, shattering his ribs and splitting his spinal cord. If not that, then maybe the surging of electricity through his broken body, as he was thrown onto the track, caused his heart to stop.

Or perhaps it is possible – *just* possible – that he was still conscious when he lay with his chin beyond the far track and his throat pressing against it. Perhaps he was aware of the wheel slicing his head from his body; perhaps he felt the sensation of falling into the dark pit below the rails; perhaps, for one brief moment before life was extinguished, he felt the blood from his body dripping onto his cheeks and forehead.

Who knows?

CHAPTER TWENTY-SEVEN

EPILOGUE

Ashley had a number of tasks to perform over the next fortnight. On the Monday, he took Edward back to the Tower, where they lunched with Yeoman Warder Gillick and the Deputy Constable. Gillick was plunged into gloom by the news of Barker's strangulation: 'Not the way a gentleman would choose to go, Mr Ashley, not the right thing at all.' Nor did the news of Dutton's decapitation cheer him: 'Too good for him, sir, too good. He should have been the one that got strangled.'

On Wednesday, Ashley attended Barker's funeral. Dutton had left a note taking on himself as much of the blame for Cooper's death as was possible. He said nothing of Cooper blackmailing Barker and much of his own forcing the gunner to be an accomplice. Ashley felt that this was probably fairly near the truth, and was pleased when Benson announced that Barker was to be given a military funeral. Several of the soldiers who had been on duty at Horse Guards fourteen days before acted as his pallbearers: Green and Lang were there, as were the Smith twins, carrying their friend on their shoulders.

Chadwick played the cavalry Last Post over the open grave. Nobody knew how he managed to get through it when, all around him, friends and relations were crying, freely and openly. But somehow, he played on, the songbird singing while the thorn pierced its chest. The pure notes of his trumpet sounded across the cemetery and down into the little valley where Barker had grown up. There they fell to the earth and were absorbed. After a silence, he began the *Reveille*; somehow, its brightness made it more difficult to bear.

Barker's funeral seemed to mark a psychological turning point for Prince Albert's Troop. Things returned to normal and preparations began in earnest for the gun salute for the Commonwealth leaders. True, Dutton also had his funeral but his family, like Cooper's, requested no military presence. Ashley, too, stayed away.

The day after Barker's funeral, Ashley arranged to meet Jake in St James' Park. Dutton had written a second note, which he had pushed under Ashley's door before leaving the barracks. He had written a brief instruction on the envelope, asking Ashley to give it to the young gunner. The envelope itself was unsealed, so that Ashley could check that there was nothing in the contents that the police should see.

Jake was on the bridge over the lake, leaning on the rails and throwing the remains of a sandwich to a pair of swans. He was wearing the suit and tie that Ashley had seen at Cooper's funeral. Strongly contrasting with them in quality were his shoes, obviously hand-made, shining to the military standard that Ashley now took for granted. The detective introduced himself and they headed for the tea shop.

Over tea, Jake read his letter in silence. It took only a few moments: Dutton's written confession had left him with little time for this second note. When he had finished, the soldier looked up at Ashley.

'Have you read this, sir?'

Ashley nodded. 'I'm sorry – I had to. It might have contained things that the police would need to know. As it is, they aren't aware of its existence.'

Jake folded the letter away, and took a mouthful of tea. When he spoke next, there was relief in his voice, as well as a mournful tone of acceptance.

'I knew he'd done it, sir, the moment the news reached us in Osnabrück. He more or less suggested that I should help him get rid of Cooper when we were all in Germany together. When I told him where to get off, he tried to pass it off as a joke...

'He was a very obsessive, forceful person, sir. Selfish, too.

244

It would be like him to get somebody else involved with his plans, then leave them to do all the nasty stuff. He'd have happily let others take the blame as well. To be honest with you, sir, I was quite glad when he applied to transfer to London.'

Ashley was unsurprised: 'I'd assumed that the relationship was fairly one-sided.'

Jake gave an embarrassed smile. 'I was flattered, sir: he was an officer, and I was just a gunner, fresh out of basic training. He took me to exciting parties and we went on leave together a couple of times. He bought me presents as well – these shoes were from him. We had lots of fun. But – well, let's put it this way, sir – I've got a girlfriend out in Germany. He didn't know about her. We're hoping to get married next year, in the spring. In fact,' he rummaged in his pocket and pulled out a small box with the name of an expensive jeweller on it. Inside was a diamond ring, which glittered in the sunlight as the box was opened. 'I saw it in a display last Thursday, sir. He'd insisted on buying me a pair of cufflinks, and while he was inside choosing them, I was looking at engagement rings in the window. I've been saving up for some time. She'll be wearing that, this time tomorrow, sir.'

Jake's smile had lost its embarrassment. He looked directly into the detective's eyes and Ashley found himself staring at a face radiating enthusiasm and happiness. Absorbed by a pair of intense blue irises, he began to understand why the impulsive officer had fallen so completely for this young man.

*   *   *   *   *

At the beginning of the next week, Ashley called Raynham to see if he could borrow some transport. The adjutant was happy to help: 'Will the old Land Rover do? It's not glamorous, but it gets from A to B. You can have Green as a driver, if you like – just remember not to accept a drink from his thermos flask.'

So, an hour later, the Land Rover stood in Lonsdale Square, with Green holding open the door. The lance bombardier, no longer just acting, had clearly decided that the vehicle was some kind of metal horse and was dressed in full riding kit. To Ashley's disappointment, he didn't actually use his whip to start the car, but he did say, 'Come on, giddy-up!' as they drove off. Mercifully, there was no flask to be seen.

'I hope you don't mind, sir, but I've brought Sorrell with me.' Sorrell poked his head through the flap dividing the front and rear of the Land Rover and said, 'Hello, Mr Ashley, sir – I hope it's all right.'

'He doesn't get out much, sir, and being a town boy, he's never seen a cow before – he's very excited. Dorchester on Thames, wasn't it sir?'

'It was, and is. Gunner Sorrell's very welcome to come along as well. Father Rose will be delighted to see you, Sorrell – I've never yet met a clergyman who didn't have a whole load of brass to polish.'

They stopped off at Goring for a pub meal and then drove on to Dorchester. Father Rose, as predicted, leapt at the chance to have the church brass cleaned and piled up multiple candlesticks, three thuribles, an incense boat and two processional crosses on a table in the sacristy.

'By coincidence, Miss Murchison said she would look in this afternoon and do as much brass as she could – I'm sure she'll be thrilled to find two professionals already at work.'

Since they were wearing their smart uniforms, Green and Sorrell simply did what they would in the barracks, and stripped to the waist before applying themselves to their task.

'It looks as though Miss Murchison's thrill is going to be even bigger than you anticipated, Father,' said Ashley, as they crossed the road to the presbytery.

'Ah, well, she doesn't have much pleasure in life, so who are we to begrudge it her? And your boys are quite safe – Mavis is available, but not predatory.'

They relaxed in soft chairs in the sitting room, drinking tea. The conversation became more serious.

'How is Christopher?'

'Upset about his friend, of course, and wondering whether he would still be alive if he had come forward earlier. But otherwise, he's well. Thank you for bringing him back.'

'It was good to be able to help. Did he get into any trouble?'

'Not from the army; Major Benson, very decently, overlooked it. The police would have liked to be awkward, but the inspector was too busy wiping egg from his face to do anything serious.'

'How very satisfactory. The police are not what they used to be, Mr Ashley.'

'Emphatically not, in the case of this particular one. You can imagine why the poor chap didn't want to tell him what he'd seen.'

'But he told you?'

'Yes, Father, he did. That he had seen Barker coming out of the guardroom with a sword and that Barker, who was his roommate, had been having nightmares since the murder.'

'And Robert?'

'Well, as you know, he was actually in a police cell when you arrived at the barracks. Our friend, the inspector, refused to drop the assault charge at first, but then the commanding officer had the brilliant idea of threatening to make a formal complaint about the inspector's interrogation technique. They released Smith One – sorry, I mean Robert, on Saturday.'

Father Rose sighed and put down his cup and saucer. 'So, is all well that ends well, Mr Ashley?'

'No, Father, it's not. My soul aches for that dead boy. If I'd thought more quickly, I could have prevented it. He felt a dreadful guilt – I think he even wanted to be punished – but he struggled to live. Nothing he'd done merited a death like that.'

Father Rose nodded: 'I assumed it was more than just friendly news that made you telephone and ask to see me. I share your instincts. It's not given to us to judge these things, but it is difficult for us not to conclude that an essentially good life has been wasted. Are you Catholic?'

Ashley shrugged, uncomfortably: 'Not yet, Father.'

'That is a shame. The Catholic knows that the help he can give to a fellow human being does not come to an end when that other person dies. He can pray for his soul and offer Masses to be said for him. To the non-believer, these things are foolish, but the Christian belief is in a communion of all the saints, both the living and the dead. Although our relationship changes with a person when he dies, the relationship does not end. As so often, in helping others, we find help for ourselves; those who pray for the departed are always comforted. I will say Mass for this young man. What was his name?'

'Barker, Father. Gunner Adam Barker.'

Father Rose wrote the name down on a scrap of paper. He smiled: 'I'm not sure that God will be too fussed about his rank. Is there any other way in which I can help you?'

'That has helped, Father. Thank you – I shall pray for him.' Embarrassed, Ashley stumbled his way through the sentence, glad that he had said it, but glad, too, that the interview was closing. Father Rose pretended not to notice his awkwardness.

'There is nothing better that you can do. And now do you think we should carry over some tea to those soldiers of yours?'

They made one mug as strong and as orange as they could manage and four normal ones, an extra mug in case Miss Murchison was in the sacristy when they arrived. Ashley carried them on a tray, which was nearly knocked out of his hands by the lady herself, rushing out of the church door.

'Oh, Father! Tea! How *wonderful!* I was just on my way over to ask if I could make some for those two *lovely* boys, who are doing such *marvellous* work! I've never seen the church brass look so beautiful before. The candlesticks will look lovely at Mass on Sunday – positively *glistening*, like a Life Guard's helmet, they said!'

She seized the tray from Ashley and dashed back to the sacristy, anxious to spend as much time as possible with her two young heroes. As Ashley and Father Rose walked more steadily down the aisle, the priest remarked: 'I shall try very hard *not* to recall that remark when I celebrate Mass…'

*   *   *   *   *

Finally, Ashley attended the gun salute for the leaders of the Commonwealth. He wandered into Hyde Park at about twenty minutes before noon, to find the band playing and Tom guarding the entrance to a roped-off enclosure for invited guests. The other four cadets, under the watchful eye of Green, were showing people to their seats.

'Hello Tom – you're looking smarter than I've ever seen before, and that's saying something after the last couple of weeks.'

'Thanks, Uncle George. We aren't supposed to be here at all, because we're not issued with service uniform or a pair of best boots, but Lance Bombardier Green went round scrounging kit all over the place. I've got Robin's boots and spurs and Sorrell's cap and jacket.'

'You were born to wear uniform, Tom – you look marvellous.'

He left his nephew blushing and entered the enclosure. Before any of the cadets could show him where to sit, Green collared him.

'What do you think of my young gunners, sir?'

'You've done a grand job, Lance Bombardier – they look very smart in their borrowed kit.'

'Thank you, sir. Strictly speaking, they've got no real function – this is a one-man job, normally. But they're having a wonderful time: all the tourists are taking pictures of them – look there.'

And Ashley saw Toms One and Two posing in the position of attention while cameras clicked around them.

'I just hope they managed to get Tom Two's ears in. By the way, sir, are you having lunch in the Mess afterwards? Because if so, Bombardier Burdett and I are having an illegal get-together in the forge to celebrate the confirmation of our promotions. We'd be very pleased if you could look in.'

249

'I shall be delighted.'

The party atmosphere continued for another fifteen minutes. Then the band paused in its playing and somewhere in the distance a bugle sounded the charge. The band struck up a brilliant fanfare and, from over the horizon, thundering and jangling, the Troop appeared. Horses and guns roared past the enclosure. There was a dismounting of riders, a detaching and turning round of guns, then the horses withdrew as rapidly as they had arrived, leaving six guns, shining in the sunlight, waiting to bellow out their salutes. Ashley recognised Sorrell sitting at the metal seat of the gun nearest. Behind him, down on one knee, was Burdett. Two other gunners, Lang and Watson, on either side of Sorrell completed the formation and the pattern was repeated at each gun in the line.

The officer in charge of the salute was too far away for Ashley to see who it was, but he recognised Raynham's voice when the command came.

'Number one gun – Fire!'

A jet of red flame and a cloud of smoke shot from the barrel of the farthest gun; a split second later, the noise of the blast hit the spectators. There was a rustling among the trees as birds made a rapid departure.

'Number two gun – Fire!'

With each successive gun, the noise grew louder, and the time between the sight of the flash and the sound of the blast grew smaller. When Raynham called, 'Number six gun – Fire!' the brilliant flame and the deafening thunder were simultaneous, and the ground beneath the spectators shook.

Ashley watched Sorrell open the breech, tear out the spent round and pass it to the other seated soldier. The far gunner handed him a new round and he loaded it, ready for the next firing.

Round after round, the salute continued. Breezes blew the smoke first one way, then the other, so that sometimes the guns were invisible, only to appear mystically through the clouds a second later. Impassive, the soldiers kept up their task. Thirty-eight, thirty-nine, forty... Finally, Raynham called, 'Number five gun – Fire!' and the forty-first and last explosion echoed around the park.

Then there was a flurry of activity. The guns were turned round once more, the horses reappeared and the guns were hooked up. Ashley saw and admired a dozen examples of the "quickest and best" mount as soldiers vaulted back on to their horses and, in another minute, horses, riders and guns had disappeared back over the horizon.

It was a marvellous sight. It was the best of British ceremonial.

No other nation could have done it.

* * * * *

There was a small luncheon party in the Officer's Mess. Ashley felt particularly dingy in his civilian suit next to Raynham and the other officers in their full dress uniforms. Talk was of the salute and fine details of ceremonial rather than of recent events, but eventually, as guests departed and the riding master went upstairs to change, other subjects came up.

The commanding officer, Raynham and the two junior officers retired with Ashley to the more comfortable armchairs in the morning room. There was a general loosening of tunics and a passing round of cigars. As they relaxed, Benson spoke: 'Well, Mr Ashley, I need hardly say that had it not been for you, that salute may well not have taken place. Everybody in the Troop is grateful to you...'

It was one of those pompous little speeches which have to be made from time to time, with, 'hear, hear' sounding from the officers after every compliment, followed by an embarrassed nod from Ashley in acknowledgement. There were interesting moments: Ashley was enchanted to hear that any time he wanted to ride in the park, he could simply telephone and a horse would be made available – together with a second horse, ridden by somebody altogether more experienced. He was also pleased by the present of the bronze statue of a mounted gunner which he had admired in his room. Finally, at the end of the speech, he was particularly delighted to discover that no reply beyond a brief word of thanks was required.

*   *   *   *   *

Green's party was altogether a more relaxed affair. Most of the soldiers there had been taking part in the salute; they were now in curious mixtures of uniform, having removed their tunics and replaced them with a variety of rugby shirts, olive green vests or, in a couple of cases, nothing at all. The cadets, in contrast, were clinging on to their borrowed glory for as long as possible.

The bar consisted of a horse trough full of water in which cans of beer were floating. Every time the supply looked low, another crate arrived from the fridge in the cookhouse and the trough was replenished. If there had ever been food, it was gone by the time Ashley arrived.

He found himself next to Lang, who was squatting on an anvil.

'Would you like me to budge up, sir? There's room for two.' So Ashley sat as well, uncomfortable but pleased to have company.

'I enjoyed the salute, Gunner Lang – I saw you on gun number six.'

'Thank you, sir. Number six was Adam Barker's gun as well – it felt strange, him not being there. I miss him in the harness room too.'

'I can imagine. You were close to him – did it ever occur to you that he might have been one of the killers? Don't answer, if you'd rather not.'

'That's all right, sir – there's no point in keeping secrets any more. I did wonder about some things. Not when he lost it in the harness room, that day we tied him up – I was so busy

252

worrying that you suspected me, that I didn't even think about him. But there were other, odd things. For example, he was working so hard to make extra money before the murder and then he cut right down again as soon as Cooper was dead – that was funny.'

'I suppose you've no idea he was being blackmailed?'

'No, sir – but, honestly, it needn't have been anything important. Adam was going all out for promotion. Any small thing that might have stood in the way of that would have done. Cooper tried the same thing on Chadwick, but Chadwick just threatened to go straight to Captain Raynham, so he backed off.'

Ashley had heard exactly that from Chadwick himself, the day after the jumping competition. If only, he thought, Barker had shown the same strength of character as the trumpeter, or if Chadwick had carried out his threat, three people would still be alive. Lang continued: 'And after the killing, Adam was always tired. Smith Two says he was having nightmares, which would explain that.'

'Yes, I think Barker was too decent a person to make a good murderer. He had a conscience. That's why he gave himself away in the end. Being able to chop a few vegetables in half is no evidence at all, really. If he'd brazened it out, as Dutton wanted him to, we wouldn't have been able to prove anything – but then, I suppose, the police would have charged the Smiths.'

'Barker would have come forward then, sir. He was good friends with the Smiths – he wouldn't have let them go to prison for something he did.'

'No, I'm sure you're right.' There was an awkward pause. Ashley decided to turn the conversation in another, more cheerful, direction: 'So now you are the undisputed polishing champion of the Troop?'

'Well, sir, Sorrell is catching up fast. And for a beginner, your nephew – yes, we all know about that, sir – is doing rather well. Just look at those boots on him.'

Those boots, and their contents, were swaying unsteadily in the direction of Lang and Ashley. The same tottering path was being trodden by Tom Two. Green was once more cast in the role of sheepdog. He was carrying three cans of beer and threw one to Ashley, and another to Lang. The third he opened for himself.

'Tom, you're drunk,' observed Ashley indulgently. 'Just think what your mother would say.'

'Well, Uncle George, she'd start by blaming you for not keeping a proper eye on me; then she'd blame father for dying and leaving her to cope all by herself, and then she'd blame the school for allowing me to get in with a bad lot. Finally, she'd blame the army for corrupting me and say that it was a good thing that my three weeks have almost come to an end and that I'll soon be safely home with mummy. Does that sound about right?'

'It sounds entirely accurate. And are you looking forward to the "safely home with mummy" bit?'

The Toms grinned at each other and then at Ashley.

'It's not going to happen, Uncle George. That's what we've come to tell you – we're signing up. Keith's going to as well, as soon as he's seventeen. What do you think mother will say to *that?*'

Ashley looked from Tom One to Tom Two and then from Lang to Green. 'Well, as you say Tom, she'll blame me, and then your late father and then anyone else she can think of.' Ashley sighed contentedly. The warm glowing feeling might just be too much alcohol, but he liked to think that it resulted from a contemplation of his sister's wrath to come.

'And then?' He looked up at Green, expecting him to repeat his silly joke about the number two uniform. The Lance Bombardier, however, had lost his inhibitions. He said, simply: 'She'll shit herself, sir, won't she?'

Ashley nodded happily.

'She will, Lance Bombardier Green, she will.' Ashley paused to pull the ring on his can of beer. The noisy explosion which followed and the messy spray of froth which spurted out, illustrated exactly how his sister was going to behave.

THE END

Printed in Great Britain
by Amazon